DOWN HOME MURDER

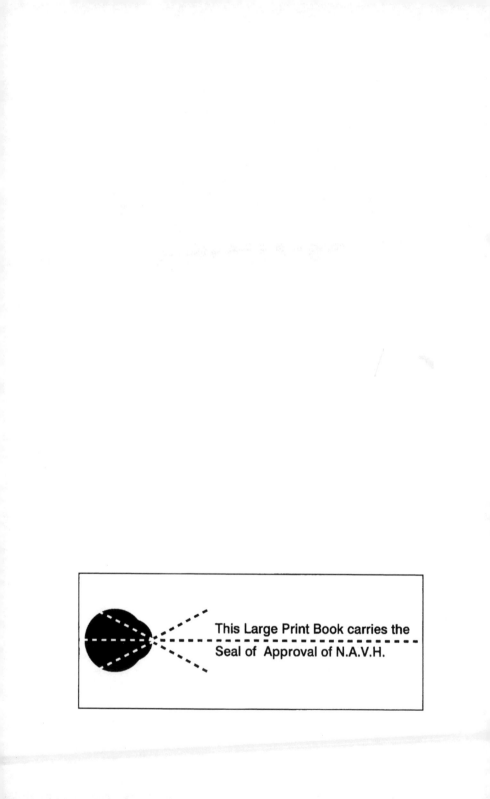

This Large Print Book carries the
Seal of Approval of N.A.V.H.

DOWN HOME MURDER

A LAURA FLEMING MYSTERY

TONI L. P. KELNER

WHEELER
PUBLISHING

Published in 2005 by arrangement with Kensington Books,
an imprint of Kensington Publishing Corp.

Wheeler Large Print Softcover.

The text of this Large Print edition is unabridged.
Other aspects of the book may vary from the original edition.

Set in 16 pt. Plantin by Minnie B. Raven.

Printed in the United States on permanent paper.

**Library of Congress Control Number: 2004117756
ISBN 1-58724-911-1 (lg. print : sc : alk. paper)**

To my Grandparents:

Alice Allen Cannon
Tony Robert Cannon

Margaret Little Perry
Acyle Everett Perry

Irene McCrary Reece
Collis Eugene Reece

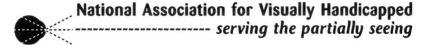
As the Founder/CEO of NAVH, the only national health agency solely devoted to those who, although not totally blind, have an eye disease which could lead to serious visual impairment, I am pleased to recognize Thorndike Press* as one of the leading publishers in the large print field.

Founded in 1954 in San Francisco to prepare large print textbooks for partially seeing children, NAVH became the pioneer and standard setting agency in the preparation of large type.

Today, those publishers who meet our standards carry the prestigious "Seal of Approval" indicating high quality large print. We are delighted that Thorndike Press is one of the publishers whose titles meet these standards. We are also pleased to recognize the significant contribution Thorndike Press is making in this important and growing field.

Lorraine H. Marchi, L.H.D.
Founder/CEO
NAVH

* Thorndike Press encompasses the following imprints: Thorndike, Wheeler, Walker and Large Print Press.

ACKNOWLEDGEMENTS

First, I want to thank my husband Stephen P. Kelner, Jr., for all the obvious reasons.

Second, I want to thank my Review Team: Janet Bosworth, Michael Luce, Richard Marek, Peggy Reece Perry, William Everett Perry, Robin Perry Schnabel, and Elizabeth Shaw. Thanks to all of y'all!

Third, I have to thank Sarah Smith, who took time away from her own writing to help me with mine.

CHAPTER 1

I saw my cousin Thaddeous as soon as I stepped into the Hickory Regional Airport, towering over everybody else.

"Hello Thaddeous," I said. "It's been a long time." My husband Richard and I hadn't been back to Byerly since the Christmas before last.

"Hey there Laurie Anne. It's good to see you."

I reached up to hug him, and then said, "How's Paw?"

"I talked to Mama just before I left work to come out here, but she said there's been no change."

I let my breath out slowly, not knowing whether I should be relieved by his answer or not. I had known that Paw was bad off when Aunt Nora called that morning because she would never have risked Uncle Buddy's wrath for a frivolous long-distance phone call. She told me that my grandfather, known to several generations as Paw, had been in an accident at the mill. When I asked how badly he had been hurt, all Aunt Nora would say was that she thought I should come home right away.

I had taken the next flight out of Boston, leaving Richard to pack and take care of the necessary details so he could join me that evening.

Thaddeous and I walked on to the parking lot, letting the hustle of the airport excuse us from making small talk. I looked at him curiously. He was even taller than I remembered. Of course Thaddeous had always been taller than me, even if I was two years older. Obviously he got his height from Uncle Buddy's side of the family.

Other than his height, he was clearly Aunt Nora's son. He had her blue eyes and solid build, and his skin burned easily just like hers. Normally his face looked cheerful and friendly, but today he just looked tired. Even if I hadn't already known about Paw, I would have been able to tell that something was wrong.

I could feel the heat rising from the parking lot when we left the air-conditioned airport. In April, the difference between the seasons in Massachusetts and North Carolina was plain. Spring had just begun to make itself felt in Boston, but here in Hickory, the first flowers were already fading to make way for the next batch of blooms.

"Isn't it awfully hot for this time of year?" I said.

"We've been having a warm spell for the last couple of weeks. It wouldn't be so bad if it would just rain. It's not the heat — it's the humidity."

Great, I thought as he opened the door of his dark blue pickup truck for me and I gingerly climbed onto the sun-warmed seat. I hadn't seen my cousin in a year and a half and all we could talk about was the weather. I sighed. I always did feel tongue-tied around my family, except for Paw.

"As soon as I get the truck going good, I'll turn the air-conditioner on," Thaddeous said.

I waited until he had pulled out of the parking lot and turned onto the highway before I asked, "What happened, Thaddeous? Aunt Nora didn't tell me much."

"Just one of those things, I guess," Thaddeous said. "Paw went up to the mill yesterday afternoon to pick up a carton of socks to pull."

I nodded. Tube socks were woven in long tubes with the junction between each sock perforated, like a sheet of stamps. The mill paid retired mill workers to take the long tubes home and pull them apart.

Thaddeous continued, "There wasn't nobody else there but Davy Sanders at the security booth. They don't run the mill on Sunday like they used to."

I knew that there hadn't been enough business to run the mill on Sundays for the past ten years, but I nodded anyway.

Thaddeous said, "Davy let Paw in and then the shift changed and Ralph Stewart came on. You remember the Stewarts, don't you, Laurie Anne? May was in your class in school."

He stopped talking long enough to pull out in front of an eighteen-wheeler with a flourish that would have done a Bostonian proud, and then went on.

"It wasn't until two, three hours later that he checked the sign-in book and realized that Paw hadn't come out. He called up to the warehouse, but when no one answered, he locked up the gate and the booth and went to take a look."

There was another pause while Thaddeous pulled a pack of Pall Malls out of his shirt-front pocket. He tapped the bottom of the pack to slide a cigarette neatly into his hand, inserted it into his mouth, lit it with a disposable lighter decorated with a Confederate flag, and inhaled deeply.

Then he politely rolled down his window a crack to draw the smoke out.

"Then what?" I prompted.

"Paw was there, all right. He must have slipped while trying to pull a box of socks off of the shelf and fell and hit his head. Ralph found him stretched out on the floor with the box of socks pulled out on top of him. He called for an ambulance, and they got him up to the hospital in Hickory."

The hospital in Hickory would have been the closest. There hadn't even been a doctor in Byerly since Dr. Spater died when I was in high school.

Thaddeous said, "The doctor said he was lucky to be alive. He had had a heart attack, and that may be what made him fall. Or maybe he had the attack after he hit his head — they can't really tell. They've got him in the coronary care unit, won't let us in to see him but for ten minutes every three hours. Mama's been up there all night. Just in case."

I knew what he meant. Just in case Paw died.

Neither of us said anything for a while, and then Thaddeous asked, "Are you still working with them computers?"

"I still am. How about you? Didn't Aunt Nora write me that you were promoted to supervisor at the mill?" I was amused when he puffed out his chest a bit at the question.

"Yeah," he answered nonchalantly. "Not all that much of a much, really. Longer hours, lots more paperwork, and a little bit more money."

"Youngest supervisor they ever had, so I hear."

"I don't know about that," he said with a small grin.

By then we had reached the hospital. We parked, stopped to pick up visitor passes from the front desk, and walked up to the second floor. Aunt Nora, a plump woman who kept her hair blond, was sitting in one of the green vinyl-covered chairs in the waiting-room. Though there was an open true confessions magazine in her lap, she was staring into space and my heart sank when I saw the forlorn expression on her face.

"Aunt Nora?" I said softly. "Is Paw . . ." I couldn't finish the question.

She jerked toward my voice, and then half-smiled. "He's still hanging on."

I found I could breathe again.

"Laurie Anne, I am so glad you're here," Aunt Nora said. She stood and held her arms out toward me. "Just let me hug your neck." She hugged me firmly, whispering,

"I swear, why is it that we only see each other when there's trouble?" I didn't say anything because I knew it was herself she was asking as much as it was me.

Aunt Nora pulled back but took both my hands in hers. "Just let me look at you. You know the older you get, the more you favor your mother. I just wish she was here now." Tears glistened in her eyes, as they always did when she spoke of my mother. She let go of my hands so she could rummage in an enormous beige, vinyl pocketbook and pull out a ragged, pink tissue to wipe her eyes.

"All right, Mama," Thaddeous said, not unkindly. "I expect Laurie Anne wants to see Paw."

"I'll take you down to his room," she said. "Thaddeous, you stay here and watch my pocketbook." She led the way down the quiet hospital hallway to a room on the corner.

"We got him a private room. The Medicare would only pay for a semi-private room, but you never know who you're going to get in your room with you that way." She raised her eyebrows at a passing black woman. I nodded, only half-offended. I knew Aunt Nora didn't mean any harm.

15

"The nurse said to let him rest," Aunt Nora went on, "but he'd have a fit if he found out you were here and we hadn't told him. You know Paw." She carefully opened the door to the room. "Just go on in," she whispered. "We'll be in the waiting-room." She tiptoed away.

The room was so quiet I had to resist the impulse to tiptoe myself. The only sound was a soft wheezing coming from an oxygen machine attached to a tube leading into Paw's nose. Standing next to the oxygen machine was a rack holding an IV bottle, filled with yellowish fluid slowly seeping into his arm. This array of medical technology seemed to dwarf the man sleeping in the bed.

Damn the mill, anyway! Paw was supposed to be retired. If Walters Mill paid a decent pension, he wouldn't have to work part-time to supplement his Social Security checks.

Of course, while I was at it, I might as well blame the entire Burnette family. Paw would have savings to live on if he hadn't spent every penny he ever made bailing out Aunt Nellie and Uncle Ruben; Aunt Ruby Lee and her husbands; Aunt Nora and Uncle Buddy; Aunt Daphine; and cousins galore every time they got into trouble. My

16

parents had had enough sense to take care of themselves, at least until they died in a car accident when I was fifteen.

Paw took me in then, and made sure I never felt alone. He encouraged my college-bound ambitions, despite the opinions of the rest of the family, and helped me find my way through the maze of admissions and financial aid forms to get into MIT. When I graduated with a degree in computer science and decided to stay in Massachusetts, he never balked, only nodded and filled his station wagon with my belongings to trundle them to Boston. The last thing he said when leaving me was, "If you need anything, you just call. Collect."

I blinked back tears. Oh Paw, what are you doing here? You should be in the basement of the house, watching *Jeopardy!* on the tiny black-and-white portable because you think the color console upstairs in the living-room is too much picture for just one person. You should be telling your grandchildren what their mothers were like when they were young. You should be playing your guitar and singing sweet gospel music. You should be anywhere but in this sterilized, hush-voiced horror of a place.

As if he had heard my thoughts, Paw opened his light blue eyes and smiled a soft smile. "Laurie Anne."

"I'm here, Paw." I leaned over to carefully kiss one cheek. "How are you doing?" I asked, wondering how anyone could ask such an inane question.

"I've been better," he said, his voice only a whisper. "Where's Richard?"

"Still in Boston. He had a meeting he couldn't miss, but he'll be here tonight."

"He's a good boy." He winced, and I saw him tremble.

"Should I call for a nurse?"

He shook his head, and just stared at me for a long moment. Did I really favor my mother? Everyone knew Mama had been Paw's favorite, and sometimes I thought I could see something of her in the dark brown eyes, light brown hair, and firm jaw line reflected in my own mirror.

Seeming to sense my thoughts, he said, "Alice would be real proud of you."

"Don't talk so much," I said as lightly as I could. "You need to rest. You've had a rough couple of days."

He trembled again, clearly tiring. "Laurie Anne?"

"Yes, Paw?"

"I didn't fall."

I waited while he struggled with what he was trying to say.

"They said I fell, but I didn't."

I stared at him. "What do you mean, Paw?"

He strained, but couldn't seem to get any more words out.

"Paw, I don't understand what you mean. You didn't fall?"

He nodded, and managed to work out one word, "Hit."

"Hit? You were hit by something? Something fell on you?"

He shook his head, and I hated how frustrated he looked. I tried again. "You didn't fall, and nothing fell on you." I had a thought, but surely that wasn't it. "Did someone hit you?"

He nodded as forcefully as he could.

"On purpose? Someone hit you on purpose?"

He nodded again.

"Who? Who hit you, Paw?"

He tried to speak once more, but after a few seconds seemed to give up. His eyes fluttered shut.

"Paw?" I couldn't tell if he was breathing. "Paw!" Then I saw the blessed movement of his chest, and I felt like crying in relief. I probably would have if I hadn't heard the door open.

CHAPTER 2

A short, red-haired nurse with a bosom like the prow of an aircraft-carrier strode into the room. Without deigning to notice me, she touched Paw's wrist, then made indeterminate adjustments to the oxygen and IV tubes. Apparently satisfied, she lifted an eyebrow at me, and pointed to the door. With a last look at Paw, I followed her out of the room.

Aunt Nora was hovering in the hall. "I told her you flew in all the way from Boston," she said indignantly, "and the least she could do was let you speak to your own grandfather."

"I don't care if she flew in from Timbuktu," the nurse said in a tight voice. "I have explained to you that visitors are only allowed at ten o'clock, one o'clock, four o'clock, and seven o'clock. Mr. Burnette is *not* to be disturbed again!" With a gait that would have been stomping if she hadn't been wearing crepe-soled shoes, the nurse marched away.

"Well, I swear!" Aunt Nora said, her

hands on her hips. "You'd think she owned the hospital and the rest of the town besides."

"Never mind, Aunt Nora. She's right. Paw needs his rest." After what Paw had just said, I felt like I needed a rest, too. Surely I hadn't heard what I thought I heard.

"Was Paw awake?" Aunt Nora said.

"Barely," I said.

"Did he say anything?"

"He talked about Mama a little," I said, feeling awkward. "They've got him on a lot of medication, don't they?" I asked hesitantly.

Aunt Nora nodded. "They've kept him pretty well doped-up ever since they found him."

That explained it then. It was just the drugs talking. It had to be. There was no need to say any more and get Aunt Nora all stirred up over nothing.

Thaddeous was standing when we got back to the waiting-room. "Mama, I've got to get back to work."

"Thaddeous," Aunt Nora said, "why don't you call the mill and tell them you won't be back today. Go home and get some sleep."

He shook his head. "I've got too much

to do. Besides, I don't think I could sleep. You call Willis and wake him up when y'all want a ride home." Aunt Nora's youngest boy Willis worked second shift at the mill and usually slept until dinner time.

"Thanks for picking me up at the airport, Thaddeous," I said.

"That's all right. Mama, I may be a little late for dinner. I've got something I need to take care of after work." He kissed his mother's cheek, and headed for the stairs.

Aunt Nora shook her head ruefully as she watched him go and then said, "Well, if we're not going to be able to see Paw for another hour, let's go get something to drink."

After leaving word at the nurse's station, we went down to the snack bar on the first floor. When Aunt Nora found out that I hadn't eaten since breakfast, she insisted that I get a pimento cheese sandwich and a bag of potato chips to go with my iced tea.

I ate the impromptu meal without much interest, but I figured it was worth it if it meant that Aunt Nora would have one less thing to worry about.

"I'm surprised you're the only one up here," I said. "The rest of the family's been told, haven't they?"

Aunt Nora nodded. "The security guard

from the mill called Loman and Edna as soon as the ambulance took Paw away. Edna *said* she called me as soon as he got off of the phone, but you know she called Reverend Glass first."

I nodded. Aunt Edna's devotion to the First Baptist Church of Byerly and its preacher was old news.

"Anyway, Edna said she'd call everybody else and Buddy and I came on up here. Then they said we couldn't see Paw until this morning, so Buddy went home. There wasn't no need for us both to be sitting here."

"You're a fine one to talk about Thaddeous needing sleep."

"I only missed the one night. I don't think Thaddeous has slept since Thursday night."

"Thursday? But Paw was just hurt yesterday."

Aunt Nora held one hand up to her mouth. "I forgot you didn't know about Melanie Wilson."

"What about her?"

"She's missing. They found her car left by the side of the road Friday night, but they can't find hide nor hair of Melanie."

"No wonder Thaddeous looked so bad." Thaddeous and Melanie had been in the same grade in school and he had been carrying a torch for her as long as I could remember. "What happened?"

"They don't have any idea. There wasn't any sign of her putting up a fight, so she either left on foot or went willingly. The car was left on Johnston Road, and they've had people searching the woods, but they haven't found a thing. Thaddeous heard about it that night on his CB, and went right over to join the search party. He kept looking all Friday night and Saturday, and he'd probably still be at it if I hadn't sent Willis to tell him about Paw."

I stared at my iced tea glass. "You know, I hear about this kind of thing all the time in Boston but I never expected it here." I felt oddly guilty that I hadn't even bothered to read similar stories in the *Boston Globe*.

"Her being missing like that was bad enough, but yesterday someone called up the police. He wouldn't leave his name, but he said he had seen her Friday night in Marley."

"In Marley? That's miles from there." Marley was actually part of Byerly, though there were plenty who would rather renounce any connection with the largely black neighborhood that most white folks avoided.

Aunt Nora lowered her voice. "Whoever it was said she was in a car with a bunch of black men." She looked around, checking to make sure there were no blacks sitting near us. "Her family is just frantic, thinking about what could have happened to her."

"Maybe they just stopped to give her a ride," I said.

"A carload of blacks? Do you really think Melanie Wilson would have gotten into a car full of black men on her own steam?"

"Probably not," I said reluctantly. I didn't like to admit it, but I knew how girls were raised around here. "Still," I said, "an anonymous phone call doesn't mean much. They get all kinds of crazy tips in Boston every time something like this happens. If he really knows something, why doesn't he come forward?"

"Scared to, I imagine. You know how those people are. They look after their own."

That was too much for me. "Aunt Nora," I began, fully intending to single-handedly take on generations of prejudice, but then I remembered Paw and stopped. The last thing Aunt Nora needed was a lecture on morality. "How's the rest of the family doing?" I asked instead.

"Same as always. Well, Nellie and Ruben have been having some problems. The bank repossessed Nellie's car."

"Again?"

She nodded. "They spent the car payment buying floor polish to sell door-to-door, and they only sold just a few bottles."

"How many bottles did you buy?" I asked.

Aunt Nora looked embarrassed, but didn't answer. "Augustus is doing fine. I called him this morning to tell him about Paw."

My cousin Augustus, Aunt Nora's oldest son, was in the Army and currently stationed in Germany. He and I were the only ones out of this generation of Burnettes who had moved away from Byerly.

"He was so upset that he couldn't be here," Aunt Nora went on, "but he used up his leave at Christmas. That's what I hate about him being in the Army. He can't just come home when he wants to like you can."

Maybe I was imagining it, but I had to wonder if Aunt Nora was reminding me that I hadn't been home in over a year even though I could theoretically come down any time. Instead of making excuses about why it was I didn't visit more often, I changed the subject again. "Aunt Nora, tell me about Paw's accident."

She looked puzzled, but said, "According to Edna, he had a heart attack and fell and hit his head."

That sounded reasonable. I never would have thought twice about it if Paw hadn't whispered those few words to me. "Was he alone when it happened?"

"As far as I know. Why?"

I hesitated a minute. "When I was with Paw just now, he said that he didn't fall, that someone hit him."

"Hit him? Why on earth would anyone hit Paw?"

"I don't know, but that's what he said."

"Don't you think you must have misheard him?"

"I guess I could have," I admitted, but I wasn't convinced. "And like you said, he is on drugs."

"That's right," Aunt Nora said. "He's liable to say anything. And I know you're upset about all this, too."

I bristled at the patronizing tone in her voice, but I couldn't argue with her. I didn't really believe it myself. "I guess you're right," I started, "but still —"

A strident call stopped me cold. "Aunt

Nora!" That had to be Vasti, Aunt Daphine's only daughter and another one of my cousins. Only Vasti would yell in a hospital, and only a fool would tell Vasti something she didn't want spread all over town.

There she was, waving wildly from the doorway just in case we hadn't heard her. Her shoulder-length brown curls bounced merrily despite the red barrettes that exactly matched the color of her crisp red and white pin-striped shirt-dress, her earrings, her necklace, and her high heels.

Aunt Nora sighed. "Daphine says that child was as quiet as can be when she was a baby, but I swear she's been trying to make up for it ever since."

Vasti pushed her way through the other tables in the cafeteria toward us, her three-inch heels clicking against the tile floor. "Laurie Anne? Is that you? I just don't believe it! You look so *good!*"

I wasn't sure if her surprised delight was at my presence, or at the fact that I looked halfway decent.

Vasti threw herself into the chair between us, flung her overstuffed, red patent leather handbag onto the table, and kicked her shoes off under the table.

"Lord-a-mighty it is *so* hot out there,

and as muggy as all get out. Thank goodness my new Cadillac is air-conditioned. You have to see this car, Laurie Anne, you will not believe it. Arthur insisted on getting everything for it, you know. I told him I didn't need power windows and a sun roof, but he said, 'I won't have *my* wife driving around in a car unless it's top of the line!' and what could I say? He's just like that. Of course, he gets a discount because he owns the dealership." She paused long enough to take a quick breath. "I wouldn't have come out in the heat at all, but of course I had to see how Paw was doing. Mama wanted to come but she's booked solid at the beauty parlor and couldn't get away. Well, don't I get a hug?"

I felt a bit dizzy from this stream of Vasti's consciousness, but I dutifully reached over to embrace my cousin. As I leaned back into my chair, I was momentarily touched when I saw that Vasti's eyes were tearing up.

"*What* are you wearing?" Vasti wailed. "I must be allergic to your perfume. I'm allergic to all but the best, you know." She reached for the napkin holder, wrenched out half a dozen, scattering several on the floor in the process, and wiped her eyes carefully. "I know I've ruined my mascara."

"I'm not wearing perfume, Vasti."

"Oh. It must be all those antiseptics and things here in the hospital." The flood of water subsided and Vasti looked pointedly at the glasses on the table. "What do we have to do to get a waitress around here? I am *dying* of thirst."

"It's a snack bar, Vasti," I said. "You have to go up to the counter if you want something."

"Oh. I just hope I can get my shoes on," she said, not moving. "I just got them last week to go with this outfit, and my feet are covered with blisters." When neither Aunt Nora nor I offered to go get her a drink, Vasti, manufacturing all manner of grimace, squeezed her feet back into her shoes.

"Maybe you should get a larger size, Vasti," Aunt Nora said helpfully.

"Aunt Nora, I've *always* taken a size five-and-a-half shoe! Now if I just have some money." She dove into her handbag, peering into its depths in frustration and then finally pulling out a chubby, red wallet. "I usually just have credit cards, you know. Arthur says it's dangerous to carry cash. I know we don't have the crime Laurie

Anne's used to up North, but a woman can't be too careful. Especially after what happened to Melanie Wilson. Did y'all hear about that? Isn't it awful? That poor girl got dragged from her car by half-a-dozen blacks and they can't even find her body." She finally gave up opening compartments in her wallet. "Could one of you — ?"

"Isn't that a five-dollar bill poking out of there, Vasti?" I said.

Vasti frowned, and pulled the bill out to examine it suspiciously. "I wonder where that came from. Well, I'll be right back. Y'all don't want anything, do you?" Without waiting for an answer, she launched herself toward the counter.

Aunt Nora stood up. "Now that you've got some company, I'm going to head back upstairs. Edna said she'd try to stop by today, and I don't want to miss her."

"Wait and we'll come with you," I protested.

"No, that's all right. You sit right here and have a good talk with Vasti." She was gone before I could say anything else.

A good talk with Vasti? Talking with Vasti at all was nigh onto impossible, although listening to her was usually pretty entertaining in its own way.

31

Vasti sat back down, Diet Coke in hand. "Where's Aunt Nora?"

"She went back upstairs. She said we should come on up as soon as we finished our drinks." It was a lie, but surely no more than a white one.

Unfortunately, Vasti had kicked her shoes off again. "So Laurie Anne, how are you doing? Where's that husband of yours? You two aren't having trouble, are you?"

"Richard and I are doing fine, thank you. He's flying down this evening. He wanted to come with me this morning, but he had a meeting with the head of his department today and I didn't want him to miss it."

"Isn't that just like a man?" Vasti said, nodding sagely. "Letting his business come between him and family. Of course your husband doesn't own his own business, does he?"

"He teaches Shakespeare at Boston College, Vasti. It's kind of hard to be a free-lance academic."

"That's right, now I remember. You had to finish putting him through school when y'all first got married. I know you're glad he's finally working so you can stay home."

"I still work, Vasti," I said, annoyed that she had so quickly discounted my education and career. "In fact, I make more money than Richard does."

Vasti gasped. "Doesn't he *hate* that? Doesn't it make him feel, you know, unmanly. I mean, Arthur would just feel *impotent* if he couldn't support me."

I couldn't help it. I had to laugh. Vasti looked at me in consternation for a moment, then clucked in exasperation. "Oh, you! You know what I mean!" She took a swallow of her drink, and then said, "Well I'm glad you two are getting along anyway."

"Why do you say that? Are you and Arthur — ?"

"Oh Laurie Anne, don't be silly. I'm talking about Linwood and Sue."

I nodded. "I heard that they separated for a while, but I thought they worked things out."

"Well, they're living together again, as far as that goes, but if you ask me, the only reason she let him come back is because she's pregnant. You did know Sue was pregnant again, didn't you?"

"Of course I know. You know I call home every couple of weeks."

She went on as if I hadn't spoken. "You'd think she'd use some kind of protection. Three babies in three years is a bit much, don't you think? But maybe she thinks that's the only way she can hold onto Linwood. Considering how she got him in the first place that is."

It was no secret that Sue had already been pregnant when she and Linwood got married, but I refused to rise to the bait. "Wasn't it Sue who threw Linwood out?" I pointed out.

"I suppose," Vasti said vaguely. "But enough of that. Tell me about what you've been up to. How is your job going? That's not what you wear to work, is it?"

"Well, yes. I was just about to leave for work when Aunt Nora called." I looked down at my clothes. The suit was my favorite work outfit, a rose wool skirt and bolero jacket that I wore with a pale rose and teal paisley blouse. "Why do you ask?"

"Oh, nothing. Some women can wear that color, I suppose."

Implying that I was one of the ones who couldn't. Why did I care what she thought, anyway? Her dress had gone out of style in Boston two years ago.

I checked my watch and said, "Why don't we head on upstairs? Aunt Nora said we'd be able to see Paw at one, and it's a quarter to now."

We rode the elevator to the second floor in deference to Vasti's new shoes, and rounded the corner by the waiting room. Then I stopped dead in my tracks and stared with equal amounts of amazement and disgust. Vasti, for once, was speechless.

The chairs in the waiting-room had been rearranged to face one side of the room. Sitting with their heads bowed were Aunt Nora, Aunt Ruby Lee and Uncle Conrad, Uncle Loman, and my cousin Linwood with his wife Sue. Aunt Edna stood in front of them, holding a hefty, white-bound Bible for the tall, cadaverous man beside her.

"Shhhh," Aunt Edna hissed at us, then turned a page for the preacher as he read from the book of Job in a dreary monotone.

Behold, thou hast instructed many, and thou hast strengthened the weak hands. Thy words have upholden him that was falling, and thou has strengthened the feeble knees. But now it is come upon thee, and thou faintest; it toucheth thee, and thou art troubled. Is not this thy fear, thy confidence, thy hope, and the uprightness of thy ways? Remember, I pray thee, who ever perished, being innocent? Or where were the righteous cut off? Even as I have seen, they that plow inequity, and sow wickedness, reap the same. By the blast of God they perish, and by the breath of his nostrils are they consumed.

He finished reading, and Aunt Edna reverently closed the Bible and held it tightly against her bosom. Linwood looked up, but bowed his head again when the preacher continued.

"Oh Lord, do not take this man, this devoted father and grandfather from us. Or, if it be thy will to take him now, treat him with the honor and glory due so generous a man, a man who has thoughtfully included your church in his will, a man who wishes so much given to us, a man who would even leave his family home to us. Amen."

The "congregation" murmured amens and raised their heads, while I bit my lip to keep from laughing. I went over to Aunt Nora and whispered, "Reverend Glass didn't sneak in and bother Paw, did he?"

Aunt Nora looked exasperated. "No, I got back up here just in time. I'll tell you, it wasn't easy keeping him out, what with Edna saying how he needed a chance to make his peace with the Lord."

Something in Glass's prayer bothered me. "What was that about Paw giving the house to the church?"

"It's the first I've heard of it."

Reverend Glass approached us, slicking back his shiny, black hair as he came, and Aunt Nora and I forced smiles. Aunt Edna followed him at a respectful distance.

"Sisters, what a terrible time this is for us all," Glass said solemnly.

"It was good of you to come, Reverend Glass," Aunt Nora said. "I know Paw would appreciate it."

Actually, I thought, what Paw would really appreciate would be a chance to toss the old windbag out on his ear, or maybe on some other part of his anatomy.

He turned to me. "Laurie Anne, how are you? We haven't seen you in church lately."

"I moved to Boston three years ago, Reverend Glass."

"Ah, yes. You know Laurie Anne, even though you can't get to church regularly, you don't have to lose touch. If you'd like, I'll arrange for you to receive our church bulletin in Boston."

"That would be very nice." Just what I needed, a weekly dose of Glass's sanctimonious nonsense.

"I regret that I can't speak with Brother

Burnette," Glass said with a sad shake of his head. "It's good to clear one's conscience when one is so close to one's immortal reward."

I started to fume. Paw wasn't dead yet, damn it! And I wasn't aware that his conscience needed clearing.

Glass went on. "I am grateful that I had this chance to lend some small comfort to you and the others." He took Aunt Nora's hand and patted it. "Do let me know if there is anything I can do for you or for your father."

"We'll be sure to call," Aunt Nora said, pulling her hand back as politely as possible.

He nodded at the rest of his flock, and said to Aunt Edna, "Sister, will I see you at the prayer meeting this week?"

"Of course, Reverend," Aunt Edna gushed. "I was planning to bake some of those ginger snaps you liked so well."

"That would be most pleasant." He smiled at us all, and for a minute I was afraid that he was going to pass the collection plate before he headed for the elevator. Aunt Nora breathed an audible sigh of relief when the door slid shut.

"Wasn't it nice of him to come?" Aunt Edna asked. Her face, usually so pinched, was bright with enthusiasm, and I didn't have the heart to say anything against the man. Aunt Nora must have felt the same way, because she just nodded.

Unfortunately, Uncle Loman didn't give a hoot for his wife's feelings. He snorted loudly, and said, "Why'd you call that old fart for anyway? I've never known a man so in love with the sound of his own voice."

"Haw haw haw! In love with the sound of his own voice," Linwood cackled. "That's a good one, Daddy."

"Shut up, Linwood," Sue said automatically.

Aunt Edna bit out her words. "I thought it was very nice of Reverend Glass to take time out of his very busy schedule to come see Paw."

Cousin Linwood snorted again, but before Aunt Edna could say anything else, I hurriedly said, "Aunt Edna? Aunt Ruby Lee? Don't I get a hug?"

Exchanging hugs distracted them long enough for us to regroup by age and gender. I stayed with the three aunts while Uncle Conrad and Uncle Loman went to light cigarettes in the hall and Vasti went to visit with Linwood and Sue.

Aunt Edna looked skinnier than ever, especially wearing that shapeless, faded blue cotton shift. I knew she hadn't always looked like this; I had seen pictures from her wedding. She had been slender, but not skinny, and had worn her hair down on her shoulders instead of tied up in a tight bun. Maybe after twenty years of marriage to Uncle Loman, a man not known for giving compliments, she had lost interest in the quest for beauty.

Of course most women would look a bit scrawny next to Aunt Ruby Lee's bountiful curves. If her figure wasn't enough to make most other women jealous, her shiny blond hair, big blue eyes, and dimples would do it. Looking ten years younger than she was, despite her three children, I could see how my aunt had managed to attract all four of her husbands. And it certainly didn't hurt that she was as genuinely sweet a woman as I had ever met.

She and Uncle Conrad, a well-built man with dark, wavy hair and dark eyes, did make a handsome couple. Though I had realized the first time I met him that he wasn't the smartest man in the world, he did seem to adore Aunt Ruby Lee.

What a contrast Uncle Conrad was to Uncle Loman, even though they were first cousins. Uncle Loman was so wiry you'd think Aunt Edna didn't feed him, and his washed-out, grey eyes and light hair were nothing like his cousin's.

Even the way they stood was different. Uncle Loman was leaning back against the wall, arms folded over his chest, not even looking at Uncle Conrad. Every once in a while he'd say a word or two, but his expression never changed. Uncle Conrad, on the other hand, was waving his arms as he spoke, pacing back and forth in front of Uncle Loman, and he kept looking around as if worried he was disturbing someone.

My aunts launched into a rehash of Paw's accident, which was the last thing I wanted to hear right then. Besides, I knew darned well that I had better not leave Sue and Vasti together for too long, especially not with Linwood there to egg them on.

I walked over just in time for Vasti to smile maliciously at Sue and say, "My, you are getting big. Are you sure it's not twins?"

That was unkind, even for Vasti. Admittedly Sue looked like she was ready to give birth at any minute, but it was her third child in as many years. Sue was clearly suffering from the heat. Despite the hospital's air-conditioning and being dressed in blue jean shorts and a tank top, Sue's face was flushed and her sandy-blond hair was damp.

Before I could think of anything supportive to say to her, Sue responded to Vasti in kind.

"The doctor says it's just one, but I guess it's taking after its cousin Arthur."

I winced. Vasti's husband Arthur did tend toward the portly.

"Arthur could stand to lose a few pounds, I guess," Vasti said. "It must be all that fancy food from all the dinner parties we've been going to. Keeping up appearances is so much work, but a woman has to stand behind her husband through thick and thin, don't you think?"

Ouch! Not a nice thing to bring up with a couple that was having marital problems. "It sure is hot outside," I said hurriedly.

"Don't take no computer to figure that one out," Linwood said with his characteristic politeness. He hadn't changed a bit, although I kept hoping he would. Fleshy and freckled, Linwood had his father's nearly colorless grey eyes and straw-colored hair.

"Hey Vasti," he said, "what's this I hear about your husband? Someone I know said he was going to start selling imported cars."

"Well, it's not definite yet so I probably shouldn't say anything." Vasti looked around the room as if expecting men in trench coats to take note of her words, and then lowered her voice to a stage whisper. "Arthur's been thinking about building a Toyota dealership next door. He says it would pay for itself in the first year."

"I wouldn't own no Japanese car," Linwood said. "Daddy says that anybody who owns a foreign automobile is just taking food away from American workers."

"But driving a small car like a Toyota is better for the environment," I said before Vasti could reply.

"Shit! What's that got to do with anything?" Linwood said. "What kind of car do you drive, Laurie Anne?"

"I don't have one."

"Can't you and your husband afford a car?" Vasti asked with a look of horror.

"Of course we could afford a car if we wanted one, but we don't need a car in Boston," I said. "We take the subway."

Linwood looked a little suspicious of the idea of not needing a car, but let it pass as Vasti broke in with a description of a new party gown.

I sighed. I was already worn out from dealing with family, and this wasn't even close to the full Burnette complement. All told there were five surviving sisters with four husbands, twelve grandchildren, two grandsons-in-law, one granddaughter-in-law, and two great-grandchildren. I wasn't sure how I could feel so lonely in the midst of such a crowd, but I did.

The red-headed nurse came in and made her way to Aunt Nora. "Mr. Burnette can see visitors now," she said, "but only two of you can go in, and just for ten minutes."

"I've already seen him," I said reluctantly, hating to give up my chance, "so one of you go."

The three sisters looked at each other, no one wanting to speak.

"Actually," the nurse said, "As long as only two go in at a time and the total visit is ten minutes, several of you can see him."

There were smiles all around, and in quick succession Aunt Nora and Aunt Ruby Lee, Uncle Loman and Aunt Edna, and Sue and Linwood went into and came out of Paw's room. "That's all," the nurse said firmly to the rest of us. "No more visits until four."

"Did he say anything?" I asked when we had reassembled, wondering if he had repeated what he had told me.

"No," Aunt Ruby Lee said, "but I think he knew we were there."

44

"He looked so old," Aunt Edna said. "I never thought of Paw as old."

"I hate to see him like that," Aunt Nora said. "He looks right pitiful in that hospital gown he's in. I didn't even think to bring him a pair of pajamas."

"If you want, I can run up to the house and get him a pair." I had assumed that Richard and I would be staying at his house anyway, though it wouldn't seem right without Paw there.

"If Aunt Maggie will let you in," Aunt Edna sniffed.

"Aunt Maggie's staying at Paw's house to keep an eye on things," Aunt Nora explained. "She's got some idea that if she doesn't, there won't be anything left when Paw gets back."

For Aunt Maggie, that made sense, so I didn't question it further. "Can someone give me a ride, or can I borrow someone's car?"

"I thought you said you couldn't drive," Linwood said.

"I said I didn't have a car," I answered. "I do have a driver's license." I considered reminding him that I passed my driver's test on the first go-round, compared to the three tries it had taken him, but decided that it would be beneath me.

"Buddy and the boys have our cars,"

Aunt Nora said. "Vasti?"

"I would, Aunt Nora, but I've got to get home to get ready for tonight. Arthur and I are taking some clients out to dinner, and I have to do my hair and my nails, and I just don't have a minute to spare."

"I'll drive you over there, Laurie Anne," Uncle Conrad said.

"I thought you had to get back to work," Aunt Ruby Lee said.

"They can do without me for a little while longer," Uncle Conrad said with a touch of bravado. "It's the least I can do, considering. I want to make sure everything's all right."

Uncle Loman said, "Edna, you take Ruby Lee home. Conrad can drop me off at the mill."

"I was going to stay with Nora for a while," Aunt Edna said stiffly.

"That's fine with me," Aunt Ruby Lee said quickly.

Aunt Nora said, "Laurie Anne, why don't you come eat dinner with us tonight? There's probably nothing to eat at Paw's house. Bring Aunt Maggie, too."

"Sounds great," I said. Aunt Nora made the best biscuits I had ever eaten.

Aunt Nora suggested some other items I could bring from the house, and after assuring everyone that I'd see them later, I followed Uncle Conrad and Uncle Loman down the stairs to the parking lot and Uncle Conrad's pickup truck.

CHAPTER 3

Getting the three of us into the cab of the pickup truck was a tight squeeze and I was stuck in the middle, dodging elbows from both sides. None of us said anything for a while, and I felt a little awkward.

I finally said, "I appreciate your taking me over to Paw's, Uncle Conrad."

"That's all right. I'm glad to help out," he said.

There were several more minutes of silence.

"How are the kids doing?" I asked. Aunt Ruby Lee had three children, one from each of her previous marriages.

"They're fine."

Another period of silence. "What have you and Aunt Edna been up to, Uncle Loman?"

"Nothing you'd be interested in. I work for a living, and Edna spends all her time up at the church."

So much for a heart-to-heart talk. I snuck a look at my watch. It was not quite two, but it seemed like I had left Boston days ago instead of only hours. Paw's being in the hospital didn't seem real. And even though Aunt Nora had dismissed it, what he had said was still bothering me. "Had either of you seen Paw before his accident? Recently, I mean?"

"How come?" Uncle Loman asked.

"I was just wondering if he had been doing all right. I know his heart's not too good, but aren't there usually warning signs before a heart attack?"

Uncle Loman shrugged. "I hadn't seen him in a while."

"Me neither," Uncle Conrad said. "I don't think I'd seen or talked to Ellis in a couple of weeks. Maybe longer." He patted my knee clumsily. "Don't you worry, Laurie Anne. Ellis is going to be just fine."

"Don't lie to the girl, Conrad," Uncle Loman said. "She can see for herself that Ellis isn't going to get out of that bed on his own."

"You don't know that," I objected.

"I know he's over seventy and he's got a bad heart."

I stared at the road ahead, not saying anything. He was probably right.

After a minute, Uncle Loman said, "Watch what you're doing, Conrad. Here's the turn for the mill."

As we bumped down Mill Road, I caught

sight of Walters Mill itself. Rumor had it that Burt Walters had planned an office park, complete with hotels and restaurants, that would surround the mill. Walters had gotten as far as clearing the land around the mill when the slowdown of the textile market defeated his grandiose plans, leaving the mill, an inelegant building made of mud-brown bricks, standing alone in the midst of scraggly clumps of scrub pine.

Uncle Conrad pulled up as far as the security booth, and Uncle Loman climbed out of the truck.

"Are you coming to the hospital tonight, Loman?" Uncle Conrad asked.

"I suppose so," Uncle Loman said. "If he lasts that long. You're coming back as soon as you leave her at the house, aren't you?"

"I thought I'd take a look around first. Make sure everything's all right up there."

"I'm sure everything is all right, Conrad. You just get yourself back here. Your supervisor don't owe me that many favors."

Uncle Loman shut the door without saying anything to me, and I immediately slid over and stretched out. I didn't much miss Uncle Loman's company. Maybe he was right about Paw and maybe he was just trying to be kind in his own way, but I wasn't ready to hear Paw's eulogy yet.

"Do you really think Paw is going to make it?" I asked Uncle Conrad wistfully.

"Shoot, I don't know. Those doctors are real smart, but Ellis is pretty bad off. Your granddaddy is an old man and he's had a full life. You can't ask for more than that, can you?"

"I guess not," I said reluctantly. "It just seems so sudden. I know he has a bad heart, but he sounded fine the last time I spoke to him. I just wish that I could have been there with him when it happened."

"No, you wouldn't have wanted to be with him at a time like that. You wouldn't want to see that."

I noticed we were turning toward Highway 321, and I said, "Aren't we going to take Rock Creek Road? You can turn onto that old tobacco road and it'll take you right to Paw's house. You know the way, don't you?"

"Oh, I know the way, but that road is in such foul shape I don't take it anymore."

"It wasn't that bad last time I was —" I started to say but Uncle Conrad blurted, "Do you mind if I turn on the radio?" He switched it on before I could answer, and the plaintive voice of George Jones mourning his lost love effectively forestalled further conversation.

Oh well. If he wanted to take the long way around, that was his business, and I didn't want to talk anymore anyway.

Byerly looked the same as ever, I decided as we drove through town. There was a discount auto parts store where there had once been a full-service garage, and a couple more of the downtown stores had been boarded up as their customers took their business to the malls in Hickory, but that was about it.

As we turned down toward Paw's house, I caught sight of Mill Hill, covered with the shabby mill-houses where many of the people in Byerly still lived.

Byerly had originally been a tobacco-growing town, one of several clustered around the larger city of Hickory. Then Big Bill Walters moved in and took over. He built Walters Mill, and lured the sons and daughters of farmers from all over the county to come work for him. Since Byerly had nowhere near enough houses for three shifts of workers, he followed the path of other mill owners and built rows and rows of identical cracker-box mill houses. They were cheap and drafty, but somehow most of them were still standing. When the

North Carolina textile market started to go downhill, Walters sold off the mill houses to his workers. At a fat profit, of course. These days the houses showed some variations — different colored paint, siding on a couple, a deck or garage added on — but the family resemblance was still plain.

The Burnettes had been in Byerly long before the advent of the mill, and Paw had repeatedly refused Walters's offer of a mill house. Paw's place, the Burnette home for five generations, was not fancy or even all that pretty, but it was sturdy in the way only a house that has been carefully tended to for several lifetimes can be.

It had started out as a simple farmhouse but had been added to as the size of the family increased until now it rambled inefficiently over the lot, an architect's nightmare with no two sections looking like they belonged to the same house.

Uncle Conrad parked his truck in front of the house because there were already two cars in the driveway. One was Paw's battered old station wagon. The second was a Dodge Caravan with one bumper sticker that said "I Brake for Yard Sales" and another that said "Flea Market Nut." It had to be Aunt Maggie's.

Uncle Conrad and I were halfway to

the front door when a salmon-pink Oldsmobile with a Mary Kay logo prominently displayed pulled up. A platinum blonde dressed in pink got out, and waved at us daintily.

"Who's that?" I asked in a low voice.

"Beats me," Uncle Conrad said.

"Well, hello there!" she cooed as she came up the sidewalk. "How are you doing? I didn't have any idea that there'd be anyone here. Can you two give me a hand?" She must have noticed our blank expressions, because she put her hands on her hips and chided me, "Don't tell me you don't remember your cousin Sally?"

Sally? I climbed the family tree in my head to try to figure out the relationship. My grandmother had had three sisters, one of whom was Patsy. Wasn't Patsy's youngest granddaughter named Sally? Sally Hendon, that was it! The Mary Kay logo should have clued me in — she was the one who gave away cosmetic samples for Christmas presents.

"Of course I remember you, Sally," I said. "I just wasn't expecting to see you here."

"Is this handsome fellow your husband?" she asked, batting her eyes at Uncle Conrad.

"No, this is Conrad Randolph, Aunt Ruby Lee's husband."

"It's always a pleasure to meet one of Ruby Lee's husbands," Sally said with a sweet smile, but fortunately the dig went right over Uncle Conrad's head. "Well, what are we standing outside for?" Sally said, and walked past us, but the door opened before she could get to it.

A short, stout woman in green rubber flip-flops, blue cotton shorts, and a T-shirt boldly emblazoned "Leave Me Alone!" scowled at us and snapped, "What do you want?"

"Aunt Maggie?" I said hesitantly. Actually, as Paw's younger sister, she was my great-aunt, but that was too much of a mouthful for every day.

The old woman looked me up and down. "Laurie Anne?" It sounded more like an accusation than recognition.

"Yes, ma'am."

She turned her gaze to Uncle Conrad. "Who are you?"

"I'm Conrad Randolph," he answered, stuttering a bit. "Ruby Lee's husband."

"That's right, I heard she got married again. You're taking a chance, don't you think? She's been married three times already."

Uncle Conrad cleared his throat, and said, "Anybody can make a mistake."

Aunt Maggie snorted. Then she looked at Sally, whose smile had faded. "What do you want, Sally?"

"Aunt Maggie," Sally said in a concerned tone, "I thought you'd be at the hospital."

"Ellis is the one who's hurt, not me."

"Of course, but I thought you'd want to be by Uncle Ellis's side at a time like this."

"What did you come over for if you didn't think there was anyone here?"

"I just came by to see if I could help," Sally said.

"Help yourself, is more like it."

"I'm sure I don't know what you mean," she answered stiffly. "Aren't you going to invite us in?"

Aunt Maggie clearly wasn't enthusiastic, but she nodded. "All right. I suppose you can come inside." She led the way into the living-room, and took Paw's recliner while the three of us lined up on the couch. I hadn't felt so guilty since the time Aunt Nora rounded up all of the cousins to find out who had stolen her fresh apple pie, and at least that time I had known what it was that I was accused of.

"Is there any word about Uncle Ellis?" Sally asked.

I shook my head. "We've just come from the hospital, but there's been no change."

"Poor Uncle Ellis," she said mournfully.

Aunt Maggie snorted again. "You still haven't told me why you're here, Sally, so let me guess. Ellis promised you something from the house when you were just a little girl, right?"

"That's right," Sally said with artful amazement. "He did. Laurie Anne, you used to live with Uncle Ellis, didn't you?"

I nodded.

"Then Uncle Ellis must have told you about the figurines." She pointed at the cherrywood china cabinet against the far wall.

"I don't think Paw ever mentioned them," I said.

"Did he not?" While Aunt Maggie watched through narrowed eyes, Sally pulled me over to the china cabinet. "These figurines right here." I recognized them, of course. I had dusted them more times than I could count. There was a goose girl and boy holding hands, a delicately posed Japanese geisha, a Scottie dog with a cheerfully wagging tail, and several others.

"These were my great-grandmother's," Sally said. "The cabinet, too. They've been in the family for years. Your grandfather told me a long time ago that he wanted me to have them, if anything ever happened to him." She tried to turn the latch on the cabinet, but nothing happened.

"It's locked," Aunt Maggie said smugly, twirling a key ring with a tiny brass key.

"Do you mind, Aunt Maggie?" Sally asked pointedly.

"You're darned right I mind! Those things are going to stay locked up, where they belong."

"Really, Aunt Maggie. If I didn't know better, I'd think you were accusing me of . . . I just don't know *what* you're accusing me of." Sally poked her hands into a tiny, pink handbag and pulled out a pale pink handkerchief which she lifted to her distinctly dry eyes.

"Who do you think you're fooling?" Aunt Maggie said with obvious disgust. Stepping past Sally, she unlocked the cabinet, pulled out the Scottie dog, and closed the cabinet again before Sally could reach inside.

"Laurie Anne, look at the bottom of this statue," Aunt Maggie said and thrust the figurine into my hands. "What does it say?"

I inspected it. " 'Made in Occupied Japan.' " I handed it back.

"That's right. Ellis always said you made good grades in school — how's your history?"

I shrugged, not sure where she was going. "Okay, I guess."

"When did the United States occupy Japan?"

"Just after World War II ended in 1945."

Aunt Maggie nodded her approval. "Now our boys only occupied Japan for just a few years. Anything made there before or after that was only marked 'Made in Japan.' That makes Occupied Japan pieces rare and valuable."

"What *are* you talking about?" Sally asked.

Aunt Maggie went on as if she hadn't been interrupted. "Now I remember Ellis telling me how he regretted that our mother Molly never got to see her first grandchild. Molly was your great-grandmother, Sally. Now by the time World War II started, Ellis already had two children, which is why he didn't volunteer."

"Wait a minute!" I said as it dawned on me. "If Molly died before World War II started, how could she have owned any-

59

thing marked 'Occupied Japan'?"

Aunt Maggie grinned. "She couldn't have."

Sally jammed her handkerchief back into her handbag. "I was told they were hers," she said angrily.

"Then I guess you were told wrong. Now if you don't mind, we have some business we need to tend to." Aunt Maggie walked to the front door and opened it wide.

"What about the cabinet?" Sally asked.

Aunt Maggie didn't answer, Sally flounced out, and Aunt Maggie bolted the door behind her.

"Aunt Maggie, that was wonderful!" I said.

"Just looking after Ellis's interests," she said mildly, but she was grinning as she replaced the figurine in the cabinet. "I take it you two didn't come with her."

"No, ma'am. Aunt Nora sent us to get some of Paw's things."

Aunt Maggie's eyes narrowed again. "What kind of things are you talking about?"

"A pair of pajamas, some underwear, maybe a robe."

"No furniture?"

"No ma'am," I answered firmly. After

what I had just seen and heard, I could see why she asked.

She nodded, apparently satisfied, and led the way down the hall. "Come on into the kitchen and have a Coca-Cola. What have you been up to, Laurie Anne? I haven't seen you in I don't know how long."

"I'm still living in Boston. I flew in this morning after Aunt Nora called."

Aunt Maggie pulled three bottles of Coke from the refrigerator, popped the caps one by one using the handle of the silverware drawer, and handed one to me and another to Uncle Conrad. Then she gestured for us to have a seat around the kitchen table.

"Edna called last night and told me about Ellis," Aunt Maggie said. "I know how fast news travels around here, so I came right over. Sure enough, the first batch of vultures showed up at eight o'clock this morning. Conrad? Is that your name?"

"Yes, ma'am," he said.

"While you're here, why don't you take out the garbage? I've been afraid to leave the house for fear someone would sneak in behind my back."

Uncle Conrad complied meekly.

"Aunt Maggie," I asked, "What's going

61

on? Have other people been trying to take Paw's things?"

"Lord, yes. Something like this always brings them out of the woodwork. My brother Coulson's boy Herman showed up first thing this morning."

"Herman? He's my third cousin, I think."

"You don't want to claim him as family. That boy would steal your toilet seat right out from under you if he thought he could get away with it. He told me that Ellis had promised him that bedroom set in the spare bedroom. He probably thought I didn't know what it's worth, but I wouldn't have been dealing at flea markets all these years if I couldn't tell good pieces from junk."

"He thought you were going to let him take stuff out of Paw's house?" I said.

Aunt Maggie shrugged. "Most likely he thought there wouldn't be anyone here, just like Sally did, and he could come on in and take that and anything else he could lay his hands on."

"That's stealing!"

"Of course it's stealing! The trouble is, once he got stuff out of the house, we wouldn't be able to do a thing about it."

"What about the police?"

"He knows darned well that none of us would call the police. Only trash would put their own flesh and blood in jail. Anyway, as long as I'm here, nobody is taking anything out of this house." She took another swallow. "A death in the family does bring out the worst in folks."

"Paw's not dead!"

Aunt Maggie looked at me sharply. "Don't you think I know that?"

"I'm sorry, it's just I can't believe anyone acting that way."

"When you get to be my age, Laurie Anne, you'll come to expect it and a sight more besides. Ellis and I are all that's left of our generation, and I saw the same thing when Mama and Daddy died, and when our sisters and brothers died. If your granddaddy makes it out of the hospital, I mean to make sure he's still got a house to come back to. If not, I'll make sure his stuff goes where he wants it."

I drank down the last of my Coke. "Aunt Maggie, I don't mean to sound ugly, but have you seen Paw's will?"

She studied me. "Why do you ask?"

"Reverend Glass was at the hospital today, and he said Paw had left the house to the church."

"Like they say, that's his tale, but I'm sitting on mine. Ellis would sooner let this place rot as to give it to that hypocritical so-and-so. Don't you remember the fight they had when Glass tried to give himself a raise without telling the congregation anything about it?"

I remembered the incident well. It had been one of the few times I had seen Paw lose his temper, as well as one of the few times I had heard him swear. "So why does Glass think he's getting the house?"

Aunt Maggie ran her fingers through her shock of white hair and shook her head ruefully. "You have your Aunt Edna to thank for that. You know how Glass is always talking about building a new church, and how they need more land?"

I nodded. The church had staged its first fund-raising drive the month Glass came to Byerly, and as soon as one ended, another started. At first Paw and I had dutifully bought the doughnuts and candy bars, but when nothing ever seemed to come of these efforts, we lost our enthusiasm.

Aunt Maggie went on. "He's had his eye on this place for a long time, since we're right next door and all." She glanced out the back window, and I knew she was looking at the back of the church.

"Glass tried to sweet-talk Ellis for the longest time, saying how badly the church needed the land and how little money there was. Ellis might have believed him if it hadn't been for that stunt with Glass's salary. He figured that if there was enough money to pay Glass that much, there was enough to buy land.

"Glass finally took the hint and started trying to get to the house through Edna. I don't know if Edna volunteered to try to talk Ellis into leaving the house to the church or if Glass convinced her to try, but I do know that she talked to Ellis about it more than once."

"Why didn't Paw just tell her 'no'?"

Aunt Maggie shrugged. "You know Ellis. He hates to hurt anyone's feelings. He said he did tell her straight out once, but she didn't pay him any mind. She just kept saying how nice it would be to have a bigger church. Sometimes I think your aunt is a few bricks shy of a load." She took a final drink from the Coke, and placed the empty bottle in the carton next to the refrigerator.

"Let me go see if I can find those things you wanted for Ellis." She started up the stairs just as Uncle Conrad came back inside. "I'll be right back," Aunt Maggie

65

said, eyeing him suspiciously.

Uncle Conrad walked back and forth from the kitchen to the living-room, looking a bit uncomfortable, I thought. "Uncle Conrad? Is there anything wrong?"

"Huh? No, it's just strange being here with Ellis in the hospital and all."

I nodded in agreement, and let him continue his pacing.

It was stuffy in the kitchen. I stood and stretched, and went down the stairs into the basement where Paw spent most of his time. It was just an old root cellar that resisted the summer's heat by virtue of being halfway underground. Paw and my father had tacked up the wood paneling and laid the carpeting themselves. The furniture was cast-offs from the rest of the house, but Paw always was more interested in comfort than looks.

The brown corduroy-covered recliner, its arms covered with tiny burn holes from when Paw had still smoked cigarettes, was in front of the small black-and-white television set. Next to the recliner was the couch, its vivid red and orange floral pattern only slightly dimmed by the years. My grandmother Emma, a cheerful bird of a woman I barely remembered, had made the slipcovers herself out of material purchased from the odd lots sale at the mill, and no one had ever had the heart to tell her that they weren't the most beautiful things they had ever seen. She had finished them just before her death, and I had a hunch Paw kept them to remember her by.

I noticed a newspaper on the couch, and reached for it absently, meaning to put it into the magazine rack. Paw never could abide papers strewn about. Then the lead story caught my eye. The paper was the Sunday edition of the *Byerly Gazette*, and most of the front page was devoted to Melanie Wilson's disappearance. I sat on the arm of the couch to read it.

The facts were pretty much the same as what Aunt Nora and Vasti had told me. The article included a picture of Melanie and a description of what she had been wearing when last seen, and asked for anyone who had seen her to come forward. The paper noted that racial tensions had been high ever since the anonymous phone call, which was no big surprise.

There were heavy footsteps on the stairs. "Laurie Anne?" Uncle Conrad said. "What are you doing down there?"

"Nothing," I said, and put the newspaper in the rack. Then, noticing a carton of pulled socks next to the couch, I said,

"Somebody needs to take those back to the mill."

He nodded, and wandered through the room, picking up the book Paw had left on the coffee-table, flipping through the pad next to the phone, peering into the box of socks. I was starting to get annoyed. Was he another vulture, looking to see if there was anything of value to be had? Finally he shuffled back upstairs.

I went to where a large photo of Paw, Maw, and all six of their girls hung on the wall. Next to it was a later photo, this one of Paw and the six girls, plus assorted husbands and grandchildren, including a pig-tailed and snaggle-toothed version of me. Finally, in a third photo, Paw had his arm around me as a teenager, with the five remaining daughters and their husbands and children. My throat tightened. Please, I prayed silently, don't take Paw away from me, too.

"Laurie Anne? Are you down there?" Aunt Maggie came into the room. "I haven't been in here since I came. It just seems so funny for Ellis not to be here."

Aunt Maggie joined me by the pictures, and, to my surprise, put an arm around my shoulder. We stood there a moment, and then Aunt Maggie sniffed loudly. "That's enough of that," she said. "Come on out of here."

She led the way back to the kitchen. "I found some underwear and a robe, but the only pajamas I could find aren't fitting to wear." She reached into an immense, black pocketbook, and squirmed her hand around for a full minute before bringing forth a tight roll of bills. Then she took my hand, and pressed the money into my palm. "Now you take this and buy your grandfather a decent pair of pajamas."

"I don't need any money," I protested.

"Never mind that. You just take it. Conrad, have you got time to run Laurie Anne up to the Kmart?"

He looked at the clock on the stove, and shook his head. "No ma'am, I need to be getting back to the mill." When Aunt Maggie fixed him with her sternest look, he sputtered a few seconds, blurted, "Bye now," and exited quickly.

Aunt Maggie sniffed after him and said, "Why don't you take Ellis's station wagon, Laurie Anne? It's just sitting there, so you may as well use it while you're in town."

I started to ask if that meant that I wasn't a vulture, but decided not to push my luck. Instead I just said, "Thank you, Aunt Maggie."

"You're planning to stay here at the house, aren't you?"

"If that's all right. And Richard, too."

"I suppose that's all right. Ellis probably wouldn't mind. I have to warn you that I don't have any idea of what shape your room is in. You'll probably need to change the sheets."

"That's fine. By the way, Aunt Nora invited both of us to her house for dinner."

"You go ahead, but I've got an auction to go to. I better give you the number over there, just in case." She scribbled down a name and phone number on a piece of paper and handed it to me, and I stuck it in my pocketbook.

After fending off an offer of gas money, I left for Kmart.

CHAPTER 4

It was still awfully hot, and as soon as I started up the station wagon, I flipped the air-conditioner switch. The only result was a mechanical sigh and a small cloud of dust from the vents. I rolled down the window in resignation and consoled myself with the fact that it would not take long to get to Kmart.

At least the radio worked. As I turned the knob I heard the last few bars of an Alabama song followed by the staccato teletype theme they used to announce the news.

"As the heatwave continues, Hickory police are still searching for a local co-ed, missing since Friday evening. Melanie Wilson, a resident of Byerly and a student at the University of North Carolina at Chapel Hill, was reported missing Friday night when her car was found abandoned on Johnston Road. Her parents, who were expecting the college senior for the weekend, have heard nothing from their daughter since she called to let them know she was leaving Chapel Hill."

The announcer continued, "The police received an anonymous phone call reporting that Miss Wilson was seen in the company of several black males in the Marley area late Friday night. Though the police have been unable to confirm this report and cite the danger of placing too much trust in anonymous phone calls, they are reportedly focusing attention on the streets of Marley.

"The police are asking the caller and anyone else who may have seen Miss Wilson to come forward. She was last seen wearing a green shirt, blue jean shorts, and sneakers, and was carrying a canvas satchel embroidered with a UNC Tarheel.

"In sports —"

I didn't pay much attention to the rest of the broadcast. Melanie had been two years behind me in school, but she was one of those girls that everyone knew. She was a cheerleader, and actually seemed to enjoy the job for the chance to lead cheers rather than as a way to get dates. Not that the boys hadn't noticed her. Half the guys in school had crushes on her at any given time. Thaddeous had been among the many who had never quite found the courage to ask her out.

Poor Melanie. After three days, it didn't seem very likely that she was alive. Her parents had to be going crazy with worry.

Once I got to Kmart, it only took me a couple of minutes to find a pair of pajamas that I thought Aunt Maggie would approve of, but when I approached the long line of cash registers, I saw that only one register was actually serving customers. I sighed and joined the line, wondering why Kmart insisted on that particular combination of red and sea-green to create their corporate image.

The woman in line in front of me looked toward the latest blue light special, checked her watch, and then looked back toward the resister. She looked awfully familiar, and when I tried to get a better look at her, the contents of the woman's shopping cart caught my eye. In it were three dresses, three blouses, three skirts, and three pairs of sandals. Each set was identical except for the colors. That confirmed it — it was one of Aunt Nellie's and Uncle Ruben's daughters.

Unfortunately, I couldn't tell which sister it was. Though I had spent a fair amount of time with the triplets when we were younger, I had always had problems keeping them straight. After a couple of minutes of trying to find some clue, I took a deep breath, comforted myself with the knowledge that I had a one out of three chance, and said, "Odelle?"

The woman looked around wide-eyed, then relaxed her face into a smile when she saw me. "Laurie Anne? I heard you were coming down. It's so good to see you."

I breathed a sigh of relief that I had picked the right name, and we embraced in a manner I knew was partially calculated to preserve Odelle's carefully arranged hairstyle, but none the less sincere.

Together we moved up a stage in the line. "Where are Carlelle and Idelle?" I asked. The three sisters were seldom willingly apart.

"They're up at the mill." She glanced around us as if checking for spies. "Actually, I'm supposed to be there, too. I snuck out at afternoon break so I could get here before everything got bought up. You know how it is with a sale in here — if you don't get here the first day, there's nothing left."

We moved forward another couple of inches. "What are you doing in here, Laurie Anne? Don't they have a Kmart in Boston?"

"Paw needed a new pair of pajamas, and

Aunt Maggie sent me to pick some up."

"Aunt Edna told Mama that Aunt Maggie was staying at the house. Where's that husband of yours?"

We took another step toward the register as I wondered why everybody seemed to think that Richard and I were surgically attached.

"He had a meeting today," I said, "but he's flying down this evening."

"We'll probably see you at the hospital after work. We tried to get time off today, but you know how they are at the mill."

I nodded. "How did you slip out, anyway?"

"They don't know I'm gone. Carlelle, Idelle, and I wore the same color today, and I left my name tag with them. We're working in the dye room today, and it's always such a mess in there that no one's going to realize that there's only two of us instead of three."

"What about the guard at the gate? Didn't you have to sign out with him?"

"Well, not everybody knows this, but there's a hole in the fence at the corner of the back parking lot, just big enough for someone to get through. We parked the car outside the fence this morning, and I waited until there weren't any supervisors around and slipped out as pretty as you please."

"And you'll get back in the same way?" I asked, amused at my cousin's ingenuity.

"I will if I ever get out of this line. If that cashier was moving any slower, she'd be going backwards."

"Let's just say she's not Boston Marathon material," I agreed. We chatted amiably, avoiding mention of Paw, until we were allowed to hand our money to the cheerless cashier. Then I walked Odelle to her car.

"I've got to get back to work, but we'll see you up at the hospital tonight," Odelle said.

"Say hello to Idelle and Carlelle for me."

It was only when I got back into Paw's station wagon that I realized that I probably should have asked Odelle the best way to get back to the hospital. I leaned over and opened the glove compartment, and thumbed through the registration papers and warranties inside. That's funny, I thought. Paw always kept a map in the car. Oh well. Surely I could find my way from Byerly to Hickory without getting too lost.

My memory proved better than I expected, and I found the hospital after only one wrong turn. I left Paw's things with the nurse, then went to the waiting-room.

Aunt Nora was dozing, with her head fallen onto her chest. I lightly touched her forearm. "Aunt Nora?"

Aunt Nora started, then blinked a few times. "Is Paw all right?" she said anxiously.

"The nurse says he's fine."

"Oh good. What time is it?"

I checked my watch. "It's about a quarter to five."

Aunt Nora reached for her bag. "Goodness, I didn't mean to fall asleep. I guess I just drifted off after Ruby Lee and Edna left. How did you get back here?"

I explained and concluded with, "Since I've got Paw's car, we don't have to wake up Willis." We left a note for Aunt Daphine, who was due in at five, and headed for Aunt Nora's and Uncle Buddy's house.

CHAPTER 5

Uncle Buddy's and Aunt Nora's house was a simple ranch-style brick house, but it was in a nice neighborhood and meticulously maintained. "Willis, we're home," Aunt Nora called as we came in the back door. There was a low mumble from upstairs in response.

"He doesn't really get rolling until after supper," Aunt Nora said. She looked around the kitchen and frowned. "I'm pure ashamed for you to see the place like this, Laurie Anne."

I looked around. Almost everything was in perfect order. There were a few dirty dishes, but even these were rinsed and stacked neatly in the sink.

"Here it is after five o'clock and I haven't even touched the breakfast dishes," Aunt Nora fussed. She reached for the calico apron Thaddeous had bought her for Mother's Day when he was in sixth grade, and tied it firmly around her waist.

"Why don't you just put them in the dishwasher?" I asked.

The shiny, white appliance, placed where it could be noticed immediately when someone came in the door, looked as aloof as it had when Uncle Buddy installed it three Christmases ago.

"It wouldn't be worth running it for this few dishes."

"Then why don't you wait until after supper?"

"I've never eaten supper with the breakfast dishes dirty, and I don't mean to start now."

I gave up. There was no use trying to figure out my aunt's brand of logic.

"Is Aunt Maggie coming for dinner?" Aunt Nora asked.

"No, ma'am. She already had plans."

"And Richard won't be here in time either, will he?"

"No, ma'am. His plane isn't due until after eight. I told him to call us at the hospital when he gets in."

The kitchen door opened, and Thaddeous walked in. He looked worn out, and I could well believe he hadn't slept since Thursday night.

"Any word about Paw?" he asked as soon as he got inside.

Aunt Nora shook her head. "We got to see him for a minute this afternoon, but he looked about the same."

He nodded, hung his car keys on a brass rack on the wall, and put his lunch-box and thermos down on the counter. "Mama, is there time for me to take a shower before supper?"

"Plenty of time. You go ahead."

He trudged upstairs, and went into his room for fresh clothes. A few minutes later we heard the shower running.

"Do you want me to dry, Aunt Nora?" I asked as she put the first wet dish into the drain rack.

"That would be a big help." She pulled out a faded blue dish towel from a drawer and handed it to me. "I wonder if Thaddeous remembered the dish towels I asked him to pick up at the company store. Mine are just about worn out."

"I'll go ask him."

I went upstairs past the rows of family photos lining the stairwell, and knocked on the bathroom door. "Thaddeous? Aunt Nora wanted me to ask you about some dish towels."

"They're still in the truck," he called back over the sound of the water. "I'll go get them after I get out of here."

"Okay."

I decided I could save my cousin a few

steps, and went back to the kitchen and said, "He left them in the truck. I'll go get them." I reached for his car keys.

Aunt Nora saw what I was doing and said, "This is Byerly, Laurie Anne, not Boston. I don't imagine he locked the truck."

"I forgot." I went outside, and sure enough, both doors were unlocked. There were two paper bags on the floor of the passenger side, and I pulled out both of them and went back inside.

"Here are the towels," I said as I checked inside one bag.

"Just leave them on the table. What's the other bag?"

I looked inside. "It looks like a sheet." I pulled out one corner of the white muslin and showed it to her.

"A sheet? What in the world did he bring that home for?"

I shrugged. "Maybe he stained the one on his bed and he didn't want to tell you."

"Not hardly. That boy wouldn't notice it if his sheets turned black."

"I'll take it up to his room."

The shower was still going as I went by on the way to Thaddeous's bedroom. It wasn't nearly as messy as I had expected. True, there was a healthy layer of dust and

81

the bed was somewhat sloppily composed, but there was plenty of floor space to get around the stacks of dirty clothes and hunting equipment, and only a few Coke bottles in the corner.

The one thing dust-free was the ancient shotgun hung over the bed. It had belonged to Great-Great-Uncle Thaddeous, Thaddeous's namesake. Family legend said that the elder Thaddeous had been a half-Cherokee drifter hired to help out while most of the townsmen were off fighting for the Confederacy.

When a mess of Yankee soldiers, inspired by Sherman's march through Georgia, decided to burn Byerly, Thaddeous defeated them single-handedly. Not with the shotgun — he didn't win that from Junior Norton's great-great-grandfather until several years later. Instead he approached the soldiers with all the moonshine he could find, and kept pouring it for them until they passed out. Then he went to fetch their colonel, and let the Union Army deal with their own. As a hero, he married the prettiest girl in town, the Nora for whom Aunt Nora was named. Despite its lack of a place in history, Thaddeous revered the weapon, and kept it in perfect shooting condition.

I tossed the bag onto the bed, but somehow managed to spill out the contents onto the floor. I reached for the material to fold it, but noticed that the "sheet" was much lighter than it should have been, nowhere near heavy enough for a double-sized bed sheet. What was it? I shifted it around a couple of times, and finally located what looked like sleeves and held it up as if it were a shirt. Only it was much too long for a shirt, even for Thaddeous. A night-shirt? Thaddeous had never struck me as the type to wear a night-shirt.

I put it down, and looked in the bag. There was another piece of material in there, and I pulled it out. It was pointed on one end, and I found two holes about the right distance apart for eyeholes. A hood?

I swallowed hard. If that was a peaked hood, then the night-shirt was a robe. I only knew of one reason for having a white robe and hood.

Then Thaddeous walked in, I jumped and dropped the hood onto the bed. He saw it and said, "What the hell are you doing with that?"

I suppose I should have been more tactful, but I was too shocked for tact. "Thaddeous, does Aunt Nora know you're in the Klan?"

"Shh . . ." He closed the door quietly, then reached for the robe and the hood. Carefully he folded them, and tucked them onto the shelf of the closet.

"You haven't told her, have you? Good lord, Thaddeous, what are you doing, running with the Ku Klux Klan?"

"What do you know about it?"

I looked at him in disbelief. "Just what everybody with any sense knows! That the Klan's idea of a good time is to spray-paint swastikas on synagogues and to burn crosses on people's yards in the middle of the night."

"It's not like that, Laurie Anne, not now."

"No? Then you tell me what it's like."

"The Klan is our last hope for preserving our way of life," he said, sounding as if he were quoting.

"What way of life is that?"

"We've got a right to keep a job, don't we? Without being undercut by foreigners so bad we can't make a decent wage? We've got a right to make cloth as good as we ever did and be able to sell it, instead of having to close down for two, three weeks every year to save money. We've got a right to have our women drive down the street without being dragged off by a car full of niggers and . . ." His voice caught and he turned away from me.

"Thaddeous, is this because of Melanie? Did you join the Klan because of Melanie?"

He nodded slowly.

"I don't understand."

"I went out with the search parties when they first reported her missing, and I was with them when the report came about that phone call. The one that told us to look in Marley."

I nodded.

"A bunch of us wanted to go down to Marley right then and see what we could find out, but the county police said they'd handle it."

"So?"

"They were black."

"So?" I said more loudly.

"They protect their own, Laurie Anne. Everybody knows that."

At least he came by it honestly — he sounded just like Aunt Nora. "Are you trying to tell me that county policemen covered up a kidnapping just because the kidnappers were black? Did it ever occur to you that they didn't find anything be-cause there wasn't anything to find?"

"Then where's Melanie? I went over that

ground for a couple of miles around where they found her car. There was no sign of her — someone came and took her away."

"But you don't know that that someone was black. Thaddeous, there are a lot of sick people in this world, black and white."

"What about that phone call?"

"If that person really knows something, why doesn't he come forward?"

"We figure he must be black, too, and he's afraid to say anything because of what the others will do to him."

" 'We' meaning the Klan?"

"That's right. A bunch of us in the search party got to talking while we were searching, and a couple of the guys hinted that if the police couldn't find Melanie, maybe the Klan could. They were kind of nervous about me at first, but then they figured out that they could trust me. They're good men, Laurie Anne, men with families. They told me they were going to have a meeting Saturday night and that I should come."

"Don't tell me. They showed *Birth of a Nation*, and told you how much smarter white people are than black people, and explained that the reason this country is going to Hell in a hand basket is because of the mingling of the races. Then they told horror stories about white women getting gang-raped by black men."

He didn't say anything, so I knew my guesses had been pretty close.

"I suppose you signed up right away," I said disdainfully.

"I told them I'd think about it, but I made up my mind last night and paid the dues and picked up my robes this afternoon after work."

"Great! You're making decisions that could affect your whole life when you haven't had a decent night's sleep in days."

"I know what I'm doing."

"No, you don't. Can't you see what they're up to? They're using Melanie as an excuse for a membership drive. They don't care about Melanie. All the Klan cares about is preserving *their* way of life. If you're anything but lily-white and their brand of Christian, they don't have any use for you."

He shook his head in denial, and I saw the stubborn set to his jaw. "Thaddeous, I asked Paw about the Klan once," I said. "He took me downtown, and pointed out that big old oak tree in front of City Hall. He said he used to go by it when he brought fresh eggs into town in the morning. One day he found a black man hanging there. The Klan had lynched him because he registered to vote. I could still see the scar that the rope had left on the tree branch."

"That was a long time ago," Thaddeous protested.

"Hitler killed twelve million people a long time ago, but I still remember it."

He kept shaking his head, not meeting my eyes. "What business is it of yours anyway?"

"You're my family aren't you? I care about you! That makes it my business."

Thaddeous looked at me skeptically, and I knew how he must feel. Usually I would be the last person to pass judgment merely by virtue of being related, but this was different.

Finally he asked, "Are you going to tell Mama?"

I was damn tempted to let Aunt Nora try to talk some sense into him, but I knew he'd never forgive me if I did. "No. Not yet, anyway. I do want you to think long and hard about what you're doing. Do you really want to be involved in something you're ashamed to tell your own mother about?" I looked at the shotgun over his bed. "You know Great-Great-Uncle Thaddeous was half Cherokee."

"So?"

"The Klan wouldn't have let him in." He was staring at the shotgun when I left the room.

CHAPTER 6

I went back down to the kitchen. Aunt Nora had already finished the dishes, started frying pork chops, and put pots of potatoes and snap beans on to boil. From the oven came the unmistakable smell of fresh biscuits.

I inhaled deeply. I had yet to find a restaurant in Boston that served a decent biscuit.

"Is there anything I can do to help, Aunt Nora?"

"Not a thing. I'm so used to doing it by myself I wouldn't know what to ask you to do. How do you find time to cook, what with working all day?"

"We eat out a lot, and we order in a lot of pizza," I said and sat down to watch as Aunt Nora removed potatoes from the stove; drained them; added milk, butter, and salt; and mashed them to a creamy consistency.

"Actually, Richard does most of the cooking," I went on. "He's a better cook than I am."

"Richard cooks?" Aunt Nora asked, and I bristled.

"I work eight hours a day, just like he does. Why shouldn't he cook?"

Aunt Nora laid a hand on my arm. "I'm sorry, I didn't mean to be ugly. In my day women always did the cooking, whether they worked or not. Sometimes I forget things have changed."

I relented. Aunt Nora hadn't meant to offend me. Like she said, she was brought up in a different time.

Uncle Buddy came through the back door just then and put his lunch-box on the counter. Aunt Nora immediately went into high gear, setting the table in a swirl of silverware and china.

"Good to see you, Uncle Buddy," I said.

"Laurie Anne," he said with a nod.

I neither expected nor received a hug. Uncle Buddy was not a demonstrative man.

"How's your Paw, Nora?"

"About the same. They're doing what they can."

He nodded, and went to wash up. Aunt Nora scooped up huge bowls of snap beans and mashed potatoes, placed the last few pork chops on a platter, and slid a baking sheet full of biscuits onto a plate. She hesitated a moment to look over the table, then nodded to herself, satisfied.

"Thaddeous! Willis! Buddy! Are you going to let this food get cold?"

There wasn't much conversation over supper, which was no big surprise. Aunt Nora was worried about Paw. Thaddeous was worried about Paw and Melanie, and, I hoped, thinking about our earlier conversation. Uncle Buddy was never a man to use two words when none would do, and every time I saw Willis, he looked and acted more like his daddy. He did tell me, "Good to see you," when he came into the kitchen.

I had thought that it seemed like an awful lot of food for just the five of us, but I had forgotten just how much my uncle and cousins could eat. Not that I was any slouch myself, I admitted, surveying the ruins of two pork chops on my plate as I used my third biscuit to sop up the last of the potatoes.

"Aunt Nora," I said after swallowing the last bite, "dinner was wonderful."

She said, "Shoot, it wasn't no dinner — it was just something to eat," but she looked pleased.

There was just enough time to clear off the table before we headed for the hospital in Aunt Nora's and Uncle Buddy's Buick. There to greet us was a nearly complete contingent of Burnettes: Aunt Nellie and Uncle Ruben with Idelle, Odelle, and Carlelle; Aunt Daphine with Vasti and Vasti's husband Arthur; Aunt Edna and Uncle Loman; Linwood and Sue; Aunt Ruby Lee and Uncle Conrad with Ruby Lee's children Earl, Clifford, and Ilene. Burnettes had filled the waiting-room to the brim, and were spilling into the hallway. Of course I had to speak to everyone I hadn't seen yet, and exchange hugs.

Uncle Ruben and Aunt Nellie had that familiar distracted look which would have told me that they were in trouble again even if Aunt Nora hadn't mentioned it earlier. They were such a Mutt-and-Jeff couple. Uncle Ruben was small and slight of build, and with those wire-rimmed glasses and soft blue eyes, didn't look much like a rampaging entrepreneur.

Aunt Nellie did look the part. I was sure that those jewel-green slacks and blouse patterned with a peacock feathers design would look awful on most women, but she had the height to carry it off and the colors set off her fair skin and nearly black hair dramatically.

Looks aside, they were two of a kind

when it came to financial boondoggles. Ever since they had gotten married, they had stumbled from one catastrophe to another. They had bought swampland in Florida, indulged in pyramid schemes, even once spent over a hundred dollars printing copies of a chain letter by which they would make their fortune.

Aunt Daphine, a tall brunette with unforgettable cheekbones, was the other side of the coin. Her beauty parlor had been a success from the beginning, and she had always made a good living for herself and Vasti. Of course, she had only had herself to depend on. Aunt Daphine had eloped with John Ward Marston just before he left to fight in Vietnam. He died during his first battle, never knowing that Aunt Daphine was already pregnant with Vasti.

I had just got started visiting cousins when a middle-aged doctor in a white lab coat went into Paw's room. No one spoke as we waited for him to come out. He conferred with a nurse, and then came toward Aunt Nora.

"Mrs. Crawford? We spoke earlier today."

"Good to see you, Doctor Mason." Aunt Nora introduced her sisters and their husbands and then asked, "How is he?"

The doctor hesitated a moment, and I knew I didn't want to hear what he had to say. "There's not a lot I can tell you. Mr. Burnette is very weak. Between the blow to the head, and the heart attack, and his age . . . I really can't offer much hope."

There was silence for an interminable time, then Aunt Ruby Lee and Aunt Edna broke into tears. It was all I could do to keep from crying myself. Only Aunt Daphine retained enough composure to say, "We appreciate what you're doing, Doctor."

He nodded, and said, "You can see him now. Just two at a time, please, and try to keep it short."

Part of me wanted to go in there with Paw and stay no matter what the doctor said, and part of me didn't want to go in at all. I settled for going in with Aunt Daphine when our turn came.

Paw looked even worse than he had that afternoon. He didn't say anything, but he smiled faintly when Aunt Daphine and I lied about how much better he looked. I wasn't sure if I should bring up what he had said that afternoon or not, but I felt like I might not get another chance. "Paw," I said, "do you remember what happened to you?"

Aunt Daphine tried to catch my eye,

probably to get me to change the subject, but I ignored her. "Do you remember what you said to me this afternoon?"

He looked so confused it nearly broke my heart. I could see he was trying to remember, but he just couldn't.

"It's all right, Paw. It's not important. You just get some rest." He nodded, and seemed to relax.

"We love you, Paw," Aunt Daphine said for us both when the nurse came to usher us out.

"What was that about?" Aunt Daphine asked as soon as we were out of the room.

I hesitated. What could I say? I think someone attacked Paw? "I'll tell you later," was all I could come up with.

Willis had to leave for work after that, but no one else seemed to want to go home, and soon clusters of quietly talking Burnettes formed. The sisters gathered together, as usual, and the cousins divided by age groups. The uncles split into two camps. Uncle Ruben took Uncle Buddy aside to fill him in on the details of his latest scheme, and Uncle Conrad and Uncle Loman sat together without saying much at all. I didn't quite know where I fit in. Did I look as alien to them as they looked to me?

All I could think about was what Paw had said to me that afternoon. I replayed the whole thing in my head over and over again and I knew I had heard him right, but it still didn't make sense. Aunt Nora had said that the guard at the mill had called Aunt Edna and Uncle Loman first. Maybe they knew something I didn't. Aunt Edna was surrounded by sisters, but Uncle Loman had just stepped into the hall alone to smoke a cigarette. I went to join him.

"Uncle Loman?"

"What do you need?"

"Aunt Nora told me that you and Aunt Edna were the first ones they called last night."

"That's right."

"Did anyone say anything about the police? I mean, did the police come to investigate Paw's accident or anything?"

"What for? Plain to see it was an accident."

"I thought they would have wanted to look things over. For insurance, maybe. Don't they have to check out things like this?"

"Haw haw haw!" boomed a voice from behind me, and I turned to see Linwood.

"Damned if you ain't gone and turned into a Yankee," he said, grinning. "You people got to call the police every time you stub your toe, don't you?"

I reddened.

Linwood stuck his head back in the waiting-room and called out, "Hey Earl! Did you hear that? Laurie Anne wants the police to come 'investigate' Paw's accident."

"What on earth for?" Aunt Edna asked with some irritation.

"I didn't say that," I began. "I only asked —"

"Hey Daddy," Linwood said to Uncle Loman, "Maybe we should call in the FBI."

"How about the National Guard?" Earl suggested.

"No, I got it. We'll call Augustus and tell him to bring the Army. Haw, haw!"

I looked behind me and saw that half of the Burnette clan was laughing, and the other half was looking annoyed. I counted to ten, and then repeated the process in binary. It didn't help.

"Excuse me," I said to no one in particular, and nearly ran for the ladies' room.

CHAPTER 7

Damn, damn, damn! I faced my reflection in the ladies' room mirror, commanding the tears to stay away. I am a grown woman. I've got a husband and a home and I'm one hell of a computer programmer. I am *not* going to cry! Not this time!

Linwood had always delighted in tormenting the cousins, especially the girls. I had been a favorite target. I remembered how he had stood outside the bathroom window to watch me trying to put on makeup for the first time. He had kept quiet at first, but when I tried to apply the false eyelashes, he started that horrible "haw haw" of his. If embarrassing me in private hadn't been bad enough, he then had to entertain every family gathering for the next six months with the ever-growing tale of my trying to "glue caterpillars onto my eyelids."

I heard the bathroom door open and fled into a stall. May as well use the bathroom while I'm in here, I thought in resignation. Afterward, I remained seated for a few minutes, hoping that whoever it was would leave. No such luck. I finally put my clothes in order and went out of the stall.

Aunt Daphine was waiting for me. "Are you all right?" she asked.

"Just dandy," I answered, and went to the sink to wash my hands.

"You know Linwood doesn't mean any harm."

"Oh no, he only insults and embarrasses me because he's glad to see me."

"Linwood's always been that way, you know that."

"All too well."

"Why were you asking about the police anyway? Since when do the police investigate an accident? Nora said that you thought someone hit Paw. Is that what you were asking him about?"

I ripped a paper towel from the dispenser and dried my hands. "I don't know what I'm asking about, Aunt Daphine." I told her what Paw had said before, and finished up with, "I know it sounds crazy, but I just want to be sure that it really was an accident. That's all."

"Don't you think it's all a little far-fetched? I know you've got a good imagination —"

"I did not imagine what Paw said, and I

100

didn't hear him wrong! He said someone hit him."

Though she seemed a bit taken aback by my vehemence, Aunt Daphine nodded. "Then I guess that's what he said. But you know that when people are sick they're liable to say all kinds of things."

"I know."

"Once when Vasti was running a high fever, she kept saying that there was a giant spider trying to get in the window."

"Did you check to see if Linwood was around?"

Aunt Daphine chuckled. "I never thought of that. Anyway, the point is that Paw is on all kinds of drugs and most likely doesn't know what he's saying. He could be remembering something that happened years ago. He was in a car accident once, so maybe he's remembering that. And once he told us about how a couple of union-busters beat him up. That might be what he's talking about. There's no way of knowing."

"You're probably right. I just wanted to make sure, to do something."

"I wish I could do something, too, but it's out of our hands."

I knew what she was saying. She thought that I was so desperate to help Paw that I was making something out of nothing. Maybe she was right. I couldn't remember a time I had felt so helpless.

"Maybe you should just leave it alone, at least for now," Aunt Daphine said. "This isn't really the time or place to stir up trouble."

"I'm not trying to stir up trouble. That may be what Linwood thinks, but I'm not."

"I know you're not."

"Aunt Daphine, why is Linwood like that?"

"I expect he just wants attention. He's always had a mean streak, but what can we do? He's family, after all."

"Well, what am I?" I said. "Everyone always says not to let Linwood worry me because he's family, and not to mind Vasti's little cuts because she's family, but I'm family, too, aren't I?" I bit my lip, fighting back tears again.

"Of course you're family!" Aunt Daphine said firmly. "It's just that you're right much different from your cousins, and I don't think Linwood knows how to take you. Sometimes, I don't think any of us know how to take you."

I studied our images in the mirror, and to me the family resemblance was plain, especially around our eyes. What's to take?

I realized I had been shredding my paper towel into bits the whole time we were talking, and I tossed the remains into the trash can. "We better get on back," I said unenthusiastically.

Aunt Daphine put her arm around me as we went back to the waiting-room. Linwood was in a corner with Sue, Earl, and Ilene, and I heard him say, "I swear, I thought it was a caterpillar, one of those big, black ones." I stiffened, and thought longingly of Boston.

"Linwood," Aunt Daphine said, "the nurses said for you to keep it down a little. The noise is disturbing the patients."

"Yes, ma'am," he said, and went on in a lower tone. I looked at her questioningly. When had she spoken to a nurse? Aunt Daphine glanced around to make sure no one else was watching, then solemnly winked at me.

Aunt Daphine rejoined her sisters while I found an unoccupied chair in a relatively quiet corner and leaned back, trying not to think about what Paw had said and wondering if the day would ever end.

CHAPTER 8

I had nearly drifted into sleep when I heard a delightfully familiar voice ask, "Have you got room for one more in there?"

"Well look what the cat dragged in," Aunt Daphine said with a grin. Richard came into the waiting-room and gave me the best hug I had had all day.

"God, I missed you," I said. My husband looked a little worse for wear, but I could not think of a time when his lanky frame, strong-featured face, and ill-behaved mop of dark brown hair had looked better to me.

"How did you get here? I thought you were going to call from the airport?" I asked.

"I rented a car," he explained. "What's the good word?"

I guess my expression told it all. He pulled me closer, and I buried my face in his chest, this time not trying to hold back the tears. The rest of the Burnettes tactfully looked elsewhere until I pulled away and blew my nose on a frayed wad of tissues Richard produced from his blue jeans pocket.

I wanted to tell him about what Paw had said, but like Aunt Daphine had said, this was neither the time nor the place. "I should probably let you say hello to people," I said.

"That would be nice."

"You do remember who everyone is, don't you?"

He drew himself up with dignity. "Madame, I can name all of the major characters in every one of Shakespeare's plays, and most of the minor ones. This is a breeze."

He really did know everyone's name, although once or twice he got confused about which cousin belonged with which aunt and uncle.

We Burnettes mingled quietly for the next few hours, not referring to the reason for our vigil other than an occasional glance in the direction of Paw's room. It was well after midnight before Aunt Daphine finally said in mock exasperation, "This is just silly! Some of you people have got to go home!" There were sheepish grins all around, and people started to filter down the stairs and into cars.

"Y'all may as well go on back to Paw's

house," Aunt Nora said to me. "I know you're tired from your trip, and you can let Aunt Maggie know what's what."

"Don't you want Richard and me to keep you company?" I protested, torn between exhaustion and not wanting to be away from Paw.

"Daphine is going to stay with me, and Nellie will spell us in the morning. We'll call if there's any news."

"You be sure to." I hugged whoever was handy, and let Richard lead me to the Toyota he had rented.

"You better drive," I said to Richard. "I don't trust myself behind the wheel at this point."

"Happy to oblige," he said, opening the door for me. "Just point me in the right direction."

"For a start, turn left from the parking lot. How did your meeting go?"

"Thumbs up. Harper thinks my new course idea is wonderful. He said, and I quote, 'A course on Shakespeare in popular culture is just what we need to get these illiterate boors through their English requirements.' "

"I guess that's a compliment," I said doubtfully. "Turn right."

"Anyway, he wants me to put together a

syllabus immediately."

"Isn't it too late for next semester?"

"That's what I thought, but apparently one of our senior faculty members has a book to finish and wants to bow out of a course she was supposed to teach. I get to rush into the breach."

"That's wonderful. Now turn onto the highway."

He obeyed and said, "Did you see Paw?"

"Twice. Once this afternoon, and then for a minute this evening. Richard, he didn't hardly look like himself."

He nodded sympathetically.

I spent a few minutes guiding him through a potentially confusing set of exits and turns, and then said, "There's something else." I wasn't real eager to talk about it. What if he didn't believe me either? "You remember that when Aunt Nora called me this morning, she said that Paw had been in an accident at the mill."

"Right."

"When I saw Paw this afternoon, he told me that it wasn't an accident. He said that someone hit him. On purpose."

"Who?"

"I don't know. That's all he could get out before the nurse made me leave." I looked at his face for signs of disbelief, but was reassured to see only concern.

I went on. "Everyone else thinks it was an accident. I tried to tell Aunt Nora and Aunt Daphine about it, but they kept saying that it must have been the drugs talking. When I asked Uncle Loman if the police had looked into it, Linwood made a huge joke out of it, and everyone just stared at me. I don't know what they thought I was trying to do. Just trying to stir up trouble, I guess."

"Poor Laura. I'm sorry I didn't get here sooner," he said, reaching over to rub my shoulder.

"You'd think that I'd be used to my family not understanding me after all this time," I said sadly.

"Let me get this straight," Richard said. "Someone tried to kill your grandfather, and you're the only one who believes it. Except the attempted murderer, of course."

I looked at him in surprise, but he was serious. "I hadn't thought of it that way — as murder. I just thought someone wanted to hurt him."

"From what you told me of his condition, whoever did that was trying to kill him."

I shivered, and slid closer to him on the

seat. "That's crazy! Why would anyone want to kill Paw?"

"Why does anyone kill anyone?"

We pulled up in front of Paw's house, and trudged inside, lugging our suitcases.

There was no sign of Aunt Maggie, so I scribbled a note about Paw's condition and left it on the kitchen table. My old bedroom was a little dusty, but I was in no condition to be picky. After I sniffed the sheets to make sure they weren't too musty, we crawled into bed.

"I don't know what to *do*," I said once the lights were out. "I don't think I should go to the police, not after the way everyone reacted tonight, and I really don't have anything to tell them. But I can't just go on like he never said anything."

" 'The tongues of dying men enforce attention like deep harmony,' " Richard quoted. "*King Richard II*, Act I, Scene 1."

I winced at the word "dying" and said, "Eloquent, but not very useful."

"Sorry. I can't help it."

I swallowed hard. "If Paw dies and we don't do something, his murderer is going to get away with it. Richard, what are we going to do?"

He rubbed his eyes wearily. "I don't know, but I do know that there's nothing we can do tonight. Maybe some of this will make sense in the morning."

"You're right. Good night."

"Good night, Laura."

"Oh, say that again."

"Good night?"

"No, the Laura part. Say it for me a few times."

"Laura, Laura, Laura, Laura," he said in a variety of voices ranging from the tender to the husky to a decent Mickey Mouse imitation.

"That's better," I sighed.

"I still think that if you asked them, your family would call you Laura instead of Laurie Anne."

"No they wouldn't. Aunt Daphine would try, and Aunt Nora would call me, 'Laurie A— Laura,' but the others would just say I was trying to put on airs. There's no worse sin around here than putting on airs."

I was nearly asleep when I remembered the news I hadn't told him about. "Richard, are you asleep yet?"

"Yes."

"I forgot to tell you. Thaddeous joined the Ku Klux Klan." I was asleep before he could react.

CHAPTER 9

For just a moment when the sun poured through the window the next morning and woke me up, I forgot what year it was. I was fifteen again and school was nearly out for the year and I had a whole summer of glorious reading and dreaming ahead of me. Then I felt Richard stir beside me, and remembered that one of the dreams had already come true. Being married to Richard was even more fun than I had hoped.

When I first got to Massachusetts, every man I met was exciting merely by virtue of not being from Byerly. The problem was I never could picture myself bringing one of those fellows home to meet Paw and the rest of the Burnettes. It wasn't that he wouldn't have liked them or they wouldn't have liked him. I just couldn't put the two pieces together. With Richard it was different. Despite his Harvard education and Northern accent and his habit of quoting Shakespeare, when it came down to it, he was just plain folks.

I smiled and stroked his shoulder. It was

so odd being with him here, in the room that had been my refuge for so many years. Then I remembered why we were here, and my smile faded.

From downstairs I heard the phone ring, and then movement and a low murmur as Aunt Maggie answered it. Maybe it was news about Paw. I climbed out of bed, careful not to disturb Richard, and rummaged in my suitcase until I found my bathrobe.

Aunt Maggie, already dressed in jeans and a red tank top, was still on the phone when I came into the kitchen.

"Well Nora, I can't say that I'm surprised," she said with a sad nod. "I had pretty much given up hope already."

I stopped and stared at her.

"When are they going to have the funeral?"

It was true. Paw *had* died.

I must have made some noise, because Aunt Maggie turned toward me. She looked at me sharply, and must have realized what I had heard because she shook her head vigorously and mouthed the words, "Melanie Wilson."

Thank God, I thought in relief, and then felt a sharp stab of guilt. Don't be silly, I told myself. I was sorry about Melanie, but

Paw was my grandfather.

I found a glass and got some water while Aunt Maggie finished her phone call.

"I didn't mean to scare you like that," she said after she hung up, "but I didn't know you were behind me."

"That's all right," I said shakily. "What happened to Melanie?"

She grimaced. "She was raped and murdered. They found her early this morning in a Dumpster in Marley."

"Jesus! Do they have any idea of who did it?"

"Not yet. They're still trying to find that phone caller who told them where to look. Whoever it is must know something."

"Probably so," I agreed.

"I'm surprised they hadn't found her sooner, what with the heat and all," Aunt Maggie continued in a matter-of-fact voice. "I don't suppose they'll be having an open casket ceremony for her."

I swallowed hard. The picture Aunt Maggie was conjuring up wasn't pleasant. "Did Aunt Nora say anything about Paw?" I asked, partially to change the subject.

She shook her head. "She said the doctor had just been in with Ellis, but he was about the same."

I looked at the clock over the stove. It

was after ten. "She's not still at the hospital, is she?"

"No, she's finally gone home. I think Nellie is at the hospital now, and Ruby Lee's going to take a turn this afternoon."

"Good. Aunt Nora is going to run herself into the ground if someone doesn't make her get some sleep."

"I know it. I told her to get right into bed after I hung up, but she said she wanted to cook a ham for the Wilsons so they won't have to worry about cooking."

I sighed. That was Aunt Nora. Her own father was in the hospital, but she still had time to do something for a family in trouble. "Doesn't she ever rest?" I asked.

"Not since I've known her. I used to have the girls over to spend the night with me once in a while, and every time Nora came she wanted to clean everything."

"How did you get her to stop?"

"Why would I want her to stop? That's the only time my place got clean. Are you hungry?"

"A little," I admitted.

"There's not a thing to eat in the house, so I thought I'd run up to Hardee's and pick us up some sausage biscuits. Would that be all right?"

"Sounds wonderful."

Aunt Maggie picked up her pocketbook and said, "I'll be back in a few minutes."

After she left, I went back upstairs to take a shower and put on shorts and a raspberry-pink, short-sleeved blouse. I decided against using a blow-drier. It was already getting hot, and my shoulder-length hair would dry on its own pretty quickly.

I went back to the kitchen and turned on the radio to listen to while waiting for breakfast. The news report verified what Aunt Maggie had told me about Melanie, and added that the police were making an extra effort to defuse racial tensions.

Tensions my tail end. Even people who weren't in the Klan were going to be in a stew about this. Murder and rape were bad enough, but I couldn't think of anything that would rouse people more than the idea of a black man raping a white girl, and pretty much everyone who lived in Marley was black. I wondered what Thaddeous was going to think now.

Aunt Maggie arrived then, carrying sausage biscuits and orange juice. "I got the paper," she said, "but I guess it was too late when they found the body to get anything into this edition."

"Too bad," I said, but I didn't mean it. Reading about a murder was not the best

way to get enjoyment out of a sausage biscuit, and as long as it had been since I had
had one, I intended to enjoy it.

I opened up a biscuit, bit a corner of a
mustard packet, and squeezed a good-
sized dollop onto the patty of steaming
sausage. Then I put the biscuit back together and gloated over it just for a minute
before biting into it.

It was wonderful. I sighed, and then saw
that Aunt Maggie was watching me with a
wide grin.

"Are you enjoying that, Laurie Anne?"

"They don't have sausage biscuits in
Boston," I explained sheepishly.

"What do they eat in the morning?"

"Muffins and donuts mostly. They're
good, but it's not the same."

"I never could abide anything sweet in
the morning," Aunt Maggie said. "They
don't have grits up there either, do they?"

I shook my head. "Grits I can kind of
understand. They're an acquired taste.
When Richard tried them, he said they
tasted like buttered sand."

"I'd have asked him what he was doing
eating sand," Aunt Maggie said with a
sniff.

I grinned. "That's exactly what I said.
Then I ate his share."

"That'll learn him. Where is he, anyway?"

"Still in bed. I thought I'd let him sleep in."

Aunt Maggie finished her biscuit, wadded up the wrapper, and tossed it across the room into the trash can. "Well, I can't be sitting around here all day. Today's the day they get in the new shipment at the Thrift Store, and I've got to get there early if I want to get anything good." The Salvation Army Thrift Store was a major source of the items Aunt Maggie sold at the flea market.

"Are you going to the hospital?" she asked.

"Yes, ma'am."

"I'll call to check on Ellis later," Aunt Maggie said. She stepped out the front door, and then turned around. "Where's Ellis's station wagon?"

I had forgotten all about it. "I left it at Aunt Nora's last night."

She looked at me without speaking.

"We'll go get it and bring it back here."

She nodded. "All right then. Bye."

As soon as she was gone I looked back into the Hardee's bag. There were three biscuits left. I ate another, and looked longingly at the two remaining. Stop that, I

117

told myself firmly. Richard was going to be hungry, too. I decided I better wake him up before I lost out to temptation.

When I got back to my room, I found Richard approaching consciousness, so I kissed him in appropriate spots to speed the process.

"Mmmm. . . . That beats an alarm clock any day," he said, reaching for me. "Why are you dressed?"

"I've been up for ages," I said haughtily. "Country folk don't spend all day in bed like you city slickers."

"Then you obviously don't understand the virtues of spending time in bed." He took a moment to demonstrate his meaning.

"Maybe city living isn't so bad," I said, once I was able to speak.

"Any word about Paw?"

I shook my head. "Aunt Nora called a while ago, but she said there had been no change." He squeezed me tightly, and after a moment I said, "Are you hungry? Aunt Maggie brought some sausage biscuits."

"And you left me some? What devotion."

I stuck my tongue out at him. "You better get moving or I'll change my mind." He raced me for the kitchen, but I graciously let him win.

I kept him company during breakfast, then called the hospital while he took a shower. The hospital connected me with the nurse's station on Paw's floor, and the nurse there called Aunt Nellie to the phone.

"Aunt Nellie? This is Laura. I was just wondering how Paw's doing."

"About the same."

"Oh." It wasn't that I had expected a miraculous recovery, but I had been hoping for some improvement. "How are you doing?"

"All right, I guess." There was a pause. "Laurie Anne, do you know anything about how they run hospitals?"

"No, ma'am."

"I was just thinking that as shiny as they keep all these floors, they must go through an awful lot of floor polish."

"I imagine they do," I said with some amusement, remembering Aunt Nellie's and Uncle Ruben's latest scheme. "You might try tracking down one of the janitors and asking him who's in charge of buying supplies."

"That's a good idea! I better go now. Bye."

I was still grinning over Aunt Nellie's entrepreneurial spirit when I went back up-

119

stairs to wait for Richard.

It was the first chance I had had to really look around my old bedroom. The furniture was different from when I had lived there, because Paw had given me all my stuff to take to Boston, but the walls were still covered with the maps I had collected as a teenager. There was one of Middle Earth and another of Narnia, but the rest I had pulled out of *National Geographic*. Back then, the real-life lands had seemed just as fantastic to me as the imaginary ones.

My favorite map was the huge map of the world Paw had given me for Christmas one year. I had stuck blue push pins into the location of every place I wanted to go, and then replaced the blue pins with red ones when I actually got a chance to go there. I had marked Boston in red after my first semester at MIT, but it had been years since I had updated the map.

I opened the top drawer on the dresser, and sure enough, the two plastic boxes of push pins were still there. I was cheerfully replacing blue pins with red ones when Richard came back in, wrapped in a towel.

"What are you doing?"

I explained the method to my madness.

"Don't forget London," he said.

"I got that one first off." We had spent our honeymoon in England. "I got Stratford-on-Avon, too."

"What about Newark?" he asked.

"We've only been in the airport, so that doesn't count. Besides, I'm not sure I want to admit going to Newark."

He helped me pick out Chicago; New York; Orlando; Washington, DC; and New Orleans.

"I'd say we've done pretty well in three years of marriage."

"I'm surprised you left all these maps here," Richard said as he pulled on jeans and a Harvard T-shirt. "Why didn't you bring them with you to Boston?"

I considered it a moment. "There are two times I look at a map: to see where I'm going, and to see where I've been. I put these up so I could dream about where I was going. I guess I left them here so that when I come home I can see where I've been."

I checked my watch and saw that it was nearly eleven-thirty. "Are you about ready to head out?"

"Lead on, MacDuff."

"That's not a real quote — it doesn't count."

"Pretty swift for a computer pro-grammer."

I elbowed him gently in the ribs and said, "We've got to run by Aunt Nora's place to pick up Paw's station wagon and bring it back. I think Aunt Maggie is afraid I sold it."

"Whatever you say."

I explained about vultures on the way to Aunt Nora's house. It was a bright day outside, and that bothered me. It didn't seem right that everyone was going about their business same as ever while Paw was in the hospital. And what he had said kept sneaking into my head.

"Richard . . ." I said, and then stopped.

"You're still worried about whether or not someone tried to kill Paw."

I nodded. "This is crazy. What do I do?"

Richard shrugged. "Maybe we're worrying about nothing. When Paw recovers, he'll be able to explain everything."

The problem was, I thought unhappily, it wasn't a *when*. It was an *if*.

CHAPTER 10

"Do you want to go inside?" Richard asked when we got to Aunt Nora's house.

"For a minute, anyway."

I tapped lightly on the kitchen door, and opened it when I heard Aunt Nora call, "Come in." The kitchen smelled heavenly, and I saw Aunt Nora was wrapping a fresh-baked ham in aluminum foil. She stopped long enough to give us both hugs, and I explained why we were there.

"Is that ham for the Wilsons?" I asked.

She nodded. "You must have heard about Melanie."

"Aunt Maggie told me. How did Thaddeous take it?"

"About like you'd expect," she said. "Didn't say much, but he didn't eat a bite of breakfast."

Poor Thaddeous. Unrequited or not, he had loved that girl.

"I told him he ought to stay home from work," Aunt Nora continued, "but he went in anyway."

"Talk about the pot calling the kettle

black," I said. "You should be in bed, not in the kitchen."

"I'll take a nap as soon as I get back. I was just getting ready to change clothes and run this ham over to the Wilsons."

"I'm afraid not," Richard said. "As a doctor, I'll have to insist that you get some rest. Laura and I are quite capable of delivering a ham."

Aunt Nora opened her mouth as if to protest, shut it again, and then said, "Well, if you're sure you don't mind."

"We're sure," I said, as I untied her apron, took it from her, and pushed her toward the stairs.

"All right," she said, "but Richard, since when does being a doctor of literature give you the say-so to tell people when to go to sleep?"

He drew himself up haughtily. "Madame, men and women of my profession have put thousands of students to sleep over the years. I consider myself admirably qualified."

She was still chuckling as we carried the ham out to the car.

I let Richard drive the air-conditioned rental car and led the way to the Wilsons' house, just a five-minute drive away. He parked behind me on the street and I waited for him to join me.

"Do I look all right?" I asked doubtfully. Shorts didn't seem very appropriate for a condolence call.

"You look fine," he said. "Besides, we're just going to leave the ham and go, so they probably won't even notice what you're wearing."

I nodded, and rang the doorbell. After a moment, Mrs. Wilson opened the door. Her face was so swollen from crying that I barely recognized her. She hesitated for a moment, and then said, "It's Laurie Anne, isn't it?"

"Yes, ma'am." I was surprised she remembered me. "My aunt, Nora Crawford, sent this over." Richard held out the platter. "Mrs. Wilson, this is my husband Richard Fleming."

"I'm pleased to meet you, Richard. Why don't y'all come in for a minute?" She turned, and after looking at each other helplessly, we followed her inside.

Mr. Wilson was an engineer in Hickory, and their house was nicer than most of those in Byerly. The floor of the living-room she led us to was carpeted in pale blue and the couch and chair were uphol-stered in a matching floral pattern. The coffee-table was shiny and bare, and I could tell that they almost never used the room.

Mrs. Wilson sat in the chair, and Richard and I sat on the couch. When she didn't offer to take it from him, Richard put the ham in his lap.

"It was very nice of you to come by," Mrs. Wilson said. "I know you have your own troubles about now. How is Mr. Burnette?"

"He's not doing very well, I'm afraid," I said.

"I am sorry."

There was a pause, and I honestly didn't know what to say. I had always left condolence calls to the grownups. "I was very sorry to hear about Melanie," I finally said. "She was a very nice young woman."

"Thank you," she said. "Melanie thought a lot of you, too."

Had she? I hadn't known her all that well.

"I think you inspired her," Mrs. Wilson went on. "None of her girlfriends were planning to go on to college, but when she heard about how well you were doing up in Boston, she decided she wanted to go, too."

Funny, I didn't feel like much of an inspiration. I just felt awkward, and now I wished I had taken the time to get to know Melanie better. Come to think of it, where were Melanie's friends? She had always been popular in school.

As if she had guessed my train of thought, Mrs. Wilson said, "I suppose she lost track of most of those girls when she went away."

I nodded, wishing I could think of a way to get out of there gracefully.

"Have the police found out anything more?" I asked. I wasn't real sure it was polite to ask, under the circumstances, but I didn't have anything else to say.

Mrs. Wilson must have been used to such inquiries, because she just shook her head slowly. "Even before they found her, they came and asked all kinds of questions, but I couldn't tell them much. I'm sure Melanie couldn't have known the man who did this to her, but they kept asking about the boys she dated." She hesitated. "You don't suppose that's scared people off, do you?"

"Ma'am?"

"Being afraid they'd be involved somehow, I mean. I guess that's why no one much has come by. Wallace and I don't have any family in town, but I thought that some of the neighbors would have been over. Everyone was so nice before they found her, but now that we know for sure, it's been very quiet. Other than reporters. I guess people don't know how to act after someone's been . . . After someone dies like that."

Richard said, "Maybe they thought you would rather have the time alone."

The front door opened just then, and Mr. Wilson came in, looking ten years older than when I had seen him last. I introduced Richard, and he shook our hands and finally took the ham into the kitchen. We took the opportunity to escape.

"Can you believe that?" I fumed as soon as we got outside. "It's not bad enough that people blame the victim for a rape. Now they're blaming the family, too."

"Maybe they just wanted to give them time alone," Richard said again.

"Baloney! If Melanie had died in a car crash, that house would be filled with people trying to comfort Mrs. Wilson. But because she was raped, they think it's going to rub off or something. Sanctimonious SOB's!"

"Calm down," Richard said, taking my hand. "They'll hear you."

I took a breath, held it, and then let it out slowly. "You're right. I'm just so mad I could spit."

He stepped back in mock alarm, and I had to smile. "It's just a figure of speech, Richard."

"Another colorful Southernism, no doubt." I was itching to get back to the hospital, but it would have been silly to drive two cars all the way to Hickory. With luck, we could drive to Paw's, drop off one of the cars, and be at the hospital within the hour.

"Let's get back to the house," I said. "You can follow me."

"I know the way."

I looked at him doubtfully. "Are you sure? It's kind of tricky from here."

"Compared to Boston? This is a piece of cake."

I shrugged. "You asked for it. I'll wait for you at the house."

"Madame, are you impugning my driving ability? I'll just take that challenge! I'll be waiting for *you* at the house."

"Is that so?" I said.

His answer was to hop back into the rental car and race the motor while I got into the station wagon. Silly fellow, I thought. I grew up in Byerly, and I knew every shortcut. Besides, since the station wagon wasn't air-conditioned, I had added inducement.

CHAPTER 11

I knew that Richard was just trying to get my mind off of Paw and Melanie when he suggested the race, but I had every intention of beating him back to Paw's anyway.

Richard would no doubt be going back the way we had come, passing Aunt Nora's house, and then getting back onto Main Street, I, on the other hand, knew that if I turned right onto Garner Street, I could miss three stop lights and pick up Main Street further down. By the time Richard got there, I would be sitting on the porch drinking iced tea.

Unfortunately, there was a lot more traffic on Garner Street than I had expected. You'd think it was Boston. What on earth could be causing such congestion at this time of the afternoon? When I reached the turn-off that should have taken me to Main Street, I saw that it was so locked up I couldn't make the turn. I went a block further and turned.

There was only one car between me and Main Street, but it was stopped. Remembering that laying down on the horn wasn't considered polite in North Carolina, I resisted the impulse. Instead I stuck my head out the window and saw that the intersection was blocked by bright yellow sawhorses.

I turned off the engine and got out of the station wagon, and went up to the car in front of me. The driver had his window rolled down and was looking at a newspaper.

"Excuse me," I said. "What's going on?"

"The KKK's marching," he said with an expression of distaste.

"What for?"

"They claim the police are dragging their feet in that Wilson girl's murder investigation to protect the blacks. This is supposed to be a show of strength." He snorted. "According to the radio, they've got Main Street blocked halfway to Hickory so we can't go around."

He turned back to his newspaper.

That was just great! No one could go sit with Mrs. Wilson, but they could put on those silly hoods and march down the middle of town. Only the Ku Klux Klan would use a murder to try to drum up support. Knowing the Klan, I wouldn't have been surprised if they had killed Melanie themselves just to provide an excuse to recruit new members.

Well if they thought I was going to stand in the hot sun and watch grown men parading around in bed sheets, they had another think coming. I went back and sat determinedly in the station wagon.

A state police car drove slowly past on Main Street, lights flashing, and several other state troopers came by on foot. I didn't like it. Although I supposed it was necessary for the police to keep an eye out to prevent violence, it still smacked of their condoning the Klan's activities. Seeing two men go by with television cameras on their shoulders didn't help my mood any, either. Media attention was what the Klan wanted.

A minute after the police car passed by, a pair of Klansmen walked by carrying a banner identifying themselves in glittering letters as the Knights of the Ku Klux Klan, as if their outlandish costumes weren't enough. They were followed by what I had to admit was a well-trained troop of Klansmen marching neatly in step. The men looked straight ahead, despite the catcalls and taunts from people walking along beside them. More police officers made sure no one did anything drastic.

I was glad to see that there were a lot more people taunting than there were Klansmen marching. I was tempted to join in and tell the Klansmen exactly what I thought of them, but Paw had always said, "Men like that, they only want attention. Just don't pay them any mind."

The march went on for some time, and I started to wonder if the Klan hadn't brought in ringers from other towns. Surely there weren't that many Klansmen in Byerly. Finally the march ended as it had begun, with a slowly moving state police car accompanied by officers on foot. Two of the officers stopped long enough to move the sawhorses out of the way and wave us through.

Finally! I turned onto Main Street. I still wanted to beat Richard back to Paw's house, but I wasn't about to speed with all the policemen around. Besides, he must have been stuck behind the march too.

Richard would be going down Main Street to Florence Street, which was the way I usually went, but I was going to take Rock Creek Road to the tobacco road behind Paw's house, the shortcut Uncle Conrad had avoided. I didn't use the route often because it was as bumpy as all get out, but I had a race to win.

Traffic was heavy by Byerly standards, thanks to so many folks getting caught by the march. I saw that some of the cars and trucks were carrying Klansmen, still wearing their robes and hoods. A green pickup truck carrying at least seven of them turned onto Rock Creek Road ahead of me. As I turned, I made sure to stay far enough behind them that the dust they stirred up wouldn't pour in through the open windows of the station wagon.

I needn't have bothered. They were going a lot faster than I dared to, and I bet myself that they were heading back for the mill. They had probably snuck out at lunch, and wanted to get back before they were missed. I remembered what Odelle had told me about a hole in the fence around the mill. No doubt that's how they were planning to get in.

That started me thinking. If someone had hit Paw, then he might have snuck in through that hole in the fence. That would explain why the guard hadn't seen him. I sped up. Maybe I'd tag along with this crew long enough to see exactly where this hole in the fence was.

Now I was close enough to see the Klansmen. They were a rowdy bunch. Several were drinking beer, and the others were pounding each other on the back and jumping around, probably congratulating themselves on being such macho guys. It was a wonder none of the men in back tumbled out. It would have served them right if they had, I thought meanly.

The mill was in sight over the tops of the pine trees when I saw a beige Pontiac stopped by the side of the road. Steam was rising from the engine, and even with my limited knowledge of cars, I could tell that something had overheated. Two black men, one with hair starting to go gray and one a wiry fellow a few years younger than me, were peering under the hood.

As the Klansmen went by, they yelled comments at the two black men. I didn't need to hear the actual words to know what was said. One even spat as they went by, but it only hit the ground. The older of the two black men looked up briefly and then acted as if he hadn't seen them, but the younger one yelled something back and made a rude gesture. When the older fellow saw what his companion was doing, he pushed his hand down, but it was too late.

The pickup rattled to a stop and the Klansmen seemed to be conferring. I didn't like it. After getting all riled up by the march, this crew was nothing but trouble looking for a place to happen.

By now I was a bit beyond the Pontiac, wondering what I should do. I could get around the pickup easily enough, but then what would the Klansmen do? The pickup moved forward again, and I started to relax, but after driving forward a few yards, they turned sharply to the left and made a three-point turn.

In my rear-view mirror, I could see the black men slamming down the hood of the car, jumping back inside the car, and locking the doors. There was the grinding of gears as the driver tried to get the car moving, but it wasn't going anywhere.

By now the pickup had completed its turn, and was speeding back the other way. As it raced past the Pontiac, the men in the back tossed beer cans onto the stopped car. The driver laid down on his horn, and yelled at them, but the Klansmen only laughed, a disturbing sound when coming from the cartoon faces of the hoods. A few yards past the Pontiac, they slowed and turned.

This was crazy! They drove past the Pontiac again, throwing more beer cans and trash. This time I honked my horn as they passed me, thinking that surely they wouldn't do anything else with me sitting right there. One of the Klansmen waved at me as if to shoo me away, but I could have not been there at all for all the notice the others took of me. It occurred to me that there was no reason they should care. I wouldn't be able to identify men in hoods.

They started to turn again. What about the truck's license number? As they made the turn, I read it quickly and repeated it to myself over and over again while I scrambled in my pocketbook for a scrap of paper and a pen to scribble it down. Now I had them!

They swung past the Pontiac again, but instead of turning right away, several of them had climbed out of the truck and were bending down. What were they doing? Then one of them triumphantly held up a big chunk of granite. They were getting ammunition.

Beer cans were one thing, but rocks were another. How far were they planning to go? Damn, damn, damn! All those state troopers in Byerly, and where was a cop when I needed one? By the time I could find one, it would be too late. That license plate number wasn't going to bring anyone back to life.

Scared as I was, I couldn't just sit there.

I put the station wagon into reverse, and backed up as fast as I dared to. I stopped next to the Pontiac and yelled, "Get in!" but before the black men could get out of their car, the pickup truck returned. A couple of small rocks bounced across the top of the Pontiac, but clearly the Klansmen didn't know what to do now. All I had to do was wait them out, I told myself.

Only they didn't go away. They climbed out of the pickup, and five of the Klansmen made a circle around the Pontiac. Most were carrying rocks, and one had a thick tree limb he hefted like a baseball bat. The men inside the car watched them as if trying to gauge their chances.

One of the two remaining Klansmen, whose robe had a symbol the others didn't, started waving me on. I shook my head at him, and honked the horn.

"Get out of here!" the Klansman yelled.

"Go to Hell!"

He spat in disgust. "Get them!" he yelled to the men surrounding the Pontiac. Hesitantly, one of them stepped forward and banged on the windshield with a rock. Again, harder this time. Another one hit the passenger window.

The man I guessed was the leader put both hands on his hips, and I could tell he was smiling even if I couldn't see it. I slid to the passenger side of the station wagon and got out of the car. The Klansman who was just raising his arm to strike the driver's window stepped back.

"You leave these men alone!" I said as firmly as I could. From inside the Pontiac I heard the men telling me to get away, that I was going to get hurt.

The other Klansmen backed away from the car, but the leader pushed right up to me.

"Get out of here!" he said.

I didn't say anything. I was afraid that my voice would give away how scared I was.

"These niggers have been asking for it, and now they're going to get it."

I stared him down, if one could stare down holes in a hood.

The other Klansmen started moving restlessly. They hadn't counted on this, and I, for once in my life, was grateful that Southern men treat women differently from men.

The leader, sensing his position weakening, said, "Don't mind her. Get them niggers out of the car!"

One of the men stepped forward, but I said, "If you want them, you're going to have to go through me." The man backed off.

139

"What the hell are you, some kind of nigger-lover?" the leader said. He yelled at his men, "Are you all a bunch of nigger-lovers?" There was a murmur in response, but no one moved.

"Damn it, I'll show you." He grabbed me by the wrist, and started dragging me away from the Pontiac. "I ain't about to let this bitch get in my way," he said.

"Get your hands off of me," I said, trying to pry his grip loose, and kicking him as hard as my sandals would allow. He fended off my blows with his free hand and gripped me more tightly, still pulling me away from the car.

We were now far enough away that the other Klansmen started hitting the car again. I reached to snatch at his hood, but he pushed my hand away and backhanded me across the face. The blow brought tears to my eyes, and I tasted blood.

The other Klansman who had been holding back approached, and knowing that I could do nothing against two of them, I tried my damnedest to get loose.

"Let her go!" an oddly familiar voice said.

"Take care of them niggers," the one holding me replied. "I've got her."

The newcomer grabbed the other's arm

and pulled. "I said, let her go!"

My captor released me with a shove, and my rescuer put out his hand to steady me. I stared at him. "Thaddeous?" I whispered.

"You touch her again," my cousin said, "and I'll kill you!"

"What's the matter with you?" the leader said. "You damn well better do what I say."

"The hell I will!" Thaddeous said. He called to the other men, "This has gone far enough. Y'all go on." A couple of the men started to comply.

"Get back here!" the leader screamed, but the rest of the men started to get back into the pickup truck. He grabbed the front of Thaddeous's robe and hissed, "You listen to me, boy! You're going to have to answer for this!"

Thaddeous shook the man off. "I expect I'll have to answer for a lot of things some day, but I ain't never going to have to answer for hitting a woman. Now get the hell out of here!"

The other Klansmen were all in the pickup truck, and the driver started the engine. The leader lingered a few seconds more and then climbed into the cab of the truck, muttering underneath his hood.

CHAPTER 12

As soon as the truck drove away, Thaddeous yanked off his hood and tossed it to the ground. "Are you all right?" he asked me.

"I guess so," I answered shakily. The fear started to drain away, and I finally noticed that my mouth hurt.

"You're bleeding." Thaddeous pulled open his robe, reached inside his blue jeans pocket for a handkerchief, and with surprising gentleness touched it to my mouth. He inspected my face for a minute, then said, "I don't think it's going to bruise or anything. How's your wrist?"

I flexed it. "A little sore. That fellow has one heck of a grip."

"He should have. He's a loader at the mill."

The black men got out of their car, watching Thaddeous warily.

"Ma'am, are you hurt? Do you want us to get you to a doctor?" the driver asked.

I tried to smile, but ended up wincing at the twinge of pain it caused. "I'm fine, thanks."

"No ma'am, thank you. There's no telling what would have happened if you hadn't stepped in like that. If there hadn't been so many of them, I wouldn't have minded showing them a thing or two, but you can't fight when you're outnumbered."

"It shouldn't have come to this," Thaddeous said half-apologetically, half-defiantly. "We just got overexcited from the march."

"That's what those marches are for, aren't they? To get things stirred up," the older man said.

"That's *not* why we were marching! It was supposed to be a protest march, that's all."

The younger black man snorted, and Thaddeous reddened.

"And what were you protesting?" the driver asked.

"About Melanie Wilson, that girl that got killed in Marley."

"The way I heard it, she wasn't killed in Marley, just left there. There's no reason to think that someone there did it."

"Then why didn't anybody see anything?" Thaddeous asked heatedly. "Somebody knows something they're not saying. You tell me how a carload of blacks drove a white woman into Marley without somebody seeing something!"

"Maybe no one saw anything because there wasn't anything to see."

"What do you mean?" I asked.

"I mean that your friend is right. If a carload of blacks had come by with a white woman, it would have been seen all right. But if somebody drove into a dark alley and threw something into a Dumpster, it probably wouldn't have been."

"So you don't think anyone from Marley killed Melanie?" I asked.

He shrugged. "I don't know one way or another, but I do know that if someone else killed that girl, it wouldn't be the first time that white folks had dumped their garbage in Marley."

I could tell Thaddeous didn't like what the man was saying, but he couldn't argue with it either. He stared at him as if he could tell by looking at him whether or not he was telling the truth. After a few seconds, he seemed to make a decision. He peeled off the white robe he was still wearing, handed it to me, and put out his hand. "Mister, if you would, I'd like to shake your hand."

The man looked at Thaddeous's proffered hand, shrugged, and shook it. Thaddeous then stuck his hand out at the younger man and shook with him as well.

"Thank you," Thaddeous said. "I'm proud to have met you. Do y'all need any help with your car?"

"I think all it needs is a chance to cool down. We've got a jug of water in the trunk."

"Then I guess we better be heading on." Thaddeous took my arm and escorted me back to Paw's station wagon.

"Do you want me to drive you back to the mill?" I asked.

"No, I could use the walk. I've got some thinking to do."

"What about this?" I asked, holding the Klan robe out to him.

"I won't be needing it anymore." He took it from me and wadded it up. "I'll throw it away the first chance I get. Laurie Anne, what you did took a lot of courage."

"You, too."

"That wasn't courage — that was just me coming to my senses. You tried to tell me what the Klan was like, and I didn't believe you."

"Will there be trouble? Will the Klan try to get back at you?"

"I'd like to see them try! They aren't as tough as they think they are."

"You be careful."

"You're a fine one to talk," he said grinning. "You walk out in front of half a dozen Klansmen and then tell me to be careful."

"Didn't Aunt Nora ever tell you that just because I stick my head in an oven, that's no reason for you to?" Just for the heck of it I kissed his cheek before I got into the station wagon.

CHAPTER 13

I drove slowly the rest of the way to Paw's house. Violence never seems real to me, and I felt like I had just come out of a deep sleep. Part of me wanted to laugh, and part wanted to cry. A third part was trying to decide how in the world I was going to tell Richard what I had done.

When I got to the house, I found him on the porch swing reading a journal article that was trying to decide just how many murderers there were in *Macbeth*. This was his way of telling me that he had been back so long that he had had to find something to read.

"What took you so long?" he asked with a grin, but then he looked at my face. "What's the matter?"

"I need a hug," I said. I grabbed onto him and stayed that way for I don't know how long. I knew he had to be wondering what was wrong, but he didn't ask. He just held me, and stroked my hair. Finally, I took a deep breath and started to tell him about it.

When I told about the Klansmen threatening the black men, he took my hand in his. When I explained why I stepped out to protect them, he stared at me wonderingly. When I described how the Klan leader had grabbed me, he pulled me tight and ran his fingers lightly over my wrist. By the time I got to Thaddeous's dramatic rescue, he was up and pacing back and forth across the porch.

When I had finished, he said, "I don't know what to say. Don't you realize what could have happened? You could have been hurt!"

I shrugged my shoulders. "I don't know why I did it. I just did. There wasn't anyone else there and they were going to beat those men up at the very least. I didn't think they'd hurt a woman."

"If you had been thinking, you wouldn't have done it at all."

I looked down at my feet, feeling ridiculous.

Richard ran his hand through his hair, and said, "What am I saying?" He sat back down beside me, and sandwiched my hands between his.

"I'm sorry Laura. I was just being silly and macho, and I should know better. Please, may I start over?"

When I nodded, he said, "Laura, I cannot tell you how proud I am of you. That was an incredibly brave thing to do, and I love you for it. I just wish I had been there with you, that's all."

He leaned over and kissed me delicately, so as not to hurt my lip.

"It wasn't that wonderful," I said. "If Thaddeous hadn't been there, what I did probably wouldn't have made any difference."

"You said he knows the man who hit you? Shouldn't we call the police and bring charges?"

I was tempted, but I shook my head. "It wouldn't be worth the trouble. A few years back, a group of Klansmen were harassing one of the local black leaders. The black man recognized one of them, but when he tried to take him to court, a dozen 'respectable' citizens swore that the Klansman was with them that night. Nothing ever came of it."

"Still. . . . Maybe I should go see him myself."

"And do what? Beat him up. That's very chivalrous, but you don't want to sink to his level."

"Yes I do, but I suppose I shouldn't," he said grudgingly. "How's your lip? Do you

149

feel up to going to the hospital?"

"My lip is fine." I reached up to touch it gingerly. "I don't think it's swelling or anything. Let me wash off my face and get something to drink, and I'll be as good as new."

CHAPTER 14

I was still shaky enough that I let Richard drive to the hospital. Aunt Ruby Lee was on duty in the waiting-room, and when she looked up and saw us, she smiled like she hadn't seen us in years. I was gratified by such a joyous expression, albeit surprised, but then I saw who else was there. No wonder she was so glad to see us.

A large, curly-haired man holding a felt cowboy hat with a snakeskin hatband was in the chair next to Aunt Ruby Lee. On one wrist flashed a massive silver and bear claw bracelet that matched his belt buckle, ring, and tie-tack. Beside such massive ornamentation, his Wranglers and plaid cowboy shirt seemed superfluous.

"Hey there," Aunt Ruby Lee said to us. Then to her companion, she said, "Roger, you remember Alice's daughter Laurie Anne, don't you?"

"Well I remember a skinny little thing with pig-tails, but I don't know what I remember this pretty lady. Laurie Anne, I'll be damned if you haven't gone and grown up since I saw you last." He stood up and gave me a hug and a peck on the cheek.

"Roger, I'd like you to meet my husband Richard Fleming," I said. "Richard, this is Roger Bailey. Ilene's daddy."

The two men exchanged handshakes.

"I wasn't expecting to see you here, Roger," I said. Clearly, neither had Aunt Ruby Lee. I was pretty sure that she wasn't too thrilled about her ex-husband hanging around.

"Ilene told me about Ellis and I came to pay my respects," Roger said.

"Wasn't that nice of Roger?" Aunt Ruby Lee said, her voice showing only a little strain. "Why don't y'all have a seat? You and Richard are going to stay, aren't you?"

Richard and I pulled up a couple of chairs and I asked, "Any news about Paw?"

Aunt Ruby Lee shook her head. "Not a word. Like Daphine says, no news is good news."

Roger sighed heavily, "I'm awfully sorry Ellis is in such a bad way. Ruby Lee, you know I've always been fond of Ellis."

"Thank you, Roger," Aunt Ruby Lee said. "I'm sure Paw would appreciate your coming down like this."

"I wanted to do it, Ruby Lee. It's always

good to see you." He turned to Richard. "Now I know you must think your wife is the best thing around, but answer me this: isn't Ruby Lee about the prettiest woman a man could ask for?"

"I guess it runs in the family," Richard said.

Aunt Ruby Lee smiled, but the effort of being pleasant to her ex-husband was beginning to show. She looked at her watch, and then said brightly, "Look at the time. I have got to get going. You and Richard are going to be here, aren't you Laurie Anne?"

"Absolutely," I answered quickly. It would have taken a harder heart than mine to abandon her then.

"Then you don't mind if I go on, do you? I've got some things at home I really need to take care of. I'll see you tonight." She gathered her pocketbook and started for the elevator.

"Let me walk you down," Roger said.

"That's all right, Roger. You go ahead and visit with Laurie Anne and Richard. Thank you so much for coming by."

She was gone before he could answer, and he settled back in his chair, obviously unhappy with this turn of events.

Richard looked a little confused, but he wasn't familiar with this piece of family history. Aunt Ruby Lee had been the one who asked for that divorce, and Roger had only agreed reluctantly.

Their marriage had been a stormy one, filled with furious arguments, tearful recriminations, touching reconciliations, and inevitable repeat performances. Most of the recriminations had been on the part of Roger, who, despite his feelings for Aunt Ruby Lee, could not give up performing country music at the county's honky-tonks or the long nights of drinking and carousing that went along with it.

Aunt Ruby Lee had eventually kicked him out. Shortly after their divorce was final, she met Uncle Loman's cousin Conrad and they were married not long after that. I remembered hearing that Roger had never quite given up hope for another chance with Aunt Ruby Lee, and was known to show up unannounced at her house under the pretext of visiting his daughter.

"Tell us what you've been up to, Roger. Roger's a musician," I explained to Richard.

"Well, I don't know if you'd call it being a musician, but I do all right," Roger said with a grin.

"Don't listen to him," I said. "He and

his band have played just about every club in the county and they perform at all kinds of public functions. They're real popular around here."

Roger's grin grew wider, his good humor restored by my compliments. "I'm right proud you think so," he said. "Now since when do you call me by my Christian name? What happened to 'Uncle Roger'?"

"You did divorce Aunt Ruby Lee a while ago."

"Shoot, that don't make no never mind. Family is family, I always say, and I still consider the Burnettes part of mine. Ellis has always been like a second father to me, even after Ruby Lee and I split up. I was over there visiting with him just the other day. Nothing I like better than to spend the day singing the old songs with Ellis."

"Paw does have a nice voice," I said, wishing I had recorded more of his songs.

"Well," Roger said, "I better be getting on, too. You be sure and call if I can do anything to help out, hear?"

"I will, Roger. Thank you."

After he left, I explained to Richard what he had just been in the middle of. Then I leaned back in my chair. "Sometimes I forget how much work it is keeping up with this family."

Richard pulled my hand over to his lap and asked, "How are you holding out?"

"Not too good. Richard, Paw's not going to get better, is he?"

"We don't know that."

I nodded, but still felt that I was right. We sat together quietly for the rest of the afternoon.

CHAPTER 15

Somewhere around seven, the Burnette clan started to gather once more. Richard and I relinquished our posts to Aunt Nellie and Uncle Ruben, the first arrivals, and went down to the snack bar to get something to eat. By the time we got back, all of the aunts and uncles and most of the cousins were present. Even Aunt Maggie was there.

Richard and I sat by a cluster of older cousins including Odelle, Idelle, Carlelle, Linwood, Vasti, and Thaddeous. The triplets and Vasti started talking about Melanie Wilson, but they stopped when they noticed the forlorn expression on Thaddeous's face. Then Linwood asked me if I still knew how to drink out of a Dixie cup or if I had been up North too long. Otherwise, no one said much.

Doctor Mason came to see Paw at eight, and then asked Aunt Nora to come out into the hall for a moment. After he left, she came in and said in a flat voice, "The doctor says Paw's getting worse. We can all go in to see him."

What my aunt was telling us was that Paw was dying, and that this was our chance to say good-bye to him. The figure on the bed was noticeably shrunken since yesterday, and his eyes were closed. If he knew we were there, he gave no sign.

Slowly we all crowded into the hospital room, taking turns to make sure everyone had a chance to get close to Paw. No one said much, but there were plenty of tears.

When Richard and I approached him, I whispered, "Paw? Can you hear me?"

He didn't move.

Remembering that a nurse had once told me that a person could often still hear even when incapable of responding, I continued, "Richard's with me, Paw. He came down to see you." I stopped. I wanted to tell him so much, but my throat was too tight.

"Paw," Richard said, "we just want to tell you we love you."

I nodded, but could say nothing more. I stared at him, trying to reconcile this feeble shell with the vibrant man I had known all my life, but I couldn't. Finally, Richard tugged on my shoulder and we left the room.

No one spoke as we came into the waiting-room, and I saw my own misery mirrored on the faces of my family. Silently we exchanged hugs, and left, leaving Aunt Nora and Aunt Daphine to stand watch. I had nothing left to say as Richard and I returned to the house and went to bed.

I jerked bolt upright when the phone rang. According to the alarm clock on the nightstand, it was only four o'clock. Leaving Richard to snore, I found my robe and went downstairs. There was no light on in the hall or in the stairwell, so I felt my way toward the kitchen, where I could hear Aunt Maggie speaking quietly on the phone. She hung up as I stepped onto the chilly linoleum, and turned to see me.

"He's gone," she said. "Nora says he never woke up after we saw him, just slipped away in his sleep." She hugged me clumsily, then reached for the phone again. "I have to call Edna."

I didn't remember going back up to the bedroom, or waking up Richard. All I remembered was laying in my husband's arms while sobs ripped through me.

CHAPTER 16

I didn't realize I had gone to sleep until I woke the next morning, my eyes and face swollen from crying. I could think of no reason I should move from the bed, despite noises from downstairs that told me that Aunt Maggie was stirring. Instead, I lay next to the still sleeping Richard until there was a light tap on the bedroom door.

"Laurie Anne? Richard?" Aunt Maggie said. "Are y'all awake? Do you want something to eat?"

I nudged Richard awake. "Are you hungry?"

He rolled over and blinked his eyes. "What time is it?"

"I don't know."

He grabbed the alarm clock. "After ten. We'll be there in a couple of minutes, Aunt Maggie."

"All right." Her footsteps moved down toward the kitchen.

"Hi," Richard said to me, looking at me intently. When I didn't answer, he reached over, pulled my hand to his lips, and lightly kissed it.

"Do you want to shower before breakfast?" he asked.

"I don't care." I didn't seem to care about anything. It was as though both my brain and heart were wrapped in lambswool.

Richard slid out of the bed, pulled on his robe, and held mine out to me. "Come on. Let's get breakfast."

He escorted me to the kitchen. Aunt Maggie had a bag full of sausage and country ham biscuits.

"What kind do you two want?" she said.

"Sausage," Richard answered for us both.

Aunt Maggie looked at me, then turned away. I knew I should say something, but I couldn't think of anything to say. Instead, I reached for the newspaper on the counter and stared at it. I ate what Richard put in front of me, but I could not have honestly said whether I liked it or not.

Once she was sure that Richard and I had enough to eat, Aunt Maggie made herself a cup of instant coffee and sat down with a sigh.

"You haven't been awake since Aunt Nora called, have you?" Richard asked.

She shrugged. "I laid down for a spell, but couldn't seem to fall asleep." She glanced at the clock on the wall. "It's just as well. If I stop now, I'll be out for the duration, and your aunts are coming over in a little while to plan the funeral."

"Is there anything you need us to do?" he said.

"Not a thing."

"Then we'll go take our showers."

Content to let Richard make the decisions, I followed him back to our room, then went into the bathroom. I obediently showered and dressed, then I waited while he did the same.

The doorbell rang as we came back downstairs. Aunt Maggie answered it, spoke to a woman I recognized as one of Paw's neighbors, and came back inside with a dish covered in foil.

"Mrs. Lockard from across the street brought over some macaroni and cheese," she explained. "I guess the news about Ellis is already getting around." She was right. In the next hour, friends and neighbors dropped off ham, fried chicken, potato salad, and a couple of generic casseroles. As I tried to fit it all into the refrigerator, I couldn't help but think of Mrs. Wilson sitting alone in her house waiting for visitors that never came.

When the doorbell rang again, it was a red-eyed Aunt Edna. She was shortly followed by the rest of my aunts, and I let myself be swept away into the living-room with them while Richard called our respective offices to tell them that we would be staying in town for Paw's funeral.

As soon as we were all gathered, Aunt Maggie said, "Before you get started, I just wanted to tell you that I'm going to be reading Ellis's will tomorrow night, so everybody try to get here by six-thirty." Then she started to leave the room.

"Aunt Maggie," Aunt Nora said, "don't you want to help decide about the funeral?"

"No, thank you. I've had to put together too many funerals already. You girls can handle this one." She went upstairs.

Aunt Daphine, ever practical, pulled out a pad and pen and put them on the coffee-table. "This isn't going to be easy for any of us," she announced briskly, "but it has to be done. First we need to decide when we're going to have the funeral. I called Mrs. Funderburk up at the church office, and she said that the church is free all day tomorrow, but there's going to be a wedding the next day. I went ahead and told her we'd have it tomorrow. Is that all right with everybody?"

"What about Melanie Wilson's funeral?" Aunt Nora asked.

"Mrs. Funderburk said they haven't scheduled it yet. I guess the police aren't done with her yet, poor thing."

Everyone nodded. At least we didn't have that to deal with, I thought. Or should there have been an autopsy? What would my aunts say if I suggested it? I let the notion pass.

"Did you check to see if Reverend Glass is free?" Aunt Edna said.

"Edna, that man is *not* going to officiate at Paw's funeral," Aunt Nellie said firmly.

"He most certainly is," Aunt Edna said, just as firmly.

"Edna," Aunt Ruby Lee said in her most soothing voice, "you know Paw and Reverend Glass didn't get along. Don't you think it would be a little funny for him to speak at the funeral?"

"No, I don't. Reverend Glass would be the last man on earth to hold a grudge."

"Well, *I* hold a grudge," Aunt Nellie muttered.

Aunt Edna and Aunt Nellie glared at each other, but Aunt Nora said, "I spoke to Paw about this once. It was right after

164

Mrs. Dean's funeral. Do you remember how fancy it was? I was saying that I don't want so much fuss when I go, that it was just a waste of money. Paw said he thought that funerals were for the living more than for the dead anyway, so that if it made Mr. Dean feel better to spend the money, it was the right thing to do. Then he said that we should do whatever made us feel best when we buried him."

"See!" Aunt Edna said triumphantly.

"Having to listen to Reverend Glass is *not* going to make me feel better," Aunt Nellie said.

"I'm not finished yet," Aunt Nora said patiently. "Then he said that he thought that he would rest better if whoever it was that spoke at his funeral was someone who knew him and cared about him. Then it wouldn't matter what was said, because it would be meant."

"You mean one of us should give the service?" Aunt Ruby Lee said. "I couldn't do that. I wouldn't be able to say a word."

Aunt Daphine said, "What about Paw's cousin Yancy? He's a preacher in Granite Falls, and he and Paw used to be close. I bet he'd come."

The sisters nodded their agreement, even Aunt Edna. Aunt Daphine said,

"Nora, have you got his phone number?"

We waited while Aunt Daphine called Yancy. She spoke a few minutes, and then reported while holding her hand over the speaker. "He says he'd be proud to do the service, and would ten o'clock be all right?" The time was agreed on, and after hanging up the phone, Aunt Daphine again consulted her list.

"Now who do we want for the pall bearers?" Aunt Daphine asked.

I watched while my aunts bickered their way down Aunt Daphine's list, arguing over pall bearers, whether the casket would be open or closed during the service, what suit he should be wearing, and whether or not he should be buried with his wedding ring. Did it really matter? I didn't think the funeral was going to make me feel any better no matter how nice it was.

After all the decisions were made, Aunt Ruby Lee and Aunt Edna went upstairs to get Paw's dark gray suit and a shirt to take to the funeral home.

"Laurie Anne," Aunt Daphine said, "Nellie and I are going to ride over to the cemetery to take care of things over there. Why don't you come with us?"

I agreed unenthusiastically. It was only a short drive, and I did not speak as we drove.

The one thing about which there had been no debate was where Paw was to be buried. Paw had bought a plot at Woodgreen Acres when Maw died. He would be buried alongside his wife.

Once inside the gates of Woodgreen Acres, we followed the discreet signs to the office, housed in a low building that was buried in one of the rolling hills in order to blend in with the surroundings as much as possible. Mr. Norville, a man one assumed could not smile, greeted us at the door and escorted us to his office. Nearly one whole wall of the room was a picture window with a view of the grounds, lush and verdant despite the weather. I stared outside, letting Mr. Norville's carefully rehearsed words of sympathy wash over me.

"I understand the funeral service will be at the church," he said. "What time will the funeral party be arriving here at Woodgreen?"

"The service is set for ten," Aunt Daphine said, "So I imagine it will be about eleven or eleven-thirty when we get here." Aunt Nellie nodded. How did one estimate these things, I wondered. I had never even considered the length of a funeral.

"Have you made arrangements with the

funeral home for chairs and an awning for the graveside service?"

Aunt Daphine nodded.

"Then I'll make sure that the site is prepared. The only thing we have to take care of is the marker." He consulted a sheet of paper on his desk. "Mr. Burnette purchased a marker for his wife and himself some time ago, so all we need do is remove the marker and add his name." He picked up a pencil. "Now what is the full name of the departed?" he asked.

"Ellis Everett Burnette." Aunt Daphine spelled it out for him.

"Date of birth?"

"September 3, 1918."

"Would you like anything else on the plaque? 'Beloved Father' perhaps, or 'Loved by All'?"

Aunt Daphine looked at Aunt Nellie and shrugged. I spoke for the first time since we had left the house. " 'His cares are now all ended.' "

"That's pretty," Aunt Nellie said.

"It's a quote. From Shakespeare. *King Henry IV.*"

"We'll have that then," Aunt Daphine said. "I think he would like that. Lord knows Paw had his share of cares."

Aunt Daphine inspected the paperwork

while I continued to stare out the window at the green slopes, dimpled with bronze plaques. It wasn't true, I thought. His cares weren't all ended. If someone had killed Paw, I had to find out who.

Staring at the spot where he would be buried in the morning, I said to myself, "I'll finish it for you, Paw. Your cares *will* be all ended. I promise."

After we left Woodgreen, Aunt Daphine dropped me off at Paw's. I found Richard upstairs stretched out on the bed reading.

"How are you doing?" he asked, reaching for me as I laid down beside him.

"Not good, but better."

"Did you guys get everything taken care of?"

"I think so. Richard, I've been thinking about what Paw said. That what happened to him wasn't an accident."

"What did you decide?"

"We can't just let it go. I can't, anyway. I think we should try to find out what happened. If someone killed Paw, we have to find out who."

Richard nodded.

"Is that all right?" I asked. "Will you help?"

"Of course I'll help." He gathered me in his arms. "This is why we're married — for better or for worse, remember?"

"Thank you. I couldn't face this without you."

"Nor should you," he said.

I rested my head against his shoulder and let him stroke my hair until Aunt Maggie called us for lunch.

CHAPTER 17

The three of us ate a late lunch of peanut butter and jelly sandwiches, and then Aunt Maggie disappeared upstairs to take a nap. Richard quickly buried himself in a book, but I couldn't sit still. Or rather, every time I did, I felt like crying again and I didn't want that.

With Paw's death, the house had turned into someplace foreign. The paperback bodice-ripper romance Aunt Maggie had left on the coffee-table shouldn't have been there — one of Paw's Louis L'Amour books should have been in its place. One of my aunts had left Paw's phone book open on the kitchen table, and Paw never would have done that. Even Richard looked out of place, sipping Coke from a glass instead of from a bottle the way Paw would have.

I put Aunt Maggie's book into the book-shelf and slid the phone book back into the kitchen drawer. It didn't help. It wasn't Paw's room anymore.

"I'm going to the den," I said. Richard grunted something and I went downstairs.

As far as I could tell, Aunt Maggie still hadn't spent any time down there. The room still looked as if Paw had just left. I felt tears start to form in my eyes, but deliberately blinked them away.

I sat down in the recliner, leaned it all the way back, and closed my eyes, trying to imagine that I was a teenager again and Paw was still alive. I could almost hear his voice, almost see him sitting on the couch pulling socks, almost. . . . That's when I started to cry.

Richard must have known why I had come downstairs, because he didn't come looking for me for a while. When I heard him coming down the stairs, I hastily blew my nose.

"Are you all right?" he asked.

"Sure. I was just going to straighten up a little since everyone's coming over tomorrow night." It was a lie and he knew it, but it was a good idea.

Again noticing that the carton of socks Paw had pulled was sitting out, I said with irritation, "I thought Uncle Conrad was going to take those back to the mill. I'm surprised Burt Walters hasn't called to fuss about them yet."

"Surely he wouldn't worry about a box of socks under these circumstances."

"You don't know him like I do."

"Come to think of it, why didn't Paw take them with him when he went to the mill?"

"Walters insists that the socks be counted when they're checked in, and there wouldn't have been anyone there to take care of it on Sunday. You'd think that after all this time they'd trust Paw. They were the ones who cheated him, not the other way around."

"Oh? I haven't heard that one."

"You know they pay by the sock? Paw caught them under-counting his socks. He was helping Clifford learn to count one day, and they ended up counting a whole carton. Only when he went to check in the socks the next day, they told him there were twenty-six less than he knew there were. Of course he made them count them over, but there's no telling how much money they had cheated him out of over the years. After that, Paw always kept track of what he pulled himself."

I pulled open the drawer in the end table, and produced a blue spiral notebook. "This is his ledger." I opened it to the last entries. "May 12: Received 1 carton. May 14: Completed carton. 356 socks. That's funny."

"What's funny?"

"It usually took Paw four or five days to pull a carton of socks." I showed Richard previous entries in the ledger to illustrate my point. "It only took him two to pull this batch. I wonder what he was worried about."

"I don't follow you."

"You know how when we're worried about something, you read *Richard III* and I look at the atlas? Paw pulled socks. Once it looked like Aunt Nellie and Uncle Ruben were going to end up in jail after one of their schemes went bad, and he went through a whole carton of socks in a day. He wouldn't talk, he wouldn't eat, he wouldn't do anything but pull socks."

"Maybe he did this batch in a hurry because he needed the money for something."

"First off, Paw was never pinched for money because he was careful. Second, it was only the middle of the month, so he should still have had a good piece of his Social Security check left. No, he was worried about something." I returned the ledger to the drawer and slid it shut. "I wonder if whatever it was he was worried about had something to do with what happened. With why he was killed."

"You think that if we figure out what he was worried about," Richard said, "we'll know who killed him?" He looked doubtful.

"Maybe. Let me think this through. It would have been Sunday afternoon. No, he must have started pulling Sunday morning at the latest to get that many done."

"So something happened Sunday morning. What did Paw usually do on Sunday morning?"

"He didn't go to church anymore, not since Glass came. What about Glass?"

"As a suspect?" Richard asked.

"He had a motive. He thinks Paw left him the house."

"But he wouldn't be getting it personally — the church would own it."

"True." For a minute I considered the idea of some treasure hidden in the house and of Glass killing Paw so he could search for it, but I quickly discarded it. Too many children had explored this house for there to be anything hidden in it, and how would Glass have learned about it if there was?

"Let's go back to Sunday morning," I said. "Paw always got up at around eight, even on Sunday. Then he'd eat breakfast and read the paper."

"Then what?"

"Let's stick with the newspaper a

minute," I said. "When I came over here on Monday, Aunt Maggie said she hadn't been downstairs since she got here. Therefore everything should have been the way Paw left it."

"So?"

"So when I got here, the newspaper was on the couch, right next to where he would have been sitting to pull socks."

"Where is it now? Did Aunt Maggie throw it away?"

"Probably not." I checked the magazine rack, and pulled out the newspaper on top. Richard peered over my shoulder and we skimmed the front page.

"Is that how you found it?" he asked.

"Uh huh. Folded over to this article about Melanie Wilson."

"You think Paw had this out when he was pulling socks?"

"I don't know. Why would he have been that worried about Melanie?"

"Did he know her?"

"Of course. This is Byerly — everyone knows everyone. I suppose he would have been upset about her being missing, but it doesn't seem like a sock-puller to me."

"Maybe he was worried on Thaddeous's behalf. Since Thaddeous was out searching and all."

"Maybe. Let's hold onto this."

"Shouldn't we use tweezers to handle it, and seal it in a plastic bag?"

"I'm going to hit you upside the head if you don't behave yourself," I said, feeling oddly guilty for making even a small joke. "We may as well look around and see if we can find anything else."

Unfortunately all I found was a dirty coffee cup and an empty Coke bottle, which I carried up to the kitchen. I returned to find Richard immersed in one of Paw's westerns.

"Richard! You're supposed to be looking, not sitting there with your nose in a book."

"I thought it might be a clue."

"Give it here." He handed it over, and energetically looked under the sofa cushions while I replaced the paperback on Paw's shelf.

"How about this?" he asked.

"What?"

He handed me a local road map. "It was stuck between two of the cushions."

"So that's where it was. Paw usually kept it in the glove compartment of the station wagon. I wonder why he had it out."

"Did he share your affinity for maps?"

"Nope. I'm the only map freak in the

family." I unfolded it and spread it out on the couch beside me. "Paw marked on his maps," I said in a tone of disapproval, looking at several Xs marked in various shades of ink.

"You stick pins in yours."

"That's different. You can pull the pin out again so you can still read the map." I folded it back again. I never could understand why other people had so much trouble folding road maps. "I wonder if it's all right if I keep this. I don't have a map of the area back in Boston."

"Careful," Richard warned. "If Aunt Maggie sees you with that, you'll be demoted to vulture."

We eventually did get the den, living-room and kitchen straightened up, but found nothing else that seemed to mean anything. By then Aunt Maggie was awake, and we went to Hardee's to get dinner. Afterward we watched television until time for bed.

CHAPTER 18

I was glad we had set the funeral for early in the day so there was no time for me to dread it beforehand. By the time we showered and dressed, it was time to go to the church.

The final decision on the open casket versus closed casket service had been a compromise. The mortician brought Paw's coffin to the church early and left the lid open for a time so that those who wished to could come pay their respects before the actual service. I decided not to go. Whatever it was in that box was not my grandfather.

Instead, Richard and I waited until after the coffin had been sealed to walk over. The church would have been comfortably filled with just us Burnettes; with all of Paw's friends and more distant family connections, it was bursting at the seams. It did make me feel a little better to see that others were mourning him, too.

The flowers were glorious — sprays of roses, pots of carnations and begonias, and elaborate groupings of blooms I didn't recognize. The mill had sent an impressive display, and there was a small arrangement from my company and one from the English department at Boston College.

Paw's cousin Yancy spoke for him, of how fully he had lived and how he had given so much of himself to others. Then Aunt Nellie, Aunt Nora, Aunt Daphine, Aunt Edna, and Aunt Ruby Lee left their places and stood together like they had as girls to sing *Amazing Grace*. It had been Paw's favorite hymn, and as their voices rose sweetly, tears ran down my face without my even realizing it.

For the drive to Woodgreen Acres, most of the family rode in the fleet of black Lincoln Continentals provided by the funeral home. The graveside service was simple, no more than a chance for the mourners to pray together. My aunts openly sobbed as the casket was lowered into the ground. Then each family member gently tossed a handful of earth onto the casket.

We lingered at the cemetery to accept condolences. Feeling stifled by the heat and the press of people, I led Richard to two graves at the edge of the family plot.

"This is where my parents are buried," I said. "Alice Burnette McCrary and James Lawrence McCrary." Their bronze plaque looked so plain, marked only with their names and the dates of their births and death. I hadn't thought up any words for them. I didn't remember thinking at all, not for a long time after the accident.

"When they died," I said, "Paw never once tried to shake me out of it or cheer me up. He knew I'd get better in my own time. Now I have to get better all over again."

Richard pulled me close, and kissed my forehead lightly.

"I should have brought them some flowers. It looks so empty," I said.

"Wait here a minute." Richard walked over to where workmen were moving the myriad of flowers away from Paw's grave to begin covering it with dirt, and surreptitiously carried away a small pot of carnations. Then he returned and placed it in the center between the two graves.

"I don't think Paw would mind," he said.

We stood silently for a moment, and then an uncomfortable thought occurred to me. "Richard? Do you suppose whoever killed Paw came to the funeral?"

"I was hoping you wouldn't think of that," he said, turning to look at the people still milling in the cemetery. "If it were someone he knew, I would think there would be a good chance of it."

I shivered despite the heat. Maybe the killer was still here, expressing polite sorrow to my relatives. As I inspected the group of people, trying to decide who could be a murderer, Thaddeous walked toward us.

"Laurie Anne? The car's getting ready to go."

Richard took my hand, and the three of us walked to the waiting car and rode back to the church.

CHAPTER 19

After the funeral, all of us Burnettes and a fair number of family friends gathered at Aunt Nora's house. I knew Aunt Nora had volunteered her house so that Aunt Maggie wouldn't have the bother, but all I could think of was that it was the first family gathering I had ever been to that hadn't been at Paw's house.

Aunt Nora and Aunt Daphine managed to fit most of the vast quantities of ham, chicken, barbecued pork, casseroles, macaroni and cheese, potato salad, and fresh baked biscuits that half the town had sent on the dining-room table, and covered the kitchen table with the cakes, pies, and cobblers from the other half.

Despite myself, I joined the crowd lining up for food, covered my paper plate with a respectable meal, and ate every bite of it.

"There's something about funerals," Aunt Daphine said with a small smile. "They just make people hungry."

People wandered to and fro, chatting, hugging, even laughing when some distant cousin's little girl escaped her mother during diapering and ran buck-naked through the house.

"They almost seem to be enjoying themselves," I whispered resentfully to Richard.

"It's always like this," he whispered back. "A funeral is such a strain, and it's such a relief when it's over that it almost seems like being happy."

"I guess you're right," I admitted, and then said, "I've been so upset, I didn't even think about how anyone else felt. He was their grandfather and father and brother, too. Everyone loved Paw." I squeezed his hand. "You loved him."

"Yes, I did. I love you, too."

"I'm going to go talk to people," I said determinedly. I soon lost track of which aunts, uncles, and cousins I had spoken to. I admired Vasti's dress, brought Sue a footstool, and even managed to laugh politely when Linwood asked me how many Yankees it takes to screw in a light-bulb. After hours of hugging necks and exchanging sympathy, I noticed the crowd was beginning to thin.

When Aunt Daphine got ready to go, I walked her to her car. "I suppose you and Richard will be heading back up to Boston tomorrow," Aunt Daphine said.

"Actually, I think we're going to stay in town for a few days." There was a promise we had to keep.

"Good. Maybe we'll get a chance to talk before you go. Why don't you come by the beauty parlor tomorrow and I'll take you to lunch? About one?"

"I'd like that."

Aunt Daphine leaned back to study my face. "Laurie Anne, I know what Paw meant to you. We're going to miss him, but don't you forget that we've still got each other."

"I won't."

"We all love you. *I* love you."

"I love you, too." I watched Aunt Daphine drive off, and then went back inside.

Aunt Nora was in the kitchen stuffing dirty paper plates and cups into a trash bag.

"Let me give you a hand," I said.

"That's all right. There's not that much to do."

I helped for a while anyway, and then collected Richard to head back for Paw's house.

CHAPTER 20

Aunt Maggie had driven her own car to Aunt Nora's so she was already at the house when we got there.

"Good, I'm glad you're here," she said when she saw us. "I meant to make sure we had some time alone before the others get here, but I forgot to tell you. You two sit down and I'll be right back." She bustled upstairs.

"What's going on?" Richard asked.

I shrugged. "With Aunt Maggie, there's no telling."

A few minutes later, Aunt Maggie came back down the stairs carrying a grey, metal strongbox.

"Laurie Anne, I've got something to tell you before the rest of the crew gets here, and I want y'all to promise to keep it to yourselves."

"I promise," I said.

"You, too," Aunt Maggie said to Richard.

"I promise," he said.

"All right then. Laurie Anne, Ellis always

was better than me when it came to show-ing his feelings, so I don't have to tell you how much he thought of you."

"I know Mama was his favorite."

Aunt Maggie looked at me sharply. "You think that's why Ellis told everybody who would sit still long enough about what good grades you got in school, and how you won that scholarship for college, and what a good job you got up North? Be-cause you look like your Mama? Lord, child, he was so proud of how you made something of yourself that he wouldn't have cared if you were as plain as a mud fence.

"Now Ellis loved all of his grandchil-dren, but I think he thought you were the most like him. You did the things he wished he could have. That's why he didn't try to talk you out of moving to Boston, even though it liked to have killed him when he had to come home to this empty house. He knew you'd never be satisfied working at Walters Mill."

"There's nothing wrong with working at the mill," I protested.

"I'm not saying that there is, but you know doggone well you wouldn't have been happy working there. Isn't that so?"

"Yes, ma'am," I admitted.

"Ellis knew that, too, and he knew when to let go. The only thing he was afraid of is that he'd lose you for good, that you wouldn't remember where home was."

I squirmed a bit at that, remembering just how few and far between my visits had become.

Aunt Maggie noticed my discomfort, and patted my leg. "Now don't act like that. You done right by Ellis. You wrote letters all the time, and called every two, three weeks, and came down when you could. That's not what Ellis was worried about. He wanted you to know that this is home." She sighed. "I'm not telling it right."

" 'Where we live is home. Home that our feet may leave, but not our hearts,' " Richard said.

"That's right. That's what I'm getting at." She pulled a key from her blue jeans pocket, used it to open the strongbox, and fumbled around in it.

"What play was that from?" I whispered to Richard.

"Oliver Wendell Holmes, actually. I couldn't think of one from Shakespeare."

Aunt Maggie finally found what she was looking for, and held up a folded document. "Do you know what this is?"

"No, ma'am."

"It's the deed to this house, and the land around us. The Burnettes have owned this place for five generations. You know we used to own acres of farmland all around. My daddy had to sell off most of it during the Depression and it hurt him worse than just about anything. The day he signed the papers, he came home and pulled out the family Bible and made every one of us children put our hands on that Bible and swear that we would never sell this house. He said that unless we were pure starving to death, we should never let it go because it's that much a part of us. Ellis and I and all our brothers and sisters swore to that.

"Now we knew the house was going to go to Ellis because he was the oldest, but Daddy made us all swear because he figured that as the oldest, Ellis would be the first to go. Of course God had different ideas, and Ellis and I had to bury four brothers and two sisters. I'm the only one left, and Ellis left me the house."

I nodded, but I still didn't know why she had to get me alone to tell me this.

She went on. "Ellis told me he was doing it this way several years back. I told him that was fine, because I still remembered our promise. The problem was, what should I do with it after I was gone? I

189

never could find a man I could stand to be around for any length of time, so I never had any children. I told Ellis I wanted to leave the house to one of his children or grandchildren, but I didn't know which one. He asked me to leave it to you."

I could only stare at her. I never would have guessed that she was leading up to this. "But shouldn't it go to one of the aunts?" I finally said.

"The girls all have their own homes, except Nellie, and Nellie wouldn't have it for long with all the fool stunts she and Ruben pull."

"I don't even live in Byerly anymore."

"Ellis said the distance didn't matter. You're a Burnette, and this is the Burnette house. That's all that matters."

I couldn't think of anything to say, not one word.

"Now there's a condition," Aunt Maggie continued. "You're going to have to make that same promise Ellis and I made all those years ago. Do you know where the Bible is?"

"Yes, ma'am."

"Go get it."

I went to the oak bookshelf in the corner that held Paw's photo albums and scrapbooks, pulled out the tattered, leather-bound book, and carried it back to Aunt Maggie.

"Put your hand on it," she instructed.

I obeyed.

She looked into the distance for a minute. "You know I can't remember birthdays or anniversaries to save my life, but I can remember what Daddy made us promise like it was yesterday. Repeat after me: I promise that I will never sell this house as long as I live, and to make sure that when I'm gone, it stays in the Burnette family forever."

I repeated her words, and she nodded. "That's good enough." She looked at Richard. "I asked Ellis if I should make you swear, too, but he said he trusted you to do the right thing. You better, or dead or alive, I'll come after you."

The threat would have sounded ridiculous in almost any other circumstance, but Richard took it as it was intended and nodded.

Aunt Maggie put the deed back in the strongbox and locked it back up. "Now do you know why I made you promise not to tell anyone else?"

"Not exactly," I admitted.

"Well, I don't want to name names, but some of your cousins might not be too happy with the way we've set things up. Neither Ellis nor I wanted any hard feelings at a time like this, so we thought it would be easier this way."

She looked at the clock. "Lord, look at the time. I need you two to run up to the store and get some Coca-Colas. The whole crew is going to be here in an hour or so, and I've got things to do." She trotted upstairs before we could say anything.

I looked at Richard. "I don't know what to say."

"What's to say? Like Paw said, you're a Burnette and this is the Burnette house. Now we better change and get moving, or Aunt Maggie will get us."

I looked around as I followed him upstairs, wondering if I should feel some of that pride of ownership people talk about. I didn't. It still looked like Paw's house to me.

CHAPTER 21

Richard and I quickly changed into jeans, and drove to the grocery store. When we got back with as many cartons of Coke as we could carry, we found Sue in the midst of claiming the recliner. She pushed it back so her feet were elevated. "I hope you don't mind me taking the good chair," she said, "but my feet are swollen something terrible, what with the heat and all."

"No problem," I said. "Where's Linwood?"

"He's down in the den talking with Clifford." Then, with an unusual burst of perception, Sue said, "The house don't seem right without Paw."

"No, it doesn't," I agreed.

"I think what I liked best about Paw was that he always treated me like one of his own."

"We all think of you as one of our own," I said. She had started dating Linwood so long ago I tended to forget that she wasn't a Burnette.

Sue snorted. "Loman and Edna sure

don't. I don't know why I bother to take the kids to see them anymore. When we went last Sunday, all Edna did was fuss about us not coming to church anymore and as soon as we got there, Loman went into his den and slammed the door behind him. He didn't come out until Conrad called, and he left the house not long after that."

"I guess Uncle Loman's just not used to children anymore," I said.

"Never did like kids, if you ask me. When are you two going to have kids?"

"We haven't decided," I said. I hate it when people ask me that, and since Richard and I got married, not a trip home had passed without somebody or another bringing it up. "When are you due?" I asked, hoping to distract her.

"The first week of September. There's nothing wrong with you, is there? I mean, you two are fertile, aren't you?"

"As far as I know. Have you picked out names yet?"

"Me and Linwood can't agree on anything. You two want children, don't you?"

"Yes," I said tersely, and decided that if Sue asked how often Richard and I made love, I was going to slug her.

Fortunately even Sue didn't have that

much nerve. "I didn't know," she said. "So many women would rather work than stay home and tend to children. You shouldn't wait too long, or you'll end up with a Mongoloid."

"Actually, the latest research says that you're pretty safe until forty, so we've got a couple of years left," Richard said mildly.

Before Sue could argue the point further, the doorbell rang again. This time it was Aunt Nora, Uncle Buddy, Thaddeous, and Willis. Linwood and Clifford came upstairs to join us, and as everyone found places to sit, Richard and I brought out several cartons of cold bottles of Coke.

"Who's been driving Paw's car?" Linwood asked suddenly.

"Me," I answered.

"I thought you didn't need a car. Especially not a station wagon. It's not like you've got kids or anything. We have to squeeze two car seats in Sue's Chevette, and we don't know how we're going to get the third one in."

"Aunt Maggie just loaned it to me while I'm in town, Linwood," I explained. "I'm not planning to keep it."

"All right then."

The doorbell rang once more, and Richard opened the door to let Aunt

Daphine, Vasti, and Arthur come in. I offered Aunt Daphine my chair and went into the kitchen to keep from getting caught between Sue and Vasti. Aunt Maggie was in there talking on the phone.

"Nellie? Are y'all coming over or not? What? I don't give a hoot about that floor wax. Get on over here! We're all waiting." She hung up firmly.

"Sometimes I don't think Nellie's got sense enough to come in out of the rain," Aunt Maggie said. "Laurie Anne, do me a favor and take these stools into the living-room. We're going to run out of places to sit soon, if we haven't already."

Sure enough, by the time I wrestled the first of the heavy, pine stools into the living-room, the couch and every chair was already taken. Richard gave up his seat to help me bring in the rest of the stools, but Burnettes kept arriving faster than we could find places to put them. By the time Aunt Nellie and Uncle Ruben showed up, even the floor was nearly full.

Aunt Maggie refused all offers of chairs, choosing instead to install herself in the middle of the room where she could turn as necessary to see everyone. In her hands were several pages of notebook paper, and I recognized Paw's careful printing on it.

She waited until everyone settled down, put on a pair of half-glasses, and then said, "Y'all know why we're here, so I may as well get to it. Ellis made me his executrix and I aim to do things just like he told me to. If anyone don't like it, you can just keep it to yourself. What you like don't make one bit of difference to me."

She paused as if inviting comment, but went on when no one spoke. "Ellis wanted me to tell you that he loved every one of you, and that he felt proud to have lived long enough to see so many of you grow up. He left a piece of something for each of you. Now not every piece is worth the same, and I don't want y'all comparing. Ellis decided what he wanted to give, and that's all there is to it. Does everybody understand that?"

There were nods and a chorus of "Yes, ma'ams."

"All right then. Nora, Ellis wanted you to have the family Bible our Mama and Daddy bought when they were first married. It's got all your names and birthdays and wedding dates in it, and he wants you to keep it up. He also wanted you to have all the family pictures and things like that."

Aunt Nora looked pleased, and I had to admit that it was an appropriate bequest.

She had been keeping the family together ever since she was young, and it was only right that she keep up the job.

Aunt Maggie went on. "Buddy, Ellis said you've been doing all his odd jobs for years, so he thought it only fair that you get his tools." She peered at him over the list. "You be careful with them tools, now. Some of them were my Daddy's. They're collector's items now, bringing good prices at the flea market."

Uncle Buddy nodded.

"Thaddeous, you're the oldest grandson and Ellis wanted you to have his pocket watch. Our granddaddy gave it to him because he was the first Burnette to graduate from high school."

The list went on. Paw had chosen a fitting bequest for each one of us. Sue got the station wagon, with plenty of space for her two kids, the one on the way, and later additions. Uncle Ruben was given Paw's color television, and it did not need to be said that at last he would have one that was paid for and could not be reclaimed by irate creditors. To Idelle, Odelle, and Carlelle, Paw left three completely different gifts, saying he had never had trouble telling them apart. To Richard he gave an ancient copy of *Hamlet*, which he had read in high school and kept ever since.

My legacy was a map of the Burnette lands as they used to be, and I wondered if it was Paw's way of reminding me where I came from.

Some of the bequests surprised me because they revealed things about my family I hadn't known. Paw left his guitar to Clifford, who shared his love of music. He left Willis a beat-up bedroom set, long since consigned to the attic, saying there wasn't a piece of furniture made that Willis couldn't repair and refinish. How had I missed learning these things about my own family?

Finally Aunt Maggie finished the list, removed her glasses, and said, "That's it. Like I said before, I don't want to hear about it if anyone's unhappy."

"Aren't you forgetting something, Aunt Maggie?" Vasti asked.

"I don't believe so."

"What about the house?"

"Paw left it to the church, didn't he?" Aunt Edna said anxiously.

Aunt Maggie carefully folded her sheath of papers. "No, Edna, Ellis did not leave the house to the church."

"He said he would."

"Oh Edna," Aunt Nellie said scornfully. "He did not, and you know it."

"Well he didn't leave it to you," Aunt Edna fired back. "You'd have a second mortgage on it within six months."

"Better that than to let Glass get his slimy hands on it."

Aunt Edna glared at her sister, her cheeks high spots of red. "You watch your mouth! Reverend Glass is a man of God!"

Aunt Nellie snorted loudly in response, and I had to resist the impulse to cover my eyes. This could get ugly in a hurry.

Then Aunt Nora stood up, her hands on her hips. "I hope y'all two realize what you sound like! You would *think* grown women could show a little respect when their father is barely in his grave."

Aunt Nellie and Aunt Edna stared at each other for a minute, but then Aunt Nellie relented. "You're right, Nora. I'm sorry, Edna. This week has been hard on me."

"I've been on edge myself," Aunt Edna acknowledged. "I'm sorry, too, sister."

"Then who does get the house?" Vasti persisted.

"Me," Aunt Maggie said. "I'm the last one with the Burnette name, and Ellis figured that since it was our daddy's before it was his, I've got as good a claim to it as anyone else." I was pretty sure there could be no argument to that, and everyone else seemed to agree.

The family milled around as Aunt Maggie located and distributed bequests. I went downstairs to help Aunt Nora remove family photos from the wall, then helped carry the ancient sewing machine Paw had left to Carlelle out to her car. I was in the kitchen wrapping Vasti's legacy, the cordial glasses Paw had given his bride on their first anniversary, when the doorbell rang.

I was the closest to the door, so I called out, "Aunt Maggie, do you want me to get that?"

"Go ahead," she hollered back from somewhere.

I opened the door, and there was Reverend Glass standing on the porch. "Reverend Glass," I said stupidly. "What a surprise."

He smiled like the cat who had just swallowed the canary. "I understood that your family would be reading Brother Burnette's will tonight, and I thought it would be a good time to start making arrangements."

"Arrangements?"

"For the transfer of title."

Good lord, he still thought he was getting the house. "I think I better get my aunt." I hesitated, not wanting to be rude and just yell for Aunt Maggie but certainly not wanting to leave him alone in the house.

Fortunately, Aunt Maggie saved me from making the decision by appearing from upstairs and saying, "What is it? Another casserole?"

"Aunt Maggie, you know Reverend Glass," I said.

She looked at him with ill-disguised disgust. "I suppose you want to come in."

"If that would be all right," he said, still smiling.

"Laurie Anne, take him on into the living-room. I'll go get Edna."

"Yes, ma'am. Won't you come this way, Reverend Glass?"

The living-room was currently empty. Glass took the recliner, and I perched on the couch. Neither of us said anything. I didn't know what to say, and I think he was too busy making plans for the house.

A few minutes later, Aunt Edna came in looking more than a little flustered, her hands fluttering from smoothing her hair to fixing the belt of her dress to wiping her hands. She was followed by Aunt Maggie, who had a stern expression on her face but a gleam in her eye. She was looking forward to this.

"Why Reverend Glass," Aunt Edna said as brightly as she could, "I wasn't expecting you."

Glass rose and took her hand in his. "I heard from Mrs. Funderburk that you would be reading your father's will tonight, and while I did not wish to intrude upon your grief, I thought that it best that I be here. I hope you don't find my haste unseemly."

"No, no, of course not. Please sit down. Can I offer you a drink? A soft drink, of course. Or iced tea?"

"No, thank you."

We sat for a minute without speaking. A few other family members walked by, but crept away when they saw Glass. Aunt Edna kept a brittle smile on her face, and nodded amiably.

Glass cleared his throat a few times before saying, "Has the will been read yet?"

"Oh yes," Aunt Maggie said. "We took care of that a good hour ago."

"I see. I thought it was customary for all heirs to be present when a will is read."

"We were all here," Aunt Maggie said with a wide-eyed, innocent look. She obviously wasn't planning on making this any easier for Aunt Edna.

Glass cleared his throat again. "I'm afraid I don't understand. I realize Mr. Burnette left his house to the church and not to me personally, but shouldn't a representative of the church have been present?"

Aunt Maggie turned to Aunt Edna. "Well Edna? Are you going to tell him, or am I?"

Glass looked from one of them to the other, and I looked everywhere else. Someone was going to have to tell him, and it wasn't going to be me.

"Well, Reverend Glass," Aunt Edna finally said, "I'm afraid there's been a misunderstanding." She smiled again, as if pleased with finding the right word.

Glass waited for her to continue, but when she didn't, he prompted, "What kind of misunderstanding?"

"Though Paw and I had discussed leaving the house to the church, he never completed the paperwork. His death was quite sudden, as you know."

"Of course, of course, it must have been a terrible shock to you all." His look of deep concern lasted a full ten seconds. "Still, you and I should be able to make the title transfer easily enough. It did pass on to you as the oldest, did it not?"

"Not exactly," Aunt Edna said. "Paw left the house to Aunt Maggie."

He turned to Aunt Maggie. "Then you and I should be able to take care of it."

Aunt Maggie said, "Hold on a minute, fellow. I'm not giving this house to nobody."

Glass's eyebrows lowered, for the first time betraying his consternation. "But surely," he said, "you will want to carry out Brother Burnette's wishes."

"Oh, I'll be carrying out Ellis's wishes all right," Aunt Maggie said, "but they do not include giving this house to a —" I had a good idea of what was coming next and I could tell Aunt Edna did too because she cringed, but Aunt Maggie stopped and visibly took hold of herself. "What I mean to say, Reverend Glass, is that Ellis had changed his mind about the house. He decided he'd rather keep it in the family."

"But the church!" Glass wailed. "We had such plans."

"I sure am sorry about that," Aunt Maggie said dryly. "Ellis's decision was fairly recent, and he hadn't had a chance to tell you." She looked at Aunt Edna. "Or Edna," she added, letting her off the hook. "As Edna said,

205

Ellis's death was unexpected."

A selection of emotions played across Glass's face. He eventually cleared his throat three times and said, "I must admit that this is a disappointment, but of course Mr. Burnette had to do what he thought proper."

I noticed that now it was Mr. Burnette instead of Brother Burnette.

"I just don't know what to say, Reverend Glass," Aunt Edna said miserably. "I thought Paw's mind was made up."

Glass nodded stiffly. "Don't trouble yourself, Sister. The thought processes of the elderly can become confused, and they often change their minds suddenly. The Church is forgiving."

I could tell Aunt Maggie wanted to say something else, but what came out was, "If you don't mind, Reverend, we've got some more family business we should attend to before it gets too late."

It was a clear dismissal. "Of course," he said as he rose. "I'll be going now." He was halfway out the door when he turned to Aunt Maggie and said, "Now that you'll be living next door, Miss Burnette, perhaps you'd be interested in attending our weekly Bible study classes. Wednesday evenings at six?"

With some effort, I kept my face straight. Glass might have lost this battle, but he wasn't giving up the war.

"I'll keep it in mind," Aunt Maggie said, and closed the door firmly behind him. Then she turned to Aunt Edna and said, "Edna, you know that you're the only reason I didn't tell that so-and-so what I think of him."

"Yes, ma'am," Aunt Edna replied, hanging her head and looking more like a five-year-old child than a grown woman.

Aunt Maggie allowed herself an exasperated sigh and said, "We'll say no more about it. But if that man ever gets the idea that I'm giving him this house —"

"He won't have any reason to think that, Aunt Maggie," Aunt Edna said hurriedly.

"All right then."

Aunt Edna muttered something, and scurried away.

Aunt Maggie went back upstairs, and I found Richard to tell him what he had missed. I finished up with, "I think you're right about Glass. He was peeved about the house, but I can't believe he wanted the house badly enough to kill for it. It's just as well. I wouldn't want to be the one to have to tell Aunt Edna that he was a murderer."

After everyone gathered their inheritances, pockets of people formed throughout the house until finally Aunt Maggie announced with her characteristic tact, "Y'all can go home now."

I got caught in a last flurry of conversation with my aunts at the front door.

"We'll see y'all at church on Sunday," Aunt Nora said to everyone in general.

"Sunday? Are we not going to the outlets Saturday?" Aunt Ruby Lee said.

"I forgot all about that," Aunt Nora said. "I don't suppose we should, so soon after the funeral and all."

"I guess not," Aunt Edna agreed mournfully.

"Why not?" Aunt Daphine said. "We've been talking about going shopping together for I don't know how long, and it's taken us weeks to set a time when none of us had to work or anything. Paw would want us to go."

"Maybe you're right," Aunt Nora said.

"What are y'all talking about?" I asked.

"Why don't you come with us, Laurie Anne?" Aunt Nora said. "We were all going to drive to Burlington to be there when the outlet stores open. We're going to make a day of it, and then go someplace nice for dinner."

"Are you sure you want me to tag along?

If it's just going to be you sisters . . ."

"Of course we want you to come. Vasti's coming, too. It will be all of us girls together."

I agreed, pleased not only by the chance to go shopping, but also by the prospect of picking my aunts' brains. Maybe one of them, without realizing it, knew something about Paw's death.

After everyone else was gone, Richard and I helped Aunt Maggie straighten up.

"Well that's that," Aunt Maggie said once we were finished. "Laurie Anne, do you think you could get over to the flea market Sunday? I had a lawyer put together some papers for you to sign about the house. Not that I don't trust you after you swore, but it's best to get everything in writing."

"That makes sense to me, but wouldn't it be easier to go to the lawyer's office?"

"No, let's do it at the flea market. You see I'm not exactly paying the lawyer. I'm trading him something for his services, and this way I can give it to him as soon as we finish."

I nodded. For Aunt Maggie, the arrangement made sense.

She headed on upstairs, but I didn't feel much like going to bed yet. Instead, I unrolled the map Paw had left me to show Richard. "This is the land we used to have," I said, showing him the borders. "Then, like Aunt Maggie said, we had to sell most of it during the Depression." I outlined a much smaller area with my finger. "That's all that's left."

"How big is that?" Richard asked.

"Come outside with me, and I'll show you." We went out to the back porch, and I showed him how the landmarks corresponded with reality.

"What's that?" Richard asked, pointing to a large rectangle on the map.

"That's the tobacco curing shed. From when this was a farm. They'd cut the tobacco and then leave it to dry out there."

"Why so far from the house?"

"Whichever great-grandmother it was then didn't care for the scent of tobacco, so she made them put it far enough away from the house that she couldn't smell it." I pointed to a dusty track leading from the back of the house, and then to the same track on the map. "The tobacco road leads to the shed, and then to Rock Creek Road." I rolled the map back up, sat down on the white-painted porch swing, and patted the spot next to me. Richard took the hint.

Despite everything, I had to admit that it was a beautiful night. The humidity had subsided some, there was the hint of a breeze in the air, and the tree-frogs and crickets added their familiar songs. I snuggled closer to Richard's side, and when he put his arm around me, I realized with some surprise that I was smiling. Guilt tweaked me for a moment, but I shook it off. Like Aunt Daphine had said, Paw would want me to feel better.

"You know, I had forgotten how nice this could be," I said.

"Hmmm?"

"The crickets and the frogs, and the smell of fresh cut grass. And sitting on the porch in a swing. Look, see that!" I pointed at a yellow flicker in the air.

"One of Bush's thousand points of light?"

I elbowed him gently. "It's a lightning bug. I haven't seen a lightning bug in I don't know how long. We used to catch them in our hands to make our hands glow."

"You touched bugs?"

"Lightning bugs aren't bugs. I mean, I know they're insects, but they aren't bugs. They're different."

"Of course."

"We used to catch pocketbook ladies, too."

"Is that anything like a bag lady?"

"Did y'all not catch pocketbook ladies? Those little black bugs that roll up into a ball like an armadillo. We'd pick them up and watch them roll up. Then we'd put them down again and watch them unroll."

"I guess I had a deprived childhood."

We swung gently in companionable silence, then I surprised myself again. "You know what? Even with everything that's happened, part of me is glad to be here. To be home."

Richard kissed my forehead gently. "Of course you are."

Then very quietly I said, "I miss Paw," and Richard held me for a long time while I cried.

CHAPTER 22

It was well after midnight before Richard and I got to bed, but we made up for it by sleeping until ten o'clock the next morning. By the time we made it out of the bedroom, the house was empty, other than a note from Aunt Maggie saying that she had gone out. We had picked up cereal and milk at the store the previous night, and we took our time eating breakfast as we read the newspaper. I checked for more news about Melanie Wilson, but there was only a brief mention that the investigation was continuing.

"What do you want to do today?" Richard asked once we had washed our bowls and spoons.

"I'm supposed to meet Aunt Daphine for lunch at one, but that's all we've got planned so far." I considered the possibilities. "I think our first stop should be the mill."

"Are you sure you want to go there?"

"I don't want to, but I feel like I need to. It's been a while since I've been inside the mill, and I don't have a clear picture in my head of where it happened."

We showered and dressed, and drove to the mill. After we got through the main gate, I pulled over to the security booth.

"Can I help you, ma'am?" the guard asked.

"Could you tell me if either Davy Sanders or Ralph Stewart are working today?"

"I'm Ralph Stewart."

"I'm Laura Fleming, Ellis Burnette's granddaughter. This is my husband, Richard. If you don't mind, we'd like to talk to you about his accident."

He looked nervously toward the front of the mill where Burt Walters's office was. "I don't know. . . . I better not without Mr. Walters's say-so."

"Then we'll go see Mr. Walters," I said. Stewart directed me toward the visitor's parking lot, and retreated into the booth.

I checked with the woman at the information desk to make sure Walters's office was still on the fourth floor, and we rode the elevator up. The first thing I saw was a bolt of faded blue gingham in a glass case with a sign identifying it as the first woven at Walters Mill. The second was a sharp-faced secretary with arched eyebrows and a seemingly permanent frown. Her desk was placed directly in front of a door with a brass plate that read "Burt Walters, Chief Executive Officer."

"May I help you?" she asked stiffly.

"I'd like to see Mr. Walters. I'm Laura Fleming, Ellis Burnette's granddaughter. This is my husband, Richard."

The receptionist peered at the calendar on her desk. "Did you have an appointment?"

"No, but it shouldn't take but a minute."

Her frown deepened. "And may I ask what this pertains to?"

"I'd like to talk to the security guard who found my grandfather, and to go see where he was found."

"Oh? Why is that?"

I guess Richard saw the steam starting to come out of my ears, because he said, "You can tell Mr. Walters that we wanted to investigate further before we decide what legal steps to take."

The secretary's frown turned into a straight line.

"Legal steps? Just a moment." She went through the door, closing it firmly behind her, and stepped out a minute later. "Mr. Walters will see you now."

"Thank you so much," I said sweetly,

215

and Richard winked at me as we went in.

Burt Walters was coming out from behind the massive mahogany desk, and reached out to take my hand in a gesture that was not so much a handshake as a pat. "Why Laurie Anne. It's been an age since we've seen you. This must be your husband."

I performed introductions, and Walters shook Richard's hand in a more manly fashion.

"Come on in, have a seat," he said. He was a small man, conservatively but expensively dressed in a blue seersucker suit. His hair and mustache were jet-black, and although I knew the color was almost certainly from a bottle, it was at least skillfully applied. Though he was not unattractive, he still suffered by comparison with William "Big Bill" Walters, forever peering over his shoulder in the life-sized oil painting hung on the wall behind him.

"I cannot tell you how sorry I am about Ellis," he said once we were all seated. "What a tragedy for all of us here at Walters Mill! The Burnette family has been a mainstay of the mill since its very inception. Your grandfather, and then your aunts, and now your cousins. The Burnette girls are still a legend around here."

"Women," I said.

"I beg your pardon?"

"Since my aunts all have grown children, I thought that 'women' was a better word."

"Of course, of course." He smiled weakly. "It's just that I still remember them as they were when I first knew them, and I never saw a prettier bunch of girls . . . women. Your mother was the prettiest one, and I can see that you've inherited her good looks. Did she ever tell you that we used to keep company when we were in school?"

I said, "Yes, she did," but keeping company was not how Mama had described it. Walters had asked her out a few times, and then tried to use his father's power versus her father's job to convince her to "show him a good time." He never expected Mama to tell Paw, who promptly told Big Bill, a man of honor in such matters. They had not kept company after that.

"The reason we're here, Mr. Walters, is to find out more about what happened to my grandfather."

"Surely that would only upset you."

"Actually I think it would clear my mind to know everything. We'd like to talk with Ralph Stewart, and we want to see the place where he found my grandfather."

He clasped his hands together and nodded. "I see. To tell you the truth, I don't know if Ralph Stewart is on duty today."

"We already spoke to Ralph. He's working the front gate."

"That's right, he is. The problem is that I couldn't possibly spare time to take you down there today."

"Mr. Walters, as you just pointed out, the Burnettes have been around this mill just about as long as the Walterses. I know the way."

"Insurance regulations prohibit unescorted visitors from wandering around the mill."

"Then Ralph could take us."

He hesitated, and I guessed he was out of excuses. He leaned back, then sat up straight with a look of determination. "Let's put our cards out on the table, shall we? Does your family intend to sue Walters Mill? Because if you do, I can assure you that you would fail. There is not one shred of evidence that we have been negligent. Not one shred!"

"We're not really planning to go to court," I said soothingly.

"Then you're hoping for an out-of-court settlement, is that it? I don't know what you've heard, but Walters Mill is not made of money. What with foreign imports and inflation, we're barely keeping our heads above water. A settlement could put us into bankruptcy, and then what would happen to the people of Byerly?"

This was going too far. I had wanted to scare him a little, not throw him into a panic. "Mr. Walters, we're not planning to sue the mill, and we don't want an out-of-court settlement. My grandfather died here. I want to know why. Surely you can understand that."

He still looked suspicious, but after fidgeting a few more seconds, he finally nodded. "Well, if you're sure it won't upset you. I'll call Ralph to come show you around."

"Thank you," I said, and Richard and I stood.

"Now you be sure and let me know if there's anything else I can do."

"Yes, sir," Richard answered for us. "We certainly will."

CHAPTER 23

Ralph Stewart met us downstairs. "Sorry about putting y'all to the trouble of talking to Mr. Walters, Mrs. Fleming, Mr. Fleming," he said, "but a fellow can't be too careful. Not as hard as jobs are to come by these days."

"That's all right. Mr. Walters is an old friend of the family. And please call me Laura."

"What can I do for you, Laura?"

"Is there somewhere we can talk?"

"How about the break room? Morning coffee break is over, so we'll have it to ourselves."

Some of the "Safety On the Job" and "Punctual Employees are Happy Employees" posters were new and the old toaster oven had been replaced with a tiny microwave, but otherwise the room looked much as it had when I used to wait there for Paw's shift to end. Ralph brushed the crumbs from someone's Moon Pie off of the table nearest the window, and courteously held a chair for me to sit.

"Do either of y'all want a Coca-Cola?" he asked.

"No, thank you," I said, and Richard added, "You go ahead."

"I believe I will." He fed change into an ancient Coke machine, and I was a little surprised when it produced a bottle instead of the ubiquitous can. Ralph popped the cap off, took a long swallow, and sighed in satisfaction before sitting down.

"It gets right hot in the booth," he said. "I've got a fan, but it don't do much when it's as hot as it's been lately."

I nodded, and let him take another swallow before beginning. "I understand you were the one to find my grandfather after the accident." Or whatever it was, I added silently.

"Yes, ma'am, I was. I sure was sorry to hear he had passed on. We're going to miss him around here, and that's a fact. Everybody thought a lot of him. He was still working full-time when I first started here, and he took the time to show me around and help me get settled in. He knew my daddy from when *he* worked here years ago, and was always asking about him. Daddy had the brown lung."

I nodded sympathetically. Brown lung, long unacknowledged by the powers that be in the mill, had reduced uncounted men and women to constantly coughing wrecks. We Burnettes were unusually fortunate in that we had escaped it.

"Anyway," Ralph continued, "I don't really know what I can tell you."

"Just tell us what happened that day," Richard said.

"Let me think a minute." Ralph took another swallow of his drink. "I got here a little early that day so Davy could leave early. We're not supposed to leave the booth early like that, but he was going to take his two boys out to the movies, and he was in kind of a hurry." He looked a little uncomfortable.

"We won't tell anybody," I said.

"I'd appreciate it if you didn't. Now, this was about a quarter of three and what with Davy being in a hurry and all, he left as soon as I got there and never mentioned that Ellis had gone inside. It wasn't until about five that I was looking through the sign-in book and saw that he had come in and never signed back out again."

"Y'all keep track of everyone who comes in, don't you?" I asked.

"Yes, ma'am. Especially on weekends."

"Did anyone else come in that day?"

"Not a soul. Ellis was the only one on

that day's page in the book. I thought at first he must have just forgotten to sign out, but your grandfather was always careful because he knew we could get into trouble if he didn't follow the rules. I called the warehouse, and when I didn't get an answer, I went and looked in the parking lot and there was that old station wagon of his.

"Seeing his car still there scared me. I knew Ellis was getting on up there in years, and that his heart wasn't what it used to be. I locked up the booth and went inside to the warehouse where we keep the socks for pulling. There he was, lying face down with a tube of socks on top of him.

"At first I thought he was . . ." He hesitated, and I realized gratefully he was trying to spare my feelings. Richard took my hand under the table.

Ralph went on, "Well, I couldn't tell how bad off he was. There wasn't much blood, but there was a lump as big as a goose egg on the back of his head. I rolled him over real careful and saw that he was breathing, but he was cold as ice. I found a piece of cloth to lay over him and then called Mr. Walters and an ambulance."

He shrugged. "That's about it. I stayed right there with him until I heard the siren, and then I went to let the ambulance in."

"When you were waiting with him, did he say anything?" Richard asked.

Ralph shook his head. "Not a word. Mr. Walters showed up as they were taking him away, and followed them to the hospital. That's when I called your aunt and uncle." He finished his Coke, and stood. "If y'all still want to see where I found him, I'll be glad to show you."

The warehouse always seemed cold to me, no matter what the weather was like outside. We walked through the huge, dimly lit room, the clicking of our shoes against the concrete floor mingling eerily with echoes from other parts of the mill.

"This is it," Ralph said, stopping at a bank of high shelves. There was a rickety-looking stepladder leaned against the end of the shelves, and the shelves themselves were filled with open cartons with the word "SOCKS" scrawled on all four sides in black Magic Marker.

"He was right about here," Ralph said, using his foot to draw a circle on the floor. I looked away, the picture of Paw laying there suddenly all too clear.

Had Paw just had that heart attack his doctor had been warning him about for years, or had someone been waiting for him? I looked around the warehouse. There were plenty of places someone could have hidden. Over behind that rack of shelves, or next to that column. If Paw had known the person, he or she could have been in plain sight, with Paw suspecting nothing until it was too late.

I shook my head. Ralph hadn't really told or shown us a thing that we hadn't already known.

"Is there anything else?" Ralph asked.

"Just one more thing," I said and hesitated, wanting to word my next question carefully. "When you went looking for Paw, did you see anything odd?"

"Like what?"

"Just anything different," I said, not wanting to ask him directly if he had seen signs of someone else having been there.

He rubbed his chin for a moment. "I can't think of a thing. I came in, and there he was."

I forced myself to visualize it as it must have looked. It would have been much like today, only quieter, when Paw came in. He would have reached up to pull a carton off of the shelf, and must have gotten hold of it when he either fell or was hit, and spilled the socks on himself. Wait a minute! That didn't make sense.

"Ralph, did you say he was face *down?*"

"Yes, ma'am."

"But if the socks were on top of him, he must have been reaching up to pull a box down when the heart attack hit or he lost his balance or whatever. It was the back of his head that was hurt. So why was he face down? He should have been on his back."

Ralph shrugged. "I never thought about it. I suppose he rolled over after he fell."

"Maybe." I looked at the spot once more, and shivered.

Richard put his arm around me, and said, "Let's get you out of here," and Ralph walked us back to the front door.

"We appreciate your time, Ralph," I said.

"That's all right," he said. "I just wish I had found him sooner, and maybe things would have turned out different."

"Ralph, according to the doctor, it wouldn't have made a bit of difference," I said. I didn't know whether that was true or not, but it was at worst a white lie.

Ralph's face relaxed into a smile. We started to leave, but then I turned back. Ralph was waiting in front of the elevator. "Ralph," I said, "you're going to tell Mr. Walters what we talked about, aren't you?"

He reddened slightly, but nodded.

"Then you can tell him that I'm convinced that the mill isn't at fault, and in fact should be congratulated for your taking care of Paw the way you did. Tell him I have no intention of taking any kind of legal action."

"He'll be mighty glad to hear that," Ralph said, and stepped into the elevator.

"Do you want me to drive?" Richard asked as soon as we got outside.

I nodded, and waited until we were in the car before I said, "There is no way Paw could have fallen so that he would hit the back of his head and then land face down. Someone hit him, and poured the socks over him to make it look like an accident. It was murder."

I was almost hoping he would disagree, but instead he quoted from *Macbeth:*

Confusion now hath made his
    masterpiece!
Most sacrilegious murder has broke ope
The Lord's anointed temple, and stole
    thence
The life o' the building!

"Confusion is right. Richard, it was bad enough when I thought it *might* be murder. Now that I'm sure that it was, I don't know what to do next."

He shrugged. "We'll do what we can. 'Truth will come to light; murder cannot be hid long.' "

"It's hiding pretty well this time. What do we do now?"

"It's after twelve. Aren't you meeting Aunt Daphine for lunch?"

"That's right, I am. Did you want to come with me?"

"No, I think I'll let you Burnette women have some time alone."

"You're sweet."

"Quite right. Besides, I want to make some notes on the syllabus for my class."

We made a quick stop at the grocery store to pick up sandwich fixings for Richard's lunch, and then I left him at the house.

CHAPTER 24

It was just one o'clock when I pulled into the parking lot of the small shopping center where Aunt Daphine ran her beauty parlor. The scent of mingled perfume and chemicals that is unique to beauty parlors assailed my nose as soon as I opened the door to La Dauphin. From the elegant salon in New York where a friend had once lured me to be "made over" to the tiny studio where I get my hair styled in Boston to Aunt Daphine's medium-sized operation, they all smelled the same.

"Can I help you?" the dark-haired girl at the front desk asked.

"Could you tell Mrs. Marston that her niece Laura is here?"

"Laura?" The girl looked doubtful.

"Laurie Anne."

"Oh, Laurie Anne from Boston! Daphine told me you were coming. I'll tell her you're here." She stepped through the curtain of Mardi Gras colored beads, and I could see a row of half-a-dozen styling chairs, each occupied by a woman in some stage of beautification under the attention of a pink-smocked hair stylist. Aunt Daphine looked up from the mass of dirty-blond curls she was in the midst of and smiled.

"Hey there. Come meet everybody." She introduced me to the other stylists, and then nodded at the woman whose hair she was working with. "This is Mrs. Mintin. I'm running a little behind, because Mrs. Mintin got invited to a big to-do at the country club and we decided to do something special for her."

"Are you sure those curls aren't too tight, Daphine? I don't want them to look too tight," Mrs. Mintin said.

"I know they look tight now, but as humid as it is, I have to set them tight or there won't be any curls left for tonight."

"They won't *all* fall out, will they?"

"No, ma'am, they are going to fall out just enough to look wonderful."

"Well, if you say so."

To me, Aunt Daphine said, "Ruby Lee called a little while ago. I told her we were going to lunch, and asked her to come with us. You don't mind, do you?"

"Of course not."

"Good. She said she'd be along shortly." Aunt Daphine turned back to Mrs.

Mintin's hair. "Laurie Anne, why don't you let Gladys do your nails for you while you're waiting? She's just learning how since Margaret left to have her baby, and she needs to practice. Gladys? Come do Laurie Anne's nails for her. We can watch the front door from here."

The girl from the desk came back and grinned shyly. "Sure you don't mind me being a beginner?"

"Of course not. I'm sure you'll do fine."

"Now you sit right there," Gladys said, pointing to a pink, vinyl-covered chair, and rolled over a small manicurist's table neatly arranged with bottles, cotton balls, and orange sticks. Starting with my right hand, she carefully cleaned underneath each nail.

"Your nails are awfully short," Gladys commented. "I can build them up with this Italian stuff I have, and no one will know they aren't real."

"No thanks. I work on a keyboard all day, and long nails would just get in the way."

"How about plastic nails? I've got some French ones that come off with this solution, and you could take them off before you go to work, and put them back on for your husband at night."

"I don't think so." To head her off before

she suggested some nail care alternative from Mexico, I said, "Have you been working for Aunt Daphine long?"

"Almost two years now. I took cosmetology classes in high school and your aunt gave me a job right after I graduated. I went to school with some of your cousins, you know. Willis was in my grade, and I know Estelle, Odelle, and Carlelle, and of course Thaddeous." She sighed heavily. "Thaddeous was so good-looking. Well, he still is, but I'm engaged now." She placed my right hand in a pan of warm hand lotion and started cleaning the nails on the left.

"Did you know Melanie Wilson?"

"Wasn't what happened to her terrible? Everyone knew her on account of her being head cheerleader, but she didn't put on airs or anything. Can you switch hands?"

Once the left hand was soaking, Gladys began filing the nails and pushing back the cuticles on the right. "Someone told me Thaddeous had a really big crush on Melanie."

I nodded. So much for Thaddeous's secret passion.

Gladys went on. "One time some of the guys were messing around in his locker and found a picture of Melanie from when she was homecoming queen. He had cut it out of the newspaper and glued it to the inside of his notebook. They told everyone about it, and Thaddeous was so mad when he found out that he said he'd kill them." She pulled my left hand out of the lotion.

The chimes on the door jingled, and Aunt Ruby Lee came in. "Hey there," she said. "How are y'all doing?"

"Pretty good," I answered.

"I'm running a little late," Aunt Daphine said, "but I shouldn't be too much longer."

"Well, you know I've got more time than money," Aunt Ruby Lee said and pulled a chair over to the table to watch my manicure.

After one last buff with an emery board, Gladys surveyed her handiwork, and said, "What color do you want me to put on?" She brought forth a plastic carousel of reds, pinks, corals, and shades thereof.

"Just clear."

"Clear? If I make them clear, no one will know you've had them done." She pulled out a bottle and shook it. "Now this would go real good with that blouse you're wearing. It's Mauve Amber Frost."

I was momentarily intrigued by how they fit so much color into such a small bottle, but said, "I think I'd like clear."

Gladys shook her head in dismay, but began to comply.

"I bet your husband doesn't like nail polish," Aunt Ruby Lee said. Actually I didn't think that Richard and I had ever discussed the subject.

Aunt Ruby Lee continued, "Fred, my first husband, didn't, so I didn't wear any when I was married to him, but I always liked color on my nails. Conrad does, too." They were currently painted a cheerful strawberry color.

"Laurie Anne and I were just talking about Melanie Wilson," Gladys said.

Aunt Ruby Lee shook her head sadly. "Poor thing. You know I was listening to the radio when they first announced she was missing Friday night, and I had a feeling that something was bad wrong. The kids were all out, and I was pure scared to be alone. I checked every window in the house to make sure they were all locked good and tight, then I called Edna to make sure she was all right. Isn't it a shame when women are afraid to be alone in their own homes?"

"Where was Uncle Conrad?" I asked.

"Up at the Elk Lodge — they were having a party for new members. I knew

Loman would be there, too, so that's why I called Edna. You know Loman is the president of their chapter, and he thinks Conrad might be elected vice-president when they vote in a couple of weeks. He's been pushing for it with the other members. Loman's real smart, and he knows that holding office in the Elks can really help a man's chances at the mill. Lots of the supervisors are lodge members."

Gladys finished painting the last nail, and promptly tucked my hands into a pink plastic gadget marked Nails-So-Dry. "You just let them sit in there for a while, and you'll be all done."

"Thanks Gladys."

"Well, ladies," Aunt Daphine said as she pulled the protective plastic apron from around her client. "Aren't Mrs. Mintin's curls just perfect?"

"Not a bit tight," I said.

Mrs. Mintin seemed satisfied, and after Aunt Daphine saw her off, my aunts and I walked to the Woolworth's further down in the shopping center. We found an empty booth at the lunch counter and ordered three of the country-style steak specials, which the waitress assured us tasted home-made.

"Daphine, is there any word yet on when

they're going to have Melanie Wilson's funeral?" Aunt Ruby Lee asked. "You always hear the news at the beauty parlor first."

"Mrs. Funderburk came by this morning, and Mrs. Wilson told her the police have finished the autopsy and they're going to release the body today. It's too soon to have it tomorrow, and they can't have it on Sunday, so it will probably be Monday afternoon," Aunt Daphine said.

"Did they learn anything from the autopsy?" I asked.

"They've got to run more tests before they'll say much more, but they do know for sure she was raped."

"I didn't think there was any question about that," Aunt Ruby Lee said. "I mean, the way they found her and all. Will they be able to tell anything about who did it?"

"I don't know," Aunt Daphine said. "They can find out a lot in the labs these days."

Aunt Ruby Lee looked around to make sure no one was in hearing distance, and then whispered, "Will they be able to tell if it was blacks who did it?"

"Does it matter what color they were?" I said, more sharply than I had intended.

Aunt Ruby Lee looked abashed, and then said, "I guess not."

Our food arrived then, and we distrib-

236

uted paper napkins, salt, and pepper. The fried steak and its thick gravy were good, but Aunt Daphine noticed right off that the mashed potatoes were instant.

After we had taken a few bites each, Aunt Ruby Lee asked, "Can you believe Reverend Glass coming to the house last night? Why on earth did Edna tell him all that stuff about the house? I was so embarrassed for her."

Aunt Daphine shook her head. "I'm sure Edna meant well."

"Was Aunt Edna always that religious?" I asked. "Mama never mentioned it."

Aunt Daphine said, "She didn't used to be like she is now. She went to church on Sundays like anybody else, but she wasn't up there every day of the week at prayer meetings and Bible study classes and all that."

"I don't think she got bad until Linwood started getting into trouble at school," Aunt Ruby Lee said. "Smoking and skipping classes and all. Loman was no help, needless to say, so Edna went to Glass for advice about what to do. I don't know that he did Linwood or her any good, but that's when she started going up there all the time."

"I'll tell you one thing," Aunt Daphine

said. "Between you, me, and the gate post, if all I had to look forward to every day was spending the night with Loman, I'd find someplace else to go, too. Loman's just lucky it's the church and not another man. Edna could still be a good-looking woman if she put her mind to it."

"Is Uncle Loman that bad?" I asked. Though I had never cared much for the man, I had nothing much against him either. This lack of feeling seemed to be reciprocal.

"Got about as much personality as this counter, if you ask me," Aunt Daphine said, rapping next to her plate. "Never has a word to say to anyone when we see him, and he's the same way at home. If he'd pay a little attention to Linwood once in a while, maybe the boy wouldn't spend so much time picking on other people."

"Loman's not all bad," Aunt Ruby Lee objected. "I wouldn't have met Conrad if it weren't for him. Every time I went to see Edna, Conrad would be over there visiting Loman. Conrad's mother said they've been close ever since they were boys. What with working together and being in the lodge together, I think Loman sees more of Conrad than I do."

By then we had cleaned our plates, including the instant mashed potatoes. We were trying to decide if we had room for dessert when Aunt Ruby Lee looked up, and said, "Oh no, not again."

"What?" I said, turning to see. Roger Bailey was outside on the sidewalk looking at us through the window. When he saw we had seen him, he grinned and waved.

"He's not coming in here, is he?" Aunt Ruby Lee asked, knowing the answer already. Sure enough, a minute later he walked up to our booth. "Well, isn't this a surprise? You ladies don't mind if I join you, do you?"

Aunt Ruby Lee looked distinctly unhappy, but Aunt Daphine said, "Of course not, Roger. Have a seat." I slid over to let him squeeze into the booth next to me.

Roger called over to the waitress for a glass of iced tea, and then said, "I'm glad I ran into y'all. I wanted to tell you how sorry I am about Ellis. I wanted to go to the funeral, but I had a job down in Charlotte and couldn't get back in time."

Aunt Daphine said, "That's all right, Roger, a man's got to work. We appreciate the thought."

The waitress brought over Roger's iced tea, and Aunt Ruby Lee said, "Could we get the check please?" Then she added to us, "I've just got so much to do today, I don't know how I'm ever going to get it all done."

I hid a grin. This was a big change from her attitude earlier.

"You go ahead," Aunt Daphine said, taking pity on her sister. "I owe you for lunch last week, so I'll take care of it this time."

Aunt Ruby Lee grabbed her pocketbook, and was up before Roger could say a word.

"Say hello to the kids for me," he called after her, and then he stared forlornly into his iced tea. "I guess I can't blame her for not wanting me around," he said. "She'd probably just as soon I up and moved away so she wouldn't have to worry about running into me."

"Now Roger, it's not like that," Aunt Daphine said. "It's just kind of awkward for her, that's all. Just because she couldn't stay with you doesn't mean she doesn't care for you."

Roger looked up at her. "Do you mean that? Do you think Ruby Lee still has some feeling for me?"

"Of course she does. Not like before, but I'm sure she still considers you a friend."

"I guess that's something, anyway."

The waitress returned with our check,

but Roger took it from her before Aunt Daphine or I could reach for it. "You let me get this."

"That's not necessary Roger," Aunt Daphine objected.

"It's the least I can do," he said. He pulled out his wallet, and handed the waitress some money.

"At least let me get the tip," I said.

"No, you just put your money away."

"Thank you, Roger," I said in surrender.

He started to put his wallet back in his pocket, and then opened it back up. "Tell you what. Laurie Anne, why don't you come out to the Mustang Club tonight?" He handed me a couple of cardboard tickets. "The boys and I are playing tonight, and you can bring that husband of yours."

"That's a good idea," Aunt Daphine said, "Y'all shouldn't be moping around. It's not good for young people."

Since I couldn't very well explain that we had been doing anything but moping around, I accepted the two passes for that night's show.

"How about you, Daphine?" Roger said, holding out another pair of tickets. "You used to cut a fine figure on the dance floor."

Aunt Daphine smiled. "That's a tempting offer, but I've got plans tonight. Thanks just the same."

Roger replaced the tickets. "All right, but come on by if you change your mind." He turned to me and winked. "Maybe I've been chasing the wrong sister." He grinned, and left.

"That Roger is one character in this world," Aunt Daphine said after he was gone, but she was still smiling. "Well, this has been fun, but I have to get back to the shop." We gathered our purses, I walked her back to the beauty parlor, and she hugged me goodbye.

"Don't forget about going shopping tomorrow morning," she added as I headed for the car.

CHAPTER 25

I found Richard sprawled across the bed reading what looked like one of Paw's Louis L'Amour books. I couldn't tell for sure because as soon as he saw me, he thrust it under the pillow and started writing furiously on a pad of paper.

"How's the syllabus going?" I asked, careful not to grin.

"Very well. Lots of ideas," he said, still scribbling. "How was lunch?"

"It was nice. Aunt Ruby Lee showed up and went with us. My former uncle Roger showed up, too. He gave me two passes for his performance tonight at the Mustang Club. You don't know anyone who'd like to go with me, do you?"

"I think I could fix you up with someone, if you don't mind a man who is completely ignorant in the ways of country music."

"I can deal with that. Where's Aunt Maggie?"

"She blew in with a load of merchandise, took advantage of the sandwich stuff we bought, and blew back out on another expedition. She said she'd be eating at the auction house tonight, so we should get dinner on our own."

I stuck one manicured hand in front of his face. "What do you think?"

He kissed it absently and turned to a fresh page. "You have lovely hands."

"I got my nails done."

He inspected my hand more closely. "So you did. Very nice." He kept on writing.

Gladys would be much distressed. Maybe I should have gone for the Mauve Amber Frost.

I joined him on the bed. "I know you've been busy with that syllabus," I said, keeping a straight face when he looked at me suspiciously, "but do you have any idea of where we should go next?"

He put down the pad with a show of reluctance and said, "Not really. Obviously the killer had access to the mill."

"That doesn't help much. Almost anyone in town could have gotten into the mill. Either they work there now, or they used to work there, or someone in their family works there."

"Aren't the doors locked on the weekend?"

"Sure, but anyone who's a supervisor or

higher gets a key. Since they haven't been all that strict with changing locks when someone retires or leaves, they just keep making more copies to hand out. There's no telling how many keys are floating around town. Paw still had his key — that's how he'd get in to pick up socks."

"What about the guard at the gate?"

"I already thought about that. There's a hole in the fence in the back of the mill. Odelle told me about it, and I bet it's one of those open secrets that everyone knows about. Except Burt Walters, of course."

"Why do they bother to post a guard at all?" Richard asked, sounding exasperated.

I shrugged. "I suppose they'd do something more about security if they had to, but it's never been a problem."

"So anybody could have been there laying in wait for him," Richard said slowly, but then added, "There's a question — how did the murderer know Paw was going to be at the mill? He didn't have set times to pick up socks, did he?"

"No."

"What if he was there already? What if Paw saw something at the mill he wasn't supposed to see, and was killed so he couldn't tell anyone?"

"Like what?"

"Theft, drug dealing, an illicit rendezvous. What if someone has a secret cache of heroin hidden among the finished cloth, and sends out the drugs along with the regular shipments?"

It had a certain appeal, but I shook my head. "Much as I would like to cast Burt Walters as a drug mogul, I don't think it works."

"Why not?"

"You don't know the mill. Everyone there knows what everyone else is up to. Most of these people have known each other since they were children, and their parents are friends, and their grandparents. You can't keep a secret there."

Richard didn't look convinced.

"Could you deal drugs out of the English department at Boston College without someone noticing something?"

He relented. "Probably not."

"It's the same thing. Besides, we know that Paw was worried about something *before* he went to the mill."

"Otherwise he wouldn't have finished that batch of socks so quickly, and he wouldn't have needed more to pull. You're right."

"There's still the Melanie Wilson angle."

"No offense, but I'm not convinced

Paw's death had anything to do with Melanie's. Just because there are two murders in a short span of time doesn't mean that they're connected."

"I'm not completely convinced myself," I admitted. "I am sure Paw was worried about something, and that newspaper was the only thing out of place around here. Paw was such a man of habit."

"Maybe there was something else in the paper that we missed. Do we still have it?"

"It's around here somewhere." I rummaged around in the stuff on the dresser until I found it, and handed it to Richard.

" 'This news is old enough, yet it is every day's news.' *Measure for Measure*," he said. Knowing that he hated anyone to read over his shoulder, I gave him a few minutes and then asked, "So? Any other likely candidates?"

"I'm afraid not," he said shaking his head. "There was a very successful May Fair last week, the high school has snared someone I've never heard of as their commencement speaker, and the agenda for the next Town Council meeting includes debate over adding two traffic signals."

"I can't imagine Paw losing sleep over any of those. All that leaves us is Melanie."

"Assuming that the paper is connected at all, that is."

I stuck my tongue out at him. "What if Paw saw something Friday night, and the murderer killed him to keep him quiet?"

"So where does the newspaper come in?"

"Maybe he didn't know that Melanie had disappeared until he saw the paper Sunday morning. She went missing late Friday night, so it wouldn't have made it into the paper until then."

"As much of an uproar as it caused, don't you think someone might have mentioned it to him? Not to mention television and radio news."

I thought about it. "Actually, that fits even better. Whatever it was that Paw saw, it couldn't have been too obvious. If he had seen someone dragging off a screaming girl, he would have jumped in with both feet. He must have seen something subtle that he didn't connect with the murder until he read that story in Sunday's paper."

"It's possible," Richard conceded. "Do we have any idea of where Paw might have gone Friday night?"

"No, but we might be able to figure it out." I located the local road map Richard had found and unfolded it in front of him. "Now here's Paw's house," I said, pointing to the spot on the map. "And here's the area where Melanie's body was found. Now where was the car found again?"

Richard skimmed through the article. "It says they found it on Johnston Road, a mile past the intersection with Highway 321."

I found the intersection on the map, and followed Johnston Road with my finger. Then I stopped and stared. "Richard, look." He looked where I was pointing. There was a large red X almost exactly where the police found Melanie's car.

"Did Paw make that mark?" Richard asked.

"He must have. Aunt Maggie said she hadn't been downstairs before she and I went down there Monday afternoon."

"Is it recent?"

I held it close up to my face to look. "I don't know."

"Are there any other marks?"

"A bunch," I admitted. There were Xs and circles in at least three colors marking everything from the flea market Aunt Maggie sold at to the latest location of Aunt Nellie's and Uncle Ruben's house trailer to the tobacco shed back behind Paw's house.

"So how do you know that this one means anything?"

"It has to," I said stubbornly. "Why else would he have marked that particular spot? There's not a thing out there."

"So he was interested in the murder."

"Interested? When was the last time you marked a murder site on a road map?"

"But it wasn't the murder site. It was only where the car was left."

"Whatever it was. He must have known something, or he wouldn't have marked the map like that. Right?"

"I suppose so."

"Well I think that this is enough to talk to the police about. The county police are handling the investigation into Melanie's murder because the car was found outside of Byerly, but I bet Chief Norton will know what's going on."

"Should we call the redoubtable Chief Norton?"

"I've got a better idea," I said, reaching for my pocketbook. "Let's drive over to the police station and see what we can find out in person." Ignoring his protests, I pulled Richard off of the bed and nudged him downstairs and into the car.

CHAPTER 26

As I drove, Richard asked, "Do you know Chief Norton?"

"Sure. I went to school with Junior."

"Junior? Sounds like something out of a Burt Reynolds movie? Does he wear mirror shades?"

"Junior is a very good police chief," I said indignantly. "The Nortons have been police chiefs for generations."

"Don't tell me they inherit the post."

"Nothing that formal. The outgoing chief recommends a replacement, and the mayor and the town council generally go along. It's not a hotly contested position, so it's always worked out."

"Chief Junior Norton," Richard said, looking amused. "I love the South."

I didn't grin, but I wanted to. Richard was going to be more than a little surprised when he met Junior.

The police station was near the middle of town, next to City Hall. As usual in downtown Byerly, there weren't many people around. A brass bell hung over the door jangled as Richard and I came into the police station, which was mercifully air-conditioned, and a voice called out, "I'll be right there."

A minute later, a short woman with curly, brown hair and a sturdy figure stepped out. She was wearing battered, black cowboy boots, khaki pants with navy blue piping, a navy blue short-sleeved shirt, and a badge.

"Hey there Laurie Anne! I heard you were in town. How are you doing?"

"I'm doing all right. Junior, I want you to meet my husband Richard Fleming. Richard, this is Chief Junior Norton."

Richard didn't miss a beat. He reached for Junior's outstretched hand and met her firm grasp with his own, but gave me a look that promised vengeance. I looked innocent. Was it my fault that he had assumed that Junior was a man?

Admittedly Junior's name had caused confusion before. Her father, Chief Andy Norton, had always wanted a son to carry on the family name and profession, but after his wife had four daughters, he had just about given up hope. Then she got pregnant a fifth time, and Andy swore up and down that this time he was going to get a junior. When the baby turned out to be another girl, he stuck to his word and they named her Junior Norton.

Junior was a tomboy from day one and Andy decided that she'd do just fine as a police chief. Rumor had it that her first words were, "You have the right to remain silent." She could shoot as soon as she could walk, and could make out parking tickets as soon as she could write.

When Junior was about six, Mrs. Norton got pregnant again, and naturally, this time she had a boy. Now Andy finally had his son, but had already awarded the title of "Junior." Most men would have been stumped, but not Andy. He promptly named the boy Andrew Norton the Third and gave him Trey as a nickname. Trey was in college now, but he worked as Junior's deputy during the summer.

"Come on in. Have a seat," Junior said. "So this is Richard. I'm sorry I didn't make it to your wedding, but I was on duty."

Of course I knew that she could have gotten time off if she had wanted to, and the real reason she hadn't come to the wedding was that it would have meant putting on a dress, panty hose, and high heels.

She looked at Richard for a minute, and

then nodded. "He's just as good-looking as everyone said."

Darned if Richard didn't blush. "Thank you," I said for him. "How are you doing, Junior? You've been chief for over a year now, haven't you?"

She nodded. "I like it pretty well." She looked at Richard. "Did your wife tell you that she's the reason I got this job? The town council wasn't real thrilled with the idea of a female police chief and when they found out Daddy was training me as his replacement, they voted in a requirement that the police chief had to have a degree in law enforcement. Now considering I was just barely getting through high school at that point, there was no way I was going to get into any college.

"I got all upset and Daddy got all upset, and he was talking to Laurie Anne's granddaddy one day, and they figured that since Laurie Anne was such a brain, she could tutor me. We started studying together, and would you believe I turned into a straight-A student?"

"She got better grades than I did," I added. I never could get anything better than a C in gym class.

"Anyway, I got into college, and when I didn't flunk out, the town council decided

254

to give me a try after all. All thanks to Laurie Anne."

"You paid me back. Why don't you tell Richard how after you and I started studying together, people suddenly stopped picking on me?"

"That's true," Junior said with a grin. "They knew that if they didn't, I would whip their tail ends. Sometimes I wonder if that's what your granddaddy had in mind all along." The grin left her face. "I heard about Ellis, Laurie Anne. I can't tell you how sorry I am."

"Thank you, Junior. Actually, Paw's the reason we're here."

She straightened up in the chair. "Is this an official visit?"

"To tell you the truth, I'm not sure. You know what happened to Paw, don't you?"

She nodded, which didn't surprise me. There wasn't much that went on in Byerly that Junior didn't hear about.

"Richard and I went down to the mill this morning to see where they found him," I said.

"So I heard," she said, nodding again.

That *did* surprise me. I hadn't expected the news to travel that fast. "Let me tell you what I've found out." First I told her what Paw had said in the hospital. Then I told her about talking to Ralph, and the conclusion I had come to.

Junior put both elbows on the desk, and then cradled her head in her hands, just like she used to in high school when I asked her a history question that she was going to have to think about. After a minute or two, she said, "When I was in college, they taught me that there's three pieces to figure out for every crime: means, motive, and opportunity. Now means would be easy enough in this case. According to the doctor, just about any object with a decent-sized flat surface could have been used to hit Ellis."

"You talked to the doctor?" I asked.

She shrugged. "When I heard about it, I made a few phone calls, nothing much. Now opportunity doesn't help us much either. No offense to Ralph, but it wouldn't take any great shakes of a criminal to sneak past him. Just wait until he goes to the bathroom and you can waltz right in."

"There's a hole in the fence around back, too," I said.

Junior looked disgusted. "Have they not fixed that yet? Anyway, getting onto the grounds is easy. Of course the building itself would be locked, but you know how easy it would be to get a key."

I nodded.

"That gives us our opportunity," Junior went on. "Now we have to figure out a motive. Is there any reason anybody would have wanted your grandfather dead?"

I shook my head slowly. "I can't think of one. He didn't have any enemies that I know of, and he didn't have a whole lot of money. The house can't be worth all that much, and I can't imagine that the land would be worth killing for either, unless someone was planning some kind of construction."

"Nothing like that going on in Byerly," Junior said.

That settled that. If Junior hadn't heard about it, it wasn't happening. "There's one thing," I said slowly. "I know that this is going to sound silly but I think Paw's death had something to do with Melanie Wilson's death."

Junior cocked her head to one side. "How do you figure that?"

"Paw was worried about something that Sunday," I said, avoiding the sock-pulling explanation, "and we found a copy of the *Gazette* opened to a story about Melanie." I could see Junior was having a tough time keeping a straight face. "Then we found

Paw's map, and he had marked the spot where Melanie's car was found. That got me to wondering if he knew something about Melanie's death, and that's why he was killed."

"Sounds a little thin," Junior said kindly.

"I know."

Junior stayed quiet for long enough to make me nervous, and then she leaned back in her chair. "Here's the way I see it. The most likely possibility is that your grandfather had a heart attack while he was reaching for a box, fell, and hit his head. We don't have any evidence to the contrary."

"But he was lying face down," I objected. "If he had just fallen, why wasn't he on his back?"

"Because he rolled over — it's as simple as that." I started to say more, but Junior held up one hand to stop me. "I said that was the most likely possibility. A less likely possibility is that someone was waiting for him, hit him from behind, and left him for dead. The problem is we don't have any evidence to support that."

Richard pointed out, "We don't have any evidence against it, either."

"That brings us back to motive," Junior said, "and the only thing you can give me for motive is that you *think* that Ellis was worried about Melanie. Now, I can believe that Ellis was worried about Melanie, but what I can't believe is that Ellis would sit on information about her disappearance."

"We figured that out," I said. "Paw didn't realize that what he saw was important until he read that article in the paper Sunday morning."

"Do you know what time Ellis got up in the morning?"

"About eight, most mornings. Why?"

"Then the paper would have been there when he got up. Would he have read it right away?"

"Probably," I said, still not sure where she was heading.

"So even assuming he was a slow reader, he was probably finished reading it by ten. Right?"

"Right."

"So he's just realized he has a crucial piece of information about a girl who's disappeared, but he doesn't call the police. Instead he goes to the mill to pick up socks."

"I never thought about it that way," I said, feeling stupid.

Junior went on. "You also haven't explained how the killer knew that Ellis knew who he was, or why he waited until Sunday afternoon to kill Ellis. If this were a mystery on television, I'd say Ellis attempted blackmail, but knowing him the way I did, I wouldn't even suggest such a thing. Do you see what I'm saying? Your pieces don't fit together."

"You don't think it's worth investigating," I said.

She shook her head slowly. "Laurie Anne, you haven't given me anything to investigate. If I started to ask too many questions when I don't have anything more than this to go on, I could lose my job."

"Burt Walters called you, didn't he?"

She nodded. "Burt Walters is still on the town council and he's got a lot of pull with the mayor."

"So you're willing to let a murderer go free? Is that the kind of police chief you are?"

Junior took a deep breath, and I knew that she was probably as angry as I was, but she kept her voice calm. "Laurie Anne, if you had anything I could use, I'd use it come hell or high water. I thought a lot of Ellis Burnette, and there's no way I'd let anyone get away with hurting him. Don't you ever say anything different! But you know damn well that it's not been easy for me to keep this job. I'm not going to risk it for no good reason."

Neither of us said anything for a while, but then I said, "I'm sorry, Junior. You're right. I don't know anything for sure, and I don't want you to lose your job." I gave her a small smile. "I'd hate for all that tutoring to go to waste."

She smiled back. "Now Walters also told me to run you out of town, but I explained that there was no legal way for me to do that."

"Isn't his calling you kind of suspicious?" Richard said. "Maybe he's hiding something. Why else would he be so nervous?"

"Walters was born nervous," Junior said. "Of course if Big Bill was my father, I might be nervous, too. In this case, I suspect he's worried about the newspaper getting wind of this. Business at the mill hasn't been too good lately, and he's running scared. If people started to think he was negligent, he'd lose customers and workers both."

A thought occurred to me. "I don't suppose you know where Burt Walters was the night Melanie Wilson was killed, do you?"

"He was at his daddy's birthday party. I know that for a fact, because I was there, too."

So much for that idea.

"Might I assume that you're not giving up this investigation?" Junior asked.

I looked at Richard, and when he nodded, I said, "That would be a safe assumption."

"I suppose I couldn't talk you out of it if I tried."

"Probably not," I agreed.

"Then I won't bother. Try not to get into too much trouble."

"We'll try. Can I ask you a favor? I know this stuff about Melanie may not mean anything, but could we look at your file about her? I've read what's in the paper, but maybe you've got something else that would help."

Junior stood, shaking her head. "I'm sorry, Laurie Anne. I couldn't do that. It's against regulations." She walked to a file cabinet, pulled out a file folder, and gestured with it as she continued. "This file is restricted, and I can't let just anyone look at it." She laid it on top of her desk.

"Now if you'll excuse me, I've got to go into the back room for about fifteen minutes. You two let yourselves out. It's been good seeing you again, Laurie Anne, and it's been a pleasure meeting you, Richard. If you do find out anything definite, you let me know right away."

She started toward the door to the back, and then stopped. "Laurie Anne, did you notice our new photocopier there in the corner?" She pointed. "It makes real good copies and the instructions are printed on the top. Bye now."

CHAPTER 27

Richard reached for the file as soon as Junior was out of sight, but I put my hand over his.

"Are you sure you want to go through with this?" I asked.

"Don't you?"

"Maybe Junior's right. Our pieces don't seem to fit."

He shrugged. "So we don't have all the pieces yet. We'll just keep on looking. If you still want to, that is."

I hesitated for a minute more, and then remembered how hard Paw had worked to tell me someone had hit him. He *had* known what he was saying — I was sure of it. I picked up the folder.

Despite the moment of soul-searching, it only took us ten of the allotted minutes to make photocopies of everything in the folder and put it back on Junior's desk. Then I drove back to the house, letting Richard read the file on the way.

"Well?" I asked, once we were sitting at the kitchen table with bottles of Coke beside us.

"These guys don't write very well."

"I don't think taking creative license is encouraged when writing police reports. What do they say?"

"They put most of what they know in the newspaper. A county policeman found Melanie Wilson's car by the side of the road Friday night. The car was out of gas, explaining why she had stopped there. The registration was in the car, so the policeman called up Melanie's parents to see if she had called or found her way home. When he found out that she wasn't there, the police started searching for her. No trace of her was found that night. The search continued into the next afternoon, when the anonymous call came telling them to look in Marley.

"Though the police questioned a number of people in Marley, no one could tell them anything. They made a brief drive-by search, but finally decided the phone call had been a hoax and kept searching the area around Melanie's car for some clue."

"Thaddeous thought they were just protecting the blacks," I put in.

Richard shrugged. "Cynical of him. Anyway, the search continued until a woman in Marley went to take her trash out to the

Dumpster on Tuesday morning and noticed the smell and lots of flies. She had enough presence of mind not to look inside the Dumpster, and called the police instead. Though Melanie was last seen wearing a green shirt and blue jean shorts, plus the usual complement of underthings, the body was nude."

I shivered despite myself. Though rationally it shouldn't have mattered, being left naked made Melanie's death seem much more brutal.

Richard went on. "They sifted through the trash in the Dumpster and through everything else in the alley, but didn't find her clothes, her pocketbook, or anything else significant. They also searched all the nearby apartments and questioned a fair number of people, but no one saw or knew anything."

"Was she killed there?"

"They don't think so. In fact, that's been the sticking point in the investigation. They don't know where she was killed. It wasn't near the Dumpster and it wasn't by her car. The theory is that when her car ran out of gas, someone stopped to give her a ride. She probably got into the other car under her own steam because there were no signs of violence."

"That means the Klan has it all wrong," I said thoughtfully.

"What do you mean?"

"Thanks to that phone call, everyone thinks that black men killed Melanie. But no white girl raised around here would willingly have gotten into a car with a bunch of black men."

"Methinks I detect prejudice."

I shrugged. "I know it sounds awful, but it's true."

"What if she knew one of them?"

"White girls aren't encouraged to make friends with black men."

"That's scary."

"What's really scary is that I don't think I would have gotten into a car driven by a black man, either. Of course after living in Boston, I wouldn't get into a car driven by any man."

Richard looked injured. "What about a perfectly respectable WASP?"

"Those are the worst. Now, if it was white men who killed her, they must have dumped her in Marley to make it look like blacks did it. To divert suspicion."

"This notion has occurred to the police as well, but they don't know where else to look."

"What about the autopsy?"

"The cause of death was a blow to the head, probably with a stick or a club or some other piece of wood. They can't get too close on the time of death because of the time lapse before the body was found, but it was sometime Friday night. She was somewhat bruised, probably as a result of the rape. By the way, despite popular opinion, she was only raped by one man."

"How can they tell?"

He grimaced. "They only found one man's semen."

"Oh." I wished I hadn't asked. "So much for the gang bang everyone has been whispering about. Where did that idea come from, anyway?"

"It was that anonymous phone call, the one that told them to look in Marley."

"That's right. You know, the more I think about it, the more I think that that call was made by the killer himself."

"Again, the police agree with you. They would very much like to talk to this tipster, but they can't find him."

"Who received the call? Was it Junior or the county police?"

Richard thumbed through the photocopies. "The county police. Why?"

"Just a thought. If the caller was a local, he might have done it that way to make sure that Junior didn't recognize his voice."

"Maybe," Richard said. "Or if it wasn't a local, maybe it was easier to find the phone number for the county police."

"True. It's a shame that the car was out of gas. Almost any other kind of car trouble would have been better."

"Why?"

"Because if Melanie knew she was out of gas, the man probably never touched the car. Meaning no fingerprints. If it had been anything else, wouldn't he have looked under the hood? Most men would, even if they don't know a carburetor from a hole in the wall."

Richard gathered his dignity around him. "I think I would be able to admit my ignorance in this matter."

"You are a scholar and a gentleman — a rare and precious commodity."

"True. Anyway, the police checked the car for prints. Nothing. Besides, if he had left prints, he could have wiped them."

"With her standing there? Don't you think she would have been a little suspicious?"

"He could have come back later."

"That would have been a big risk. What if someone had seen him? For that matter, didn't anyone else see him when he picked up Melanie?"

"No such luck. They've found a few people who saw Melanie's car by the side of the road so they can approximate the time she was picked up, but they have no witnesses who actually saw her with anyone."

"Except for maybe Paw." I thought about it. "This sounds unpremeditated to me. This guy just happened to come along when she just happened to run out of gas and it just so happened that no one saw him. How could anyone have planned it that way?"

"I suppose someone could have siphoned gas out of her car in hopes that she'd stall somewhere isolated," Richard said, but I could tell that he didn't take it seriously.

"I suppose the police looked into her background to make sure there wasn't someone with a motive lurking around," I said.

"Of course. She had a devoted boyfriend who has an ironclad alibi, no enemies that anyone can think of, and has never been in anything remotely resembling trouble."

"So it wasn't premeditated."

"The police concur."

I put my hands behind my head, and leaned back. Though I suppose I wouldn't have felt very safe if I had come up with something that trained police investigators had missed, it would have been gratifying if I had.

"So where does all this lead us?" Richard asked.

"Nowhere, really. We still have all the questions Junior asked. Why Paw didn't call the police right away? How did the killer find out Paw knew? Why did the killer wait until Sunday to come after Paw?"

"Try this on for size," Richard said. "Since Paw wasn't killed sooner, the killer must not have known that Paw knew anything until Sunday, which is when Paw himself realized what he knew."

I nodded. If I had all that straight, it seemed reasonable.

"So either Paw told the killer, or Paw told someone who told the killer."

I nodded again.

"Let's keep it simple, and assume Paw told the killer."

"That means Paw not only knew who the murderer was, he knew him personally."

"Right," Richard said triumphantly.

"Since he knew the murderer, he wanted to give the man a chance to confess and turn himself in to the police. To do the honorable thing. The problem is, the murderer didn't do the honorable thing. Instead, he went to the mill to wait for Paw."

"How did he know Paw was going to the mill?"

"Good question. Could he have followed him?"

"I suppose so, at least long enough to figure out where Paw was going. Then he could sneak around the back to get there ahead of him. Paw wasn't a fast driver, and he would have signed in with the guard. And he usually spent a few minutes talking with the guard. So, yes, I think someone could have gotten there ahead of him."

"Then that's our answer."

I didn't say anything.

Richard said, "You don't agree?"

I shrugged. "I just find it hard to accept that Paw would give a murderer a chance like that. Even if Paw didn't think the man would come after him, he must have realized that he might run away. Would you let a murderer get away?"

"But Melanie's body hadn't been found yet, so Paw didn't know that she was dead. Maybe the murderer lied to him, told him that Melanie was fine when he saw her last. Why else would Paw wait to call the police?"

The phone rang before I could answer. "Maybe it's the murderer calling to confess," I joked.

It wasn't, of course. It was Aunt Nora calling to invite us to dinner. After a quick consultation with Richard, I accepted and told her we'd be at her house at six.

Though I spent the rest of the afternoon reading and rereading the police report while Richard finished up with Louis L'Amour, I could have twiddled my thumbs for all the good it did. By the time we had to leave for Aunt Nora's, I was eager for an excuse to quit.

CHAPTER 28

We got to Aunt Nora's just in time for dinner. This time it was fried chicken, boiled new potatoes, snap beans, and plenty of biscuits. Dessert was a pecan pie that had somehow escaped yesterday's feast.

Despite Aunt Nora's cooking, it wasn't exactly a festive meal. Willis was half-asleep, Thaddeous was clearly still mourning Melanie, and Uncle Buddy was even quieter than usual.

After dinner, Thaddeous took Richard upstairs, insisting that he had to find him something more appropriate for the Mustang Club than the Izod shirt he was wearing. I stayed in the kitchen to help Aunt Nora with the dishes, but we were only halfway through when Uncle Buddy came into the kitchen and said, "Laurie Anne, I need to talk with you for a minute."

I looked questioningly at Aunt Nora, but she looked just as mystified as I was. "Sure, Uncle Buddy," I answered, and followed him into the den.

He closed the door behind us, waited

until I sat down on the couch, then sat in the armchair opposite me. "Burt Walters called me up to his office today. He said you had come to see him, asking all kinds of questions about Paw's accident and talking about a lawsuit."

I should have known better than to expect Walters to keep anything to himself.

Uncle Buddy went on, "Walters said you seemed to think there was something funny going on. I want you to tell me just what you're trying to do."

I didn't like his tone, but I tried hard to keep my voice even. "I think there was something odd about Paw's death, and I've been trying to find out what happened."

"Now you listen here! I've been working at that mill for over twenty years and I don't mean to lose my job because of you sticking your nose in where it don't belong."

"Uncle Buddy, you don't understand."

"Oh I understand all right. You think you can come down here with one of them fancy-talking Boston lawyers and make the mill give you a bunch of money. Then when Walters fires the rest of us, you can go on back North and leave us with no jobs and no way to make a living. Well, that ain't the way it's going to be. You're going to leave it alone, and quit trying to make money from your granddaddy's death. Accidents happen, and that's all it was — an accident."

I made myself take a deep breath before I spoke, because I knew that I was as mad as I had ever been. "It wasn't an accident," I said coldly.

"Did your computer tell you that?" he asked scornfully.

"No. Paw told me that."

"What are you talking about?"

"When I went in to see Paw the day I got here, he told me that what happened at the mill wasn't an accident."

"Then what the hell was it?"

"It was murder. Paw told me that someone hit him."

"Who?"

"I don't know. The nurse chased me out before he could say more then, and he was never strong enough later." I gave him a minute for that to sink in, and then said, "I'm going to find out who killed Paw, no matter what you say or think. If that bothers you, I don't give a damn!" I stood, and walked straight past him to the front door and outside.

I couldn't leave, of course. Richard was still upstairs with Thaddeous, oblivious to what was going on, and I wasn't about to go back inside to get him. I couldn't even go sit in the car, because the keys were in the house with my pocketbook, so I sat down on the front steps and stared away from the house. A few minutes later I heard the front door open, and a quiet step behind me.

"Laurie Anne?" It was Aunt Nora. "Can I talk to you?"

Why not? Hit me with both barrels. "Sure," I said.

Aunt Nora closed the front door gently behind her, and sat down next to me. She was wringing a tired-looking handkerchief in her hands.

"You don't really think someone killed Paw, do you?" she asked.

"I tried to tell you before. Paw told me that what happened to him wasn't an accident. I have to believe him."

"He was dying when you saw him, on all kinds of drugs. He didn't know what he was saying."

"I think he did."

"Then why tell you? Why not Daphine or Nellie or me?"

I heard the pain in Aunt Nora's voice. "Is that what this is about? Are you jealous because Paw told me, and not you?"

"Why should he tell you? I'm the one who took care of him, made sure that his house was clean and that he had something to eat. I'm the one who stops the family from fighting every other day. I'm the one who . . ." Her voice caught in a sob.

I looked at her with new eyes. "Oh, Aunt Nora, I'm sorry. I didn't know."

"Of course you didn't know! You got out of this place just as fast as you could. First you had to go to school in Massachusetts because Lenoir-Rhyne in Hickory wasn't good enough for you. Then you hadn't been out of school a month before you hightailed it back to Boston because North Carolina wasn't good enough for you. How would you know anything about us?"

My own anger flared. "So now I'm too good for you? When I was growing up, I wasn't even good *enough*. All y'all could do was make fun of me. Laurie Anne's always reading. Laurie Anne's never going to get a husband if she doesn't start fixing her hair and wearing make-up. Laurie Anne's crazy if she thinks she can get into college. Laurie Anne's never going to find a job in Boston. Laurie Anne's going to be back home with her tail between her legs in six months." I glared at her and kept right on going.

"Well if I'm not what you think I should be, that's too damn bad, and if you don't understand what I'm trying to do, that's too damn bad, too. If you really think that all I'm after is money, then I don't imagine we've got a whole lot to say to one another."

We glared at each other for a full minute, and I would have been hard pressed to say whether I felt more angry than Aunt Nora looked, or the other way around. Finally Aunt Nora shook her head, and even smiled.

"You know we've been saying how much you favor Alice all these years, that I don't think I ever noticed how much like Paw you are."

I just sat there, not knowing what to say.

"Laurie Anne, did Paw ever tell you about Charlie Baxter?"

"No, ma'am."

"Mama told me this story once and I never forgot it. Charlie Baxter and Paw grew up together, like two peas in a pod. When they got old enough, they went to work at the mill together. Then Charlie's brother Pete had an accident at the mill. Pete lost his hand, and they didn't have insurance and workman's compensation like they do now. Bill Walters cut him off without a cent and when Pete couldn't get another job, he shot himself."

I flinched.

Aunt Nora went on. "Charlie never was the same after that. Mama said he was always talking about how Walters had to pay for it, how he'd get even. He got drunk one night and told Paw that he had made a bomb that would blow the mill off the map. Now you have to remember that the mill ran three shifts then, so no matter when he set it off, a lot of people were going to get hurt or, more than likely, killed."

I nodded, but I still had no idea of why she was telling me this.

"Paw tried as hard as he could to talk him out of it, and when that didn't work, he tried to find out where Charlie had hidden that bomb. Charlie wouldn't tell him, so Paw had no choice — he called the police. They put Charlie in jail."

Aunt Nora shook her head ruefully. "A lot of people never understood how Paw could turn in his best friend like that. They thought he had betrayed Charlie. Of course, you know how Paw was. He never paid them any mind, because he knew he had done the right thing."

"What happened to him? To Charlie, I

mean," I asked, interested in spite of myself.

"He served his time, and afterwards he moved somewhere out west to make a new start. He sent Paw a letter."

"Was he mad at Paw?"

"No he wasn't. He said he was glad things had turned out the way they did, because he had met a lot of killers in prison and he didn't want to have to see another one every time he looked in the mirror. Even so, he said, he didn't think he could ever trust Paw again, so it was probably best that they not see each other again."

"Poor Paw," I said.

"That's what I said when Mama told me this story," Aunt Nora said, "but she said that wasn't the point. She said Paw had done what he had to, and that was what was important."

" 'If it be aught toward the general good, set honor in one eye and death in the other, and I will look on both indifferently.' *Julius Caesar*," Richard said quietly. I hadn't even heard him come out.

Aunt Nora nodded. "As far as this business with Paw having been killed goes, I just don't know what to think, but if you really think someone killed him, then you have to do what you think best.

Just like Paw would have."

"What about Uncle Buddy?"

"Never you mind about Buddy. I'll speak to him. Now about being good enough for us. Laurie Anne, I never meant to make you feel like you should be anything but what you are. I'm proud of what you've done, and I think we all are, even if we don't say it as often as we should."

"Thank you," was all I could say. Feeling clumsy, I hugged her tightly.

"Aunt Nora, can I ask you something?" I asked when we let go. "Why do you call me Laurie Anne?"

"It's your name, isn't it?"

"No, ma'am. My name is Laura. Anne is my middle name."

"Alice always called you Laurie Anne."

"No, Mama called me Laura. She said she used to try to correct y'all when I was little, but after a while she gave up."

Aunt Nora looked at the wadded handkerchief in her hand and absently straightened it. "I guess I always thought of you as Laurie Anne," she said. "Does it bother you?"

I considered it for a moment. "I'm not sure. I've always thought of myself as Laura."

"Maybe you're both," Aunt Nora ventured.

I smiled. "Maybe I am."

Aunt Nora wiped her eyes then and said, "I better let you get ready to go."

I wiped my own eyes and said, "Aunt Nora, I'd rather you not tell anyone about this, about why we're asking questions. Until we know something more definite, I don't want to upset anyone else."

"That's probably a good idea. I'll tell Buddy, too. Of course you know that if Walters talked to Buddy, he most likely spoke to others, too."

She went back inside, but Richard held me back for a second. "Is everything okay?"

"I think so," I said, "but I could use a hug."

As he squeezed me reassuringly, I said, "I don't know how much of that you heard, but I'll explain later." After expressing I don't know how many years of hurt feelings, not to mention learning an awful lot about Aunt Nora, I wanted a few minutes to sort it out myself.

CHAPTER 29

We went back inside to get my pocketbook, and I finally noticed what Richard was wearing. In place of his polo shirt, he had on a blue and red western-style shirt with bright red trim. On his head he sported a straw cowboy hat adorned with a flock of garish feathers.

"Where did you get those clothes?" I asked.

He twirled with a flourish. "Do you like it?"

I searched for an honest, yet tactful reply. "You're positively resplendent," was what I finally decided on, and this seemed to please him.

"Thaddeous said that this was just what I needed for the Mustang Club. He doesn't have any boots that fit me, but he thought my sneakers would get by at night."

"I bow to Thaddeous's superior fashion sense," I said with a grin, and an evil thought occurred to me. "Wait a minute."

I thought I remembered seeing Aunt Nora's camera, familiar from years of family parties. I picked it up and asked, "Aunt Nora, can I borrow your camera?"

"Sure," she said.

"Richard, get over there against the door. I want a picture of your ensemble." Otherwise no one in Boston would believe it.

Aunt Nora watched as Richard posed, and I could tell she was fighting off laughter. I took a couple of pictures, and said, "I'll get this roll developed to pay you back for the film."

Aunt Nora nodded. "I wouldn't mind a copy of that picture myself."

"Am I country, or what?" Richard said.

"Mostly what," I said, "but I love you anyway." I was just glad Thaddeous hadn't come up with something for me to wear. "We better get going," I said, and Richard added, "See y'all later."

Aunt Nora snickered.

"What?" Richard asked.

"I love the way you say that," she said.

"Say what?"

"Y'all."

"I said it right, didn't I?"

"It just doesn't sound right coming from you, you being from the North." When he looked injured, she said, "Just keep practicing. You'll get it."

I told Richard about what had happened with Uncle Buddy as soon as we got in the car.

"Are you sure you still want to go out?" he asked.

"I think so. Some loud music is just what I need. A beer wouldn't hurt, either." Actually I felt oddly lighthearted in spite of what had happened. Or maybe it was because of what had happened. It wasn't that I had enjoyed the confrontation, but it had been a long time coming. Maybe it wouldn't make a difference in how my family saw me, but then again, maybe it would.

The Mustang Club's parking lot was nearly full when we arrived, even though the show wasn't scheduled to start for another hour. I guessed that we would not have been able to get in without the passes from Roger. Already people were being turned away at the door.

A cheerful waitress in a green-checked gingham shirt and a denim miniskirt showed us to a tiny table near the front of the room, and brought a beer for me and a Coke for Richard.

The club's decor was western in motif, but not obnoxiously so. Along the walls were hung branding-irons, each labeled with the name of the ranch it had been designed to represent. Above the bar was a painting of a herd of wild horses led by a white stallion with a flowing mane and flared nostrils.

The crowd was mostly in jeans and cowboy shirts, and I had to admit that Richard's outfit, however uncharacteristic it might be, fit in better than my Indian-print sundress.

Although I had heard Roger sing a number of times at family gatherings while he and Aunt Ruby Lee were married, this would be the first time I had seen him perform in public. He was such an exuberant character in everyday life, I was surprised when he and the other band members came on stage dressed neatly in matching maroon cavalry shirts, Levi's, and string ties. There was not a sequin or a ten-gallon hat between them.

Roger waited for the applause to quiet and said, "Good evening, everybody. We're mighty glad to see y'all here tonight. I'm especially proud to see my niece Laurie Anne and her husband Richard out there. They live up in Boston, Massachusetts, so y'all be sure and show them a little Southern hospitality."

There was a polite spatter of applause.

"The first song we're going to sing for

you tonight was made famous by the late, great Mr. Hank Williams."

As the strains of *Your Cheatin' Heart* filled the bar, I was pleased to note that Roger was as good as I remembered. At first, they played mostly country music standards, but as the set progressed, they snuck in some newer material I recognized as part of the New Traditionalist school — country music stripped of the rhinestones and soft-rock influence.

As the set drew to a close, Roger said, "I'm going to let the boys go get a beer now, but I'd like to sing one more song if you don't mind." The applause as the other musicians went off-stage must have reassured him, and he dragged a stool up close to the microphone.

"I'd like to dedicate this song to a man I knew. He wasn't rich or famous, but he was a good man and his family will miss him. His name was Ellis Burnette, and some of you probably know that he died this past week. He taught me this song a long time ago."

I recognized the song as soon as he started to play. I had heard Paw sing it so often, I could have sung along with Roger had I not been so close to tears. Richard took my hand under the table.

This world is not my home, I'm just
a-passing through
My treasures are laid up somewhere
beyond the blue
The angels beckon me from heaven's
open door
And I can't feel at home in this world
anymore.

The audience was quiet for a minute when Roger finished the song, but I thought it was a show of respect rather than of disinterest. Then they applauded quietly as he went backstage.

CHAPTER 30

I washed down the lump in my throat with the last of my beer, and then said to Richard, "What do you think of the music?"

"I like it. It's not my usual thing, but live music has its own charm. I really liked that next to last song. It sounded very country."

"I hate to disillusion you, but that was a cover of an Elvis Costello song."

"Elvis Costello? The king of nerd rock? He's British."

"He's also a big country music fan. He's appeared at the Grand Ole Opry, and his *Almost Blue* album won a Country Music Award."

He looked at me suspiciously. "How do you know these things?"

"You remember Michelle? The receptionist at work? She listens to country music, and when she heard I was from North Carolina she assumed I did, too. I've never had the heart to tell her anything different, so I let her tell me all about it at lunch."

"Some Southerner you are."

"Not all Southerners listen to country music. Some of the best rock-and-roll comes from Southerners. How about the other Elvis, and Lynyrd Skynyrd, and R.E.M., and the Allman Brothers? I even know Southerners who listen to Punk and New Wave."

"Don't say that too loud in here," Roger said, coming up behind us. "This is a dyed-in-the-wool country and western crowd. How are y'all doing?" He hugged me, and reached over the table to shake Richard's hand.

"Y'all want something to drink? Hey Wanda! Bring me a beer and give these two a round on me!"

"You don't have to do that Roger," Richard said.

"That's all right. The band gets ours free. So what did you think of the set?"

"I really enjoyed it," I answered. "I never realized how good you are."

Roger beamed.

"Laura says that one of the songs you played was written by Elvis Costello," Richard said.

"Shh . . ." Roger looked around in mock alarm. "Don't tell anyone! Some of these people think that country music begins and ends with George Jones and Porter

Wagonner. Not that I don't like their stuff, but a musician has to stretch himself some."

Our drinks arrived, and Roger allowed Richard to tip the waitress.

"Laurie Anne, I wanted to tell you again how sorry I am about Ellis. He was a good man."

"Thank you, Roger. That song you sang was awfully sweet."

"He taught that to me just after I started dating Ruby Lee. You know your grand-daddy had a fine singing voice. I used to take my guitar over there and we'd sing and play for hours. I think he could have made it in the music business, but once he and your grandmamma started having babies, he couldn't afford to take a chance. It's hard to have a family when you're on the road all the time. That's what split me and Ruby Lee up, you know. If I had it all to do over again, I'd do it different, I can tell you that."

He stared into his beer for a minute, and I decided I'd better distract him before he got maudlin.

"You said at the hospital that you saw Paw last week."

"Yep, Saturday afternoon, and now I'm awfully glad I stopped by. You just never know, do you? He looked fine then." He paused a moment, and then asked, "Laurie Anne, are Ruby Lee and Conrad getting along all right?"

"As far as I know," I said. "Why do you ask?"

"Oh nothing," he said unconvincingly. "Just something your granddaddy said."

"Roger, if you've heard something about Uncle Conrad . . ." I started, but he shook his head firmly.

"I shouldn't have said anything. I don't want you to think I'm making trouble for Ruby Lee." He finished his beer, looked at his watch, and said, "I've got to go get ready for the next set. I'll see y'all after the show."

After he left, Richard said, "What do you think? Should we tell Aunt Ruby Lee about this?"

"I don't think so. Keep in mind that Roger is still crazy about Aunt Ruby Lee, and would like nothing better than to get back together with her. Uncle Conrad doesn't seem like the unfaithful type to me, but if he is sleeping around, it'll come out sooner or later. We've got other problems to worry about for now."

Like what it was Paw had seen, and why he hadn't called the police as soon as he realized what it was he knew, and how the murderer had found out he knew. I rubbed my forehead as if trying to coax some answers out of it.

"Hey," Richard said, tapping the side of my head. "Anybody home? We're supposed to be having fun, remember?"

"Sorry," I said. "I guess I'm not the best company in the world tonight."

"You'll just have to make it up to me," he said.

Roger and the band returned to the stage, and the songs in this set leaned toward dance music. After a minimum of coaxing, Richard got me to dance. The set grew longer and longer with encores, until finally the band and audience called it quits from mutual exhaustion.

Once the enthusiastic clapping died down, there was a last call from the bar, and I realized it was well after one. "I'm worn out," I said.

"Let's head on out, then."

"What about Roger? He said he'd come by after the show."

"I think his plans have changed," Richard said. I looked in the direction he was watching, and saw Roger with his arm around a blonde with skin-tight jeans and a remarkably well-filled blouse. Roger saw us, grinned, and waved.

"And I thought he was still crazy about Aunt Ruby Lee," I said.

"He'd have to be crazy to pass that up," Richard said admiringly, still watching them.

Too admiringly, I thought, and I "accidentally" nudged him with my foot. Richard kept watching. I nudged him again, a little harder, and he finally looked back at me.

"Not my type, of course," he said, and offered me his arm as we left.

CHAPTER 31

My ears were still ringing from the music as we drove home, and I was content to lean back and stare idly out the window. I glanced once or twice in the side-view mirror, and flinched from the reflection of the headlights from a car traveling too closely behind us. After a few minutes, it sank in that those lights had been with us for a while. I looked behind us. It looked like a light-colored pickup truck, but it was too far away for me to see any details.

"Richard, how long has that pickup been behind us?"

He checked the rear-view mirror. "Since we left the club, I think. Why?"

"Do you think he's following us?"

"Why would anyone be following us?"

"I was thinking about what Aunt Nora said. If Burt Walters talked to Uncle Buddy, he probably talked to other people, too. Maybe the murderer has heard that we're asking questions." I looked around to get my bearings. "Get off at this exit."

Richard did so, but said, "He's still with us."

"Damn!"

"We're probably all right as long as we keep going. I mean, he can't be planning to ram us or anything like that."

"You're probably right, but I don't like it. Turn right at the end of the ramp. There's a Hardee's that stays open all night at this exit."

He followed my directions, and pulled into the parking lot. "Now what?"

"Head for the drive-through."

"Why are we doing this?"

"To make him think we got off at this exit to get something to eat. Otherwise he'll know that we know he's following us."

"Why do we care if he knows that we know?"

"I'm not sure, but I'd rather he didn't."

"Whatever you say." We pulled up to the brightly lit menu board. "What should I order?"

"Just a Coke. Actually, while we're here, get me some french fries. And a chocolate milkshake."

He gave the order to the faceless voice warbling through the speaker, then pulled around to the window to pay for and accept our food.

"Are you sure you didn't just want an excuse to get food?" he asked as he handed me the cardboard tray.

I stuffed a french fry in his mouth in answer, and we turned back onto the highway. Our tail appeared behind us on the access ramp, and stayed with us until a few blocks before we reached the house.

We looked around cautiously before leaving the car, but everything seemed normal as we went inside.

"Maybe he wasn't following us after all," Richard suggested.

"Or maybe he knew where we were staying, and that we must be heading here." The idea that a murderer was watching us wasn't a comfortable one. Maybe it was that thought combined with the story Aunt Nora had told me about Paw that caused a dreadful suspicion to shake loose.

As soon as we closed the bedroom door, I said, "Richard, I think I've come up with the reason why Paw didn't go to the police, something that fits with his personality. It seems fairly obvious that Paw must have known the murderer."

"I brought that up earlier, but you said you didn't think that would slow Paw down."

"I know, and after what Aunt Nora told

me about Charlie Baxter, I'm even more convinced," I said, and took a few minutes to slip out of my clothes and into a night-gown. I was stalling, and Richard knew it, but he let me get away with it until we were in bed and had the lights turned out. Finally I said, "What if the person who killed Melanie was family?"

"That's a possibility we have to consider," he said quietly.

"Good lord, Richard, how could it have been family? I mean, they aren't all angels and maybe I haven't gotten along with everyone all that well, but they are my family! Are you telling me that someone in my own family raped and killed Melanie, and then killed Paw to cover it up?" I knew I wasn't being fair. He wasn't telling me a thing — I was telling myself. It was the only explanation that fit.

"Why me?" I demanded. "Why do I have to play Judas? Aunt Maggie said that only trash would turn in someone in their own family."

"Turning in a rapist and a murderer isn't playing Judas!" Richard said. "Paw knew that. Whoever it was must have known that Paw wouldn't keep quiet about it, no matter what speaking up cost him."

"Can't we just go home to Boston?" I

asked in a small voice.

"We'll do whatever you want."

It would be so much easier to leave it alone. Of course, it would have been easier for Paw to let Charlie Baxter set off his bomb, too. I took a deep breath and said, "We'll do what has to be done. For Paw."

Richard held me for a while, and then said, "I don't know if now is a good time to mention this or not, but this puts a new light on what Roger said about Uncle Conrad."

"I suppose it does." I tried to picture Uncle Conrad killing Paw, but I couldn't. But then, who could I picture doing it. Uncle Buddy? Willis? Clifford? "I don't want to think about this tonight."

"Of course not. We'll talk tomorrow." Richard kissed me good night, and was soon asleep.

It wasn't that easy for me. Paw had always taught me to do the right thing, but now I wasn't sure what the right thing was. No, that wasn't true. I knew what the right thing was, but I wasn't sure I could do it.

If I sent a Burnette to prison, would anyone ever speak to me again? For so long I had tried to convince myself that I didn't care what the family thought of me. Now I was beginning to see that I cared a lot.

CHAPTER 32

I woke to a knock at the bedroom door.

"Who is it?"

"Laurie Anne?" Aunt Maggie said. "Nora's on the phone."

I peered at the clock on the nightstand. It was six o'clock. What did Aunt Nora want at this hour of the morning?

"I'll be right there," I said, and stumbled downstairs to the phone. "Hello?"

"Good morning," Aunt Nora said brightly. When I didn't answer in kind, she asked, "Did you still want to come shopping with us today?"

I had forgotten all about the shopping trip, and for a moment I considered telling my aunt that I was too tired. I changed my mind for two reasons. First, I wanted to make sure that all fences with Aunt Nora were mended from last night. And second, awful though it was, I needed to see if I could track down alibis for my family. "I've been looking forward to it," I lied.

"Good. Ruby Lee is going to drive her van so we can all ride together. We'll be

301

there to pick you up in about half an hour. Is that all right?"

"Sounds fine. I'll see you then."

I quickly took my shower, ran a brush through my hair, and pulled on a pair of jeans and a shirt. Richard slept blissfully through it all.

"Richard?" I said.

"Hmmm . . . ?" he mumbled, not quite waking up.

"I'm going shopping with the aunts and Vasti. Is that all right?"

"Sure. Anything you want."

"I probably won't get back until this evening."

"Sure. Anything you want."

"I might get some new clothes."

"Sure. Anything you want."

This has possibilities, I said to myself as I bent to kiss him good-bye.

Aunt Maggie was in the kitchen drinking a cup of coffee. "I was just on my way to the flea market," she said. "Y'all must have been out late last night. What time did you get in?"

"About four and a half hours ago."

"No wonder you look like you've been rode hard and put away wet. Well, you can sleep in the car on the way to Burlington."

"Good."

Aunt Ruby Lee picked me up a few minutes later, and drove me, the other four aunts, and Vasti to Hardee's where I choked down a sausage biscuit and coffee. Then I crawled into the back of the van to grab the proverbial forty winks during the trip to Burlington. Unfortunately, I soon realized that Aunt Maggie had been hopelessly optimistic. I had more chance of sleeping in the middle of a hurricane than I did in a car with my five aunts talking a mile a minute. Not to mention Vasti. After ten minutes, I gave up.

Aunt Nellie was in the middle of a story about Uncle Ruben. "Now he's just spent twenty minutes on the phone, half an hour looking at a movie he said he wasn't interested in, and fifteen minutes with his nose in the refrigerator looking for something to eat, and he says he doesn't have time to mow the lawn."

"I think it's all men," I said with a yawn. "They have different priorities. Richard always has time to discuss Shakespeare, but never enough to pick up our clothes from the dry-cleaner."

"Conrad is the same way," Aunt Ruby Lee said. "He bought the lumber to add a deck onto the house three months ago. He finally got around to starting on it last

Sunday, but the second I turned around, he was halfway out the door to go somewhere with Loman. I put my foot down, let me tell you! I told him, 'I know he's your cousin, but you're at work with him five days a week *and* spend at least one night a week with him at the lodge, and today you're staying home with us.' He was *so* put out, but he called Loman back and told him he couldn't go. I made sure he didn't step one foot out of our yard all day long."

"Where in the world did they want to go?" Vasti asked.

"He never did say. Did Loman tell you, Edna?"

"No," Aunt Edna answered shortly, and there was a painful silence in the car. From what I had heard of their marriage, Aunt Edna was the last person Uncle Loman would tell of his plans.

At least this took Uncle Conrad off of my list of suspects. He couldn't have attacked Paw if Aunt Ruby Lee kept him at home Sunday. Besides, Aunt Ruby Lee had said that Uncle Conrad was at the lodge when Melanie's car was found.

I decided I was fairly safe in ignoring all of my female relatives. Melanie had been raped, after all. That left Uncle Buddy,

Uncle Ruben, Uncle Loman, Thaddeous, Augustus, Willis, Vasti's husband Arthur, Linwood, Earl, and Clifford. Of course Paw had had a number of more distant male relatives. I considered the vultures Aunt Maggie chased off from Paw's house, but decided that Paw wouldn't have been so reluctant to turn in someone from that crew.

There were a few more I could cross off of the list right away. Aunt Ruby Lee had mentioned that Uncle Loman was also at the lodge Friday night. Augustus was in Germany, and Aunt Nora said Willis had been working the late shift for several months, so he would have been at work when Melanie was killed. Earl was only fifteen, and since he couldn't very well have carried off Melanie on his bicycle, he was off the hook as well.

What about Thaddeous? The way he had reacted to news of Melanie's death and spent so much time helping to search for her, surely he wasn't the murderer himself. But then again, hadn't I heard about men who would set fires and then come running to play hero? I couldn't eliminate him yet, much as I wanted to.

At least I had most of the Burnette women in one place and with a little prodding, I should be able to learn enough to take a few more off of the list. Unless, of course, one of my aunts knew about the murders. No, even if I could swallow the notion that one of the sisters had condoned rape and murder, I refused to believe that any of them would have had anything to do with killing Paw.

We reached Burlington a few minutes after ten, and parked at the outlet mall to begin shopping with a vengeance. While trying on silk-look blouses with Aunt Ruby Lee, I found out that Clifford had been at a guitar lesson on Friday night and that he had helped Uncle Conrad work on the deck on Sunday.

As Aunt Nora and I went through endless racks of dresses on clearance, she complained that Uncle Buddy spent more time asleep in front of the TV than watching it. One of the times he had dozed off was during a movie Aunt Nora wanted to watch last Friday night, and she couldn't even hear it for his snoring.

Aunt Edna verified that Uncle Loman had gone to the lodge meeting, but had no idea of how Linwood spent his time. Fortunately, in bemoaning her son's lack of religious fervor as we browsed through artificial flower arrangements, she mentioned that she had given him a stern talking to last Sunday afternoon.

By the time we reached the Western Sizzlin' Steak House for dinner, I had two blisters on my right foot and one on my left, stiff shoulders from lugging bags around, and a pocketbook full of sales receipts, including one for a violet silk-look blouse. Filene's Basement in Boston had nothing on this place.

More importantly, I had crossed off all but three of my relatives from the list of suspects: Arthur, Uncle Ruben, and Thaddeous. Vasti had talked a lot, of course, but gave me no useful information. According to Aunt Nellie, Uncle Ruben had been out trying to sell floor polish every night last week, but she didn't know exactly where. Thaddeous was the most worrisome, because Aunt Nora said he had been gone several times during the past week, and that she didn't know where he had been. He said he had been out searching for Melanie part of the time, but that would have been easy to fake.

Working at it from the other direction, no one knew where Paw had been Friday night. Aunt Daphine had called his house and received no answer, which confirmed the fact that he had gone somewhere, but that didn't help much.

The waitress came over with our food, and I looked at my steak greedily. I cut a generous piece, and had it halfway to my mouth when Aunt Edna asked, "Aren't we going to give the blessing?"

The rest of us looked startled, but Aunt Daphine said smoothly, "Edna, would you do the honors?"

I put my fork back down and bowed my head obediently, if unwillingly.

Aunt Edna hesitated a moment, then said solemnly, "Good bread. Good meat. Good God, let's eat."

She broke into helpless giggles, and after a moment of astonishment, the rest of us joined in and laughed until tears ran down our faces. Aunt Edna had made a joke!

The light-hearted feeling lasted all through the meal. As we lingered over coffee and cigarettes, Aunt Nora smiled and said, "This has really been nice, us spending the day together. We ought to do this more often."

There were nods and murmurs of assent, but Vasti said, "I wish we could, Aunt Nora, but you know I'm running around like a chicken with my head cut off all the time. What with the Garden Club and the

Junior Women's League and the Country Club, I don't have time to catch my breath, but if Arthur wants to run for City Council, I have to get to know the right people." She sighed, as if exhausted just from thinking about it all, then looked sideways at me. "Besides, Laurie Anne's never home anymore."

Why couldn't Vasti have bragged some more instead of bringing me into this? Now I had to say *something.*

"It's so hard to get away," I said, knowing how lame that sounded. "Plane fares are just outrageous, and it is an eighteen-hour drive."

"Boston's an awful long way," Aunt Daphine agreed.

I added, "I'd love to have any of y'all come up to see me so I could show you around Boston. It's a beautiful city, and I know you'd enjoy it."

"Do you like it better up there than down here?" Aunt Nellie asked.

Ouch! That was a sticky one. If I said yes, I'd be insulting their home. If I said no, they'd want to know why I didn't move back.

"It's not that I like it *more,*" I said cautiously, "but I do like it." I tried to think of a way to tell them how it felt to live in a city where so much history had been made; where the computer industry was growing and changing every day; where I could go to a circus one night, a Pops concert the next, and a Bullwinkle and Rocky cartoon festival the third. Finally, all I said was, "Besides it's where my job is, and Richard's."

This seemed to satisfy them, and Aunt Daphine promptly steered the conversation toward Sue's new baby. Why was it always like this? Why did people think my decision to leave North Carolina had been a rejection? Granted, I had been eager to move, but I didn't hate my home. There were parts of life here I didn't like — the Klan, for instance — but there were also a lot of things I didn't like about Boston. The traffic was horrendous, the weather atrocious, and there was just as much prejudice in the North. I still loved living there, just like I still loved North Carolina.

Paw had understood, I thought sadly.

The drive back to Byerly was relatively quiet, interrupted only by Vasti adding up the money she had spent and anticipating Arthur's reaction when he found out. I slept most of the way.

Aunt Maggie was snoring softly in front of the television when Aunt Ruby Lee dropped me off at the house, and there was a note from Richard waiting for me.

Dear Laura,

Roger called to invite us to a pig picking (or is that pickin'?) where he's playing tonight. Apparently our fancy footwork on the dance floor last night impressed him. Since I had nothing better to do (having been abandoned by my wife), I accepted. I also thought I should try to find out more about what Paw had told him about Uncle Conrad. Given our current suspicions, it might be important. I didn't think he would tell me with you there, but as the Bard said, " 'Tis ever common that men are merriest when they are from home." *King Henry V,* I, ii. Don't wait up — I expect the revelry will last for some time.

Love,
Richard

It serves me right, I thought philosophically. I woke up Aunt Maggie and sent her to bed, and spent what was left of the evening letting what I had learned about Paw's murder slosh around in my head, interrupted only by a phone call from Aunt

Nora inviting me and Richard to Sunday dinner after church. Despite Richard's warning that I shouldn't wait up for him, I fiddled around until after midnight before I went to bed.

CHAPTER 33

I stirred sleepily as the door opened and light streamed in from the hall.

"Richard?"

He closed the door behind him, sauntered into the room, and fell onto the bed.

"Are you all right?" I asked, switching on the bedside lamp.

"Of course. Why wouldn't I be?"

I sniffed suspiciously, and wrinkled my nose when I caught the unmistakable aroma of beer.

"You're drunk!"

"Of course. Why wouldn't I be?" He tittered. " 'Doth it not show vilely in me to desire small beer?' *King Henry IV, Part II,* Act II, . . ." He suddenly looked stricken. "Oh no! I forgot the scene number!"

"Get up off of the bed and take those clothes off," I said. "You smell like a brewery."

He stood unsteadily, leaned over to pull off his left sneaker, and toppled over onto the floor. I jumped up to see if he was hurt, then shook my head ruefully. He had curled into a ball, one hand still around his left sneaker, and was grinning up at me.

"Ooops," he said.

With an exasperated sigh, I got down on the floor with him, yanked off his shoes, and peeled off his jeans and shirt. He stood there grinning for a moment, clad only in his jockey shorts. Then he jumped into the bed, rolled to the center, flung his arms wide, and said, "Come to Papa!"

I couldn't stand it any longer. I started laughing. Richard joined in loudly, though I would have bet that he didn't know what he was laughing at. Finally I remembered that Aunt Maggie might not appreciate the humor of the situation, and stifled my giggles. Richard, released by the alcohol from such concerns, continued unabated until I placed my hand over his mouth.

His eyes filled with injury, but this was replaced with a licentious gleam when I joined him in bed and removed my hand from his mouth so I could kiss him. He returned the kiss with uncertain accuracy and sidled up to me, his intent plain.

"Good night, Richard," I said firmly.

"Good night? Don't you want to . . . ?"

"Not tonight."

His brow wrinkled in concern. "Headache?"

"Not as bad as the one you're going to have in the morning. I'm just tired."

"Maybe later?"

"Good night, Richard."

"Good night."

I woke the next morning to the sounds of piteous moans. Richard was sitting on the side of the bed, his head buried in his hands.

"What's the matter?"

"My head is trying to come off," he whispered.

As I had predicted, Richard had one heck of a hangover. I didn't know whether I should be concerned about or amused by his condition.

"I'll be right back," I said, grabbing my bathrobe. Aunt Maggie was in the kitchen, the ubiquitous Hardee's bag by her side.

"You're up bright and early," Aunt Maggie said.

"Richard woke me. Aunt Maggie, what do you do for a hangover?"

She chuckled and said, "I thought I heard him stumbling by in the wee hours."

"He came in as drunk as a skunk."

"Well he's going to suffer for it. Get him some aspirin out of the medicine cabinet and give him lots of coffee. He probably won't want anything to eat." She turned back to her biscuit. "Maybe next time he'll know better."

I poured two cups of coffee, grabbed a sausage biscuit, and stopped in the bathroom for aspirin. When I got back to our room, I saw that Richard's condition hadn't improved.

"Take these," I said, handing him two aspirin and one of the coffee cups. He washed down the tablets with the entire cup.

"Better?" I asked.

"A little. Any more coffee?"

I handed him my cup, and he drained it, too.

"Want a biscuit?" I asked.

He shuddered, and I ate it myself on the way back to the kitchen for more coffee.

"How's he doing?" Aunt Maggie asked.

" 'He receives comfort like cold porridge'," I quoted with a grin. "*The Tempest.*"

"Well, I've got to get going. You're still coming out to the flea market this afternoon, aren't you?"

"Yes, ma'am."

"I'll see you then."

After the third cup of coffee, Richard was well on his way back up the evolutionary ladder.

"So?" I asked. "What did you find out?"

"To *never* drink that much again."

"Richard! What did Paw tell Roger about Uncle Conrad?"

He leaned back on the bed. "Can't it wait?"

"No!"

He sighed heavily but started speaking in his most professorial tone. "I spent most of yesterday slaving over my syllabus, wondering what havoc my wife was wreaking on our credit cards." At this, he regarded me reproachfully for a few seconds before going on. "At about three, Roger called. He said he and the boys were playing at a pig picking, and asked if we would like to come. Admittedly I had no idea of what a pig picking might be, but I thought it might be a good time to find out exactly what it was that Paw had said to him. One of us had to keep the investigation moving."

"I *was* investigating," I said, but Richard looked pointedly at the pile of shopping bags on top of my suitcase before continuing.

"I found out from Aunt Maggie why it was we were going to pick on this pig, and Roger and his band of merry men picked me up at around five. There was an enormous cooler in the band's minibus, and by the time we reached the festivities, a number of cold beers had already been consumed. Once we arrived, kegs were available to accompany the roast beast."

"Obviously you found it necessary to share in this bounty."

"I had to blend in, didn't I?"

"I suppose if everyone got so drunk they couldn't see straight, you would indeed blend in."

He sniffed loudly.

"Do you remember whether or not you talked to Roger?"

"Of course I remember. I pulled Roger away between sets and asked him, man-to-man, whether he really had reason to believe Uncle Conrad was being unfaithful. At first he objected that he didn't want to spread dirt about a fellow lodge brother, but after about thirty seconds of persuasion, he gave in."

"And?"

"He told me that Paw had asked him whether or not Uncle Conrad had spent the entire evening at the lodge Friday night. Roger told him that Uncle Conrad had been absent for a good while. This was a welcome meeting for new members, and the lodge brother in charge of procurement woefully underestimated the amount of beer required. Uncle Conrad volunteered to go pick up more, but he called some time later and asked for Uncle Loman. His car had broken down, and Uncle Loman had to go and help get it started. Uncle Loman and he were gone an additional hour or two. During this time another lodge brother was dispatched for and returned with more beer, so the two were barely missed."

"Did Roger say where Uncle Conrad's car broke down?"

"Yes, and he said that Paw asked the same question. Uncle Loman told them it broke down on Russell Avenue, but when Roger told this to Paw, Paw did not look relieved. Roger tried to get more information from Paw, but did not succeed. This is when he decided that Paw must have seen Uncle Conrad somewhere suspicious, and Roger jumped to the conclusion that Uncle Conrad was sleeping around."

"Russell Avenue," I said thoughtfully, and pulled Paw's map from my pocketbook. "Rats!" I said after a minute. "It's a dead end."

"Literally or figuratively?"

"Figuratively. Russell Avenue is nowhere

near where Melanie's car was found, and it's not close to Marley, either."

"Maybe Uncle Conrad lied. I'd say he's a pretty hot suspect, all the way around," he said with more than a little satisfaction.

I should have felt guilty about bursting his bubble, but I didn't. "Sorry, love. Uncle Conrad's already been cleared. I don't know what he was up to Friday, but he never left his house Sunday."

"What?"

I gave him a quick rundown of everyone's alibis, and finished up with, "That only leaves Uncle Ruben, Arthur, and Thaddeous."

"What about Uncle Loman? According to Roger, he was also out of the lodge for a while Friday night."

"I don't know where he was Sunday," I said, "but I don't think he was gone long enough Friday night. He would have had to pick up Melanie, take her somewhere and attack her, dump her body in Marley, and get back to Uncle Conrad. You said he was only gone an hour or two."

"That's what Roger said."

"You're not convinced?"

"I just don't like Uncle Loman. 'A man whose blood is very snow-broth; one who never feels the wanton stings and motions of the sense.' *Measure for Measure*, Act I, Scene II."

"I don't care for him much myself," I admitted, "but he's such a cold fish that I don't think he could have done it. Melanie's murder was a crime of passion, and Uncle Loman's not got enough passion to jaywalk."

Something dawned on Richard. "If you verified Uncle Conrad's innocence yesterday, then I have this headache for nothing."

"Not at all," I said quickly. "This helps pinpoint Paw's location. We know he saw Uncle Conrad somewhere Friday night, and we have an idea of where he could have seen him. That could be important."

"I guess so," he said, only partially mollified.

I checked the clock. "I'm afraid we better get a move on and get ready for church."

"You're kidding."

"Nope. You know Aunt Nora expects us to be there and we're having Sunday dinner at her place, too. I'll be nice and take my shower first."

His ungrateful response to my generosity was to fling a pillow at me.

CHAPTER 34

Though I hadn't attended church regularly since I started college, I usually ended up going when I was in Byerly. Enough Burnettes still attended services next door to make it seem like a family outing. Aunt Nora, Uncle Buddy, Thaddeous, and Willis arrived just as Richard and I got to church.

"Don't you two look nice," Aunt Nora said, tactfully ignoring the obvious signs that Richard was more concerned with trials of the flesh than in joys of the spirit. Come to think of it, I thought, he had enjoyed his share of spirits last night.

On the lawn of the church was a large sign with a ladder painted on it. Apparently it was supposed to represent Jacob's ladder, with rungs filled in as the church approached its heavenly goal: a new organ. Reverend Glass was famous for fund-raising drives, and Paw had once complained that he used larger collection plates to encourage donations.

I had been in no mood to notice at Paw's funeral, but the church looked the same as ever, despite Glass's constant money-making schemes. The outside was white clapboard with a respectable steeple, while the inside was light pine paneling and deep maroon carpet. The lines of the furnishings were clean and simple, the only ornamentation the large vases of fresh flowers donated weekly by a local florist and church member.

One thing Glass had added was an expensive sound system whose high-pitched whines ensured that no one dozed off during his sermons. It was probably a good thing. Otherwise his droning would have put me to sleep in about ten minutes.

Aunt Edna was sitting proudly in the front pew, and we went to sit with her. We chatted until the organist started playing and Reverend Glass came out. Before beginning his sermon, Glass mentioned Paw's death and praised his long-standing support of the church. Unfortunately this message clashed with the sermon, which was titled "The Wages of Sin Are Death." Forgiveness might be divine, but I suspected that Glass was holding a grudge for missing out on the Burnette house.

After the service ended, Aunt Edna headed for Reverend Glass and engaged him in earnest conversation. Uncle Buddy,

Thaddeous, and Willis went to talk with a neighbor while Aunt Nora, Richard, and I went on outside. An older woman wearing a neat blue pillbox hat stopped us on the steps of the church.

"Nora, I just wanted to tell you how sorry I was to hear about your father. I've known Ellis since he and my late husband worked together."

"I appreciate it, Mrs. Harper. I've been meaning to call and thank you for that pecan pie you sent us. It was real good."

Mrs. Harper waved the compliment aside. "That wasn't anything. I just happened to have made an extra one, that's all."

"Do you know my niece Laurie Anne and her husband Richard? They're down from Boston."

We exchanged smiles and nods.

"Nora, are you going to be talking to Nellie or Ruben anytime soon?" Mrs. Harper asked.

"I expect so. Why do you ask?"

"Well, Ruben stopped by my house last week and sold me some floor polish. I guess I wasn't paying attention when he told me how to use it because I was watching the tail end of *America's Most Wanted*, but I don't think it worked the way it's supposed to."

"Did it not get your floor clean?"

"It's not that, it's just that I've got my kitchen all done in light blue. That polish turned my floor tiles bright green and now they don't match."

Aunt Nora sighed. "I'll be sure and tell Ruben to call you," she promised.

"Did you hear that?" I whispered to Richard.

"I sure did. Remind me never to buy anything from your Uncle Ruben."

"Anybody with a lick of sense already knows that. What I mean is that we can take Uncle Ruben off of our list."

"How do you figure that?"

"Mrs. Harper said she was watching *America's Most Wanted*, and if I remember correctly, *America's Most Wanted* is on from eight to nine on Friday. If Uncle Ruben was selling Mrs. Harper floor polish at nine o'clock, he couldn't have killed Melanie."

"Aunt Nora! Laurie Anne!" Vasti, following her habit of yelling in inappropriate places, was at the top of the church steps. After we waved to let her know she had been heard, she came clattering down the steps to join us, followed by Arthur at a more sedate pace.

"I didn't get a chance to say hello before the sermon," Vasti said. "We were running late because Arthur had to stop and get gas." She gave him a disapproving glance, and then said, "I didn't think you went to church anymore, Laurie Anne."

"I make it in occasionally."

"Anyway, I wanted to show you our new car. The one I told you about."

"They don't want to see that," Arthur said with a trace of embarrassment.

"Yes they do." Catching sight of Aunt Edna still inside, she yelled, "Aunt Edna, come on out here. I want to show you something." She took hold of my right arm and Aunt Nora's left, and pulled us into the parking lot.

I spotted the new Cadillac long before we got to it. First off, it was parked in the plainly marked "NO PARKING" zone near the entrance to the parking lot, making it nigh onto impossible for other church members to maneuver past it. Second, it was the reddest car I had ever seen. A candy apple would have looked pale beside it.

Vasti brought us to a halt in front of it. "Now isn't that something?"

"It certainly is," I said truthfully.

"That is one nice-looking automobile,"

Aunt Nora said, and if there was the slightest speck of sarcasm in her voice, I couldn't detect it.

Richard and Arthur caught up with us, along with the rest of the available Burnettes. While the men followed tradition and lifted the hood so they could admire the car's technical points, Vasti opened up the front door, and waved her arms wide in the manner of a game show hostess displaying a particularly grand prize. "All leather interior, and look at how thick the carpet is. Isn't it just beautiful?"

"Beautiful," Aunt Nora agreed.

Aunt Edna joined us and at Vasti's insistence, we all climbed into the car to fully experience the comfort of the upholstery.

"What kind of mileage does it get?" I asked.

"Oh, Arthur takes care of all that for me. Let me show you how the sun-roof works."

Once everyone had admired the new Cadillac, Aunt Edna left and Aunt Nora said, "Well, we better go on so I can get dinner on the table."

"I guess Arthur and I need to get going, too," Vasti said. "We're going out for Sunday dinner because I haven't had two minutes to do my shopping this week. We'll probably have to wait in line forever.

All the good places fill up so quickly after church, and Arthur just hates to wait." She sighed heavily. "Maybe we'll just get us a hamburger at Hardee's."

"Why don't y'all come over and have a bite to eat with us, Vasti?" Aunt Nora said. "I cooked a whole ham so there's plenty for two more."

"Oh, we don't want to be a bother," Vasti said.

Of course you do, I thought, or you wouldn't have mentioned it. After a few minutes of polite protests counteracted by equally polite encouragement, it was agreed. Aunt Nora and Willis rode with Vasti and Arthur to sample more of the Cadillac's charms, while the rest of us piled into Uncle Buddy's less flamboyant Buick.

"What do you think of that car, Daddy?" Thaddeous asked as we drove back to Aunt Nora's.

"Well," Uncle Buddy said thoughtfully, "if they'd had another nickel, they'd have bought themselves a red car." He, Thaddeous, and I chuckled, but Richard only looked mystified.

"I don't get it," he whispered to me.

"You know, if someone gets a bright-colored shirt you joke and say that if he'd had another nickel he'd have bought a brighter one."

He looked at me blankly.

"Well, Paw used to say it," I said, shrugging my shoulders. "I guess it doesn't translate."

"Not into English, it doesn't," Richard said.

"You Yankees just don't know how to talk right."

"Is that so?" he replied, and we spent the rest of the ride to Aunt Nora's debating English usage while Uncle Buddy and Thaddeous snickered.

CHAPTER 35

As usual, Aunt Nora refused all offers of help in the kitchen, insisting that everything was nearly ready. I had no trouble slipping into the living-room to check her copy of *TV Guide* to confirm that *America's Most Wanted* came on at eight o'clock Friday nights. Uncle Ruben was in the clear.

I was uncomfortably aware that this only left Arthur and Thaddeous as suspects, and that Richard and I were about to sit down to dinner with both of them. Since Aunt Nora's "bite to eat" approached feast-like proportions, I was able to subjugate my suspicions to focus on the more urgent task of eating my share of baked ham, candied yams, lima beans, fresh tomato slices, and of course, Aunt Nora's biscuits piled high with homemade strawberry jam. Dessert was apple pie topped with generous slices of cheddar cheese.

Vasti controlled the conversation with her descriptions of the parties she and Arthur would be attending for the next few months. Each guest list was a veritable

Who's Who of local notables, but Vasti had no trouble remembering every name.

Once everyone had eaten what Aunt Nora referred to as a gracious plenty and what I would have called enough to bust a gusset, we all sat back without any inclination to move.

"That was good," Uncle Buddy said with his usual flair for understatement.

"I'll say," Arthur said. "I haven't had a meal like that since I don't know when."

"Goodness, Arthur, they're going to think that I don't ever feed you," Vasti said with a touch of irritation.

"Oh honey," he said, patting her hand. "I didn't marry you for your cooking, everybody knows that." He saw the expression on her face, and realized that he had made a tactical error. "What I mean is, everyone knows you keep so busy you don't have time to cook. Now when you've got the time, you can cook like nobody's business."

Vasti was not consoled by Arthur's words. "Well, anyone can see that you're not hurting for food," she said, looking pointedly at the buttons straining across Arthur's belly. "Besides," she said to me, "how am I supposed to fix a decent meal when I never know when he's going to be home? Last Sunday I had a wonderful dinner all planned, but he left right after church and didn't come back for hours. He *said* he was going to work, but when I called the dealership, no one knew where he was."

I sat up at this mention of last Sunday, and saw that Richard was also paying closer attention.

"Now, honey," Arthur said with a trace of worry in his voice. "You know I work Sunday afternoons. I told you I must have been out on the lot and didn't hear the page."

"That's what you *said*."

There was an uncomfortable silence, and I noticed that Arthur was looking at Thaddeous. Thaddeous returned his glance, gave a slight shrug, and then looked away. What was that about?

"Well," Aunt Nora finally said, "if I sit here any longer, I'm going to take root." The bustle of clearing the table dispelled the disquiet, and Vasti and Arthur soon left.

"What are you two up to this afternoon?" Aunt Nora asked after Richard and I helped stack dishes in the dishwasher.

"We're going out to the flea market to see Aunt Maggie," I said.

"Actually," Richard said, "I thought I'd ride out to the dealership and see Arthur. Didn't he say he was going to work after he dropped off Vasti?"

"I believe he did," Aunt Nora said. "What do you want to talk to him about?"

"Laura and I have been thinking of buying a car, and I thought he might be able to give me some advice about what we should buy."

I was caught off guard, but I nodded in agreement. I wasn't sure what he was up to, but I knew that he didn't want to buy a car. Just last week he thanked our lucky stars that we didn't have to try to park in our neighborhood.

"You don't mind going to the flea market alone, do you Laura?" Richard asked.

"I wouldn't mind riding out there with you, Laurie Anne," Aunt Nora said. "I haven't been out there in a while."

"Great," I said. I wasn't sure how this would fit in with Aunt Maggie's plans for secrecy, but I figured I'd deal with that when the time came.

After making sure that no one else wanted to go with us to the flea market, Aunt Nora drove us to Paw's house. We left her downstairs while we went to change out of our Sunday-go-to-meeting clothes.

As soon as we were alone, I said, "Since when do we want to buy a car?"

"Since I saw Arthur looking at Thaddeous when Vasti complained about Arthur being gone last Sunday. You caught that, didn't you?"

I nodded. "Maybe they were together that day."

"Meaning that they were in collusion?" Richard said.

"Or that they're both innocent."

"Which would leave us back at the beginning. Arthur and Thaddeous are our last suspects."

"It was *not* Thaddeous!" I said emphatically.

"I don't want it to be him either, but the fact is we don't know where he was Friday night or Sunday afternoon."

"I don't care."

"Then you think it was Arthur?"

I frowned. "He's the only other one who has no alibi for either time. I just can't picture him killing Melanie or Paw."

"He wants to go into politics, right? Maybe he picked Melanie up as a friendly gesture, but got more friendly than he should have. He had to kill her to keep it quiet, or kiss his political aspirations good-bye. Once Paw found out, he had to go, too."

"How would he have known about the hole in the fence to get him into the mill? And how did he get in that locked door? He's one of the few people in this town who has never worked at the mill."

"You never worked there, either, but you know about the hole," he pointed out. "As for a key, he could have borrowed someone else's." He could see I wasn't convinced. "Who do *you* think it was?"

I ran my fingers through my hair. "I don't know. Maybe you were right and Paw's murder wasn't connected with Melanie's after all. All we've been going on is that map. We never did find any other connection between the two."

"Other than Thaddeous," he said evenly.

"Not Thaddeous!"

"He knew Melanie, and was infatuated with her. He knows the mill, and as a supervisor, must have a key to the door."

"But he stayed out searching for her the whole weekend. He only joined the Klan because of Melanie."

"Unrequited passion can turn into something ugly, and he could have joined the searchers to make sure they didn't find anything. Joining the Klan could have been a way to draw attention elsewhere."

"Maybe I could believe he killed Melanie, accidentally mind you, but how can I believe he killed Paw? You saw him at the funeral. He was crying as much as anyone."

"To paraphrase the Bard, one may cry, and cry, and be a villain."

I sat on the edge of the bed, looking at the toes of my sneakers. "I'm not being objective, am I?" I said. I was pretty sure that I'd rather never find out who the murderer was than to find out it was Thaddeous.

"Of course you're not, and I wouldn't expect you to be. Besides, we may have nothing to worry about. Let's hear what Arthur has to say before we get too upset." He assumed a lofty expression. "After my success with Roger last night, I have every expectation that I'll be able to wring every last bit of information from Arthur."

"How are you going to do that? By carrying along a keg of beer?"

CHAPTER 36

After Richard ignored my question and agreed to meet us back at Aunt Nora's for supper, he headed for the Cadillac place and we headed for the flea market. Though I couldn't imagine wanting anything else to eat for a week, I was interested in looking at the family photo albums Aunt Nora promised to bring out afterwards. Richard was particularly eager to see embarrassing photos of me in diapers and such.

Despite the heat, there was a good-sized crowd at the flea market and Aunt Nora had to park near the edge of the field of sun-baked red clay that passed for a parking lot.

Actually it was hard to tell where the parking lot ended and the flea market began. There were cars parked between booths, and some dealers had their merchandise displayed on the hoods of their cars or in the back of their pickup trucks.

The dealers toward the middle of the market had tables of plywood laid on sawhorses or even rough shacks from which to display their wares. They made up the larger part of the market, loosely lined up in rows across the field.

Since neither of us had any idea of where Aunt Maggie set up, we started with the first aisle, and strolled past people selling everything from tape decks to black velvet paintings of Elvis Presley, from plastic unicorns with clocks in their sides to eight-track tapes, from socket sets to collector's items like Occupied Japan figurines, Fiesta Ware dishes, and carnival glass.

After half an hour of searching, I decided I'd better ask someone. I walked up to a woman selling Harley-Davidson T-shirts who had a tan that pasty-white Bostonians would kill for. Her baseball cap had "MAMA" printed across it.

"Excuse me, ma'am," I said. "Do you know where Maggie Burnette's booth is?"

"Maggie Burnette?" the woman said, "I don't believe I know her." She called to the young man working the booth with her. His cap had "KARL" written on it. "Karl, do we know Maggie Burnette?"

"What does she sell?"

I shrugged. "I'm not sure. I think she has some paperback romances."

Karl nodded in recognition. "Oh, the Book Lady. She's got a spot inside Building 1, next to the Donut Man."

Noticing my continued confusion, the woman pointed us toward a low building made of cinder blocks covered with a corrugated aluminum roof. I thanked them, and would have gone on but Aunt Nora was fingering one of the T-shirts.

"Do you suppose Thaddeous would like a shirt like this?" she asked. "His birthday is coming up."

I looked at the shirt she was examining. It bore an exquisitely detailed rendering of a motorcycle in fluorescent colors, being ridden by a pig dressed in a leather jacket. Above the picture were the words "I Luv my Harley Hog."

"I don't think so," I said. "Maybe if they had one with a pickup truck."

Aunt Nora nodded, and we went into Building 1. It was cooler inside, and we quickly located Aunt Maggie's booth, tucked between a tattoo artist and a booth selling fresh deep-fat-fried donuts.

Half of Aunt Maggie's booth was piled high with dishes, glassware, and ceramic knick-knacks of all description. The other half was piled just as high with paperback books. Hanging on the wall between them was a trio of signs. The first said, "In God We Trust, All Others Pay Cash," the second said, "The only one who cares about what your grandmother had is your grandfather," and the third and largest said "Don't Buy Books New — Buy Them From the Book Lady."

Aunt Maggie was talking to a young woman in a green blouse when we came up, but she saw us and nodded. "This is an old piece," Aunt Maggie was saying as she and her customer examined a brown and beige striped crockery mixing bowl. "It came from my grandmother's attic, and there's no telling how long she had it." She turned it over, and showed the woman the markings on the bottom. "See, it's got McCoy written on it, and McCoy pottery is a big collector's item these days."

"How much do you want for it?" the woman asked.

"I've got it marked forty, but if you want it, you can have it for thirty-five."

The woman considered it a moment, and then asked, "I don't know. Do you have any Fenton glassware?"

"I've got a couple of pieces put back behind the counter. Come on into the booth and I'll show you."

We left them to their negotiations. Aunt Nora wandered toward a table of ruffled, gingham curtains, and I went to look at

Aunt Maggie's selection of books. Most of them were romances, divided into boxes labeled "Harlequin Temptation," "Love-swept," "Grace Livingston Hill," "Judith Krantz," and so on. The only other books were a box of Stephen King books and one small box labeled "Other."

From the box labeled "Janet Daily," I pulled out a book whose cover portrayed a buxom heroine with the obligatory flowing hair and attentive suitor, flipped through it, and grinned when it opened of its own accord to a torrid love scene.

After Aunt Maggie talked the woman into buying both the McCoy mixing bowl and a pale blue glass vase with the charac-teristic ruffled look of Fenton, I went to join her.

"How's business?" I asked.

"Not bad. Did you see that bowl I just sold? She paid thirty-five dollars for it, and I got it for two dollars last week at the Sal-vation Army Thrift Store."

"I thought you said it came out of your grandmother's attic."

"Laurie Anne, do I come up to Boston to tell you how to work your computers?"

"No, ma'am."

"Then don't try to tell me how to run my business." She looked over at Aunt

341

Nora. "What's she doing here?"

"She wanted to come along and I couldn't think of a polite way to tell her not to."

"You know there is such a thing as being too polite." She reached under the tablecloth covering the table at the back of the booth and pulled out a thick manila envelope. "I'll take care of it. Nora! Come over here."

Aunt Nora put down the curtains and came over.

"I want to show Laurie Anne something. You can watch the booth for me, can't you?" Before Aunt Nora could speak, Aunt Maggie untied the canvas money apron from around her waist, and tied it around Aunt Nora's.

"But Aunt Maggie —" Aunt Nora started.

"Everything's marked, and don't come down on anything. If they want to haggle, they'll have to wait. We'll be back in a little while. Come on, Laurie Anne." She took off down the aisle. I hurried to catch up, and then nearly ran into her when she stopped and called back to Aunt Nora. "And Nora, don't clean anything."

"Why not?" I asked as we walked.

"Whoever heard of clean antiques?" she

answered, and then said, "Shaw Stevens — he's the lawyer — said he'd be over at the snack bar. There he is now." The snack bar was a tiny counter stuck in the wall and half-a-dozen formica tables that didn't look as if they had been wiped off this week.

I had dealt with lawyers once or twice before, but this was the first time I examined and signed important papers on a sticky table at a flea market snack bar. Despite the setting, Mr. Stevens kept everything reasonably businesslike and made sure I understood what I was signing. The agreement was straightforward as legal documents go. Upon Aunt Maggie's death, ownership of the house would pass to me with the proviso that I not sell the house or allow it to pass out of the Burnette family. I read everything over twice just to be sure, and then nodded. "Should I sign now?" I asked.

"Actually," Stevens said, "it would be best if the signatures were notarized."

"I've already got that taken care of," Aunt Maggie said. "Bob at the booth next to mine is a notary. Come on over that way, and I'll get you what I owe you."

I waved at Aunt Nora as Aunt Maggie led us to the booth next door. I had assumed that Bob was the donut man, but no, the tattoo artist was a notary public. He witnessed our signatures between drawing a rose on a woman's ankle and a Confederate flag on a man's forearm.

Then we went back to Aunt Maggie's booth, and she reached under one of the tables and pulled out a large, well-wrapped object. "Here it is," she said.

"I am mighty happy to get this," Mr. Stevens said, starting to unwrap the parcel.

I don't know what I was expecting, but I was definitely not expecting a Jim Beam decanter shaped like Elvis Presley in his white jump suit and rhinestone period. Stevens looked it over carefully, his satisfaction obvious.

"I've had the other decanters of the King for a while now," he confided, "but I didn't think I'd ever find this one. Maggie, where in the world did you get it?"

"I've got my sources," she said. "Are we all square?"

"More than square. A pleasure meeting you, Mrs. Fleming." He carefully rewrapped Elvis, shook our hands, and carried the decanter away.

Aunt Nora had been watching all of this with obvious curiosity, but was too polite to ask what was going on.

"I'll take that money belt back now, Nora," Aunt Maggie said. "Did you sell anything?"

"One man bought a dozen of your books, and a woman bought that big vase with the pagoda on it."

"For what it was marked? I thought I was going to have to give that thing away. Good for you."

Aunt Nora said, "If you don't mind, I think I'm going to go look at those curtains some more."

"Let me know if you see anything you like. I'll get you a good price," Aunt Maggie said.

"I'll catch up with you in a minute, Aunt Nora," I said. As soon as she was out of earshot, I said, "Aunt Maggie, is there anything else we need to take care of?"

"That's it. It's just as well that our family never had any money — it makes settling the estate right much easier." She slid a box out from under the table, lifted out a handful of books, and started restocking the table.

I saw some writing on the outside of the box, and leaned down to get a better look. "Isn't that Paw's handwriting?"

"Sure is. Ellis was at Red Clark's auction with me last Friday night."

I started to nod, and then what she had said sank in. "You were with Paw Friday night?"

She nodded, and said, "Ellis never bought anything at the auction, but he'd come every once in a while to help me load boxes."

"What time was the auction?"

"About seven, I guess."

"How long did it last?"

"It usually runs until eleven or so, but they didn't have much that night, so I think it was over by nine."

"Did y'all leave right away?"

"Ellis did, but I hung around a while to try to talk Willie Bell out of some glassware he outbid me on. Why?"

"Where is this auction house?" I asked, ignoring her question.

"It's not in a house. It's in Red Clark's barn."

"Where?"

"Off of Gibson Drive. Why do you want to know? He won't be having another sale until next month. Now if you want to go to a good auction, I'll take you to Bob and Barbara's place. They sell some good pieces there."

I rooted around in my pocketbook, found Paw's map, and thrust it in front of her. "Which way would Paw have gone that night?"

"Laurie Anne, what on earth is the matter with you?"

"Please Aunt Maggie, I can't explain right now, but it's important."

"All right." Aunt Maggie pulled her half-glasses from her apron pocket, perched them on top of her nose, and looked at the map. "Now that's Gilmore, where the house is." She pointed it out. "And Red's place is about there." She pointed again.

"So Paw would have gone this way?" I followed the straightest route with my finger.

"Probably not. He would most likely have taken the old tobacco road behind the house to Rock Creek Road. That's not on this map."

"It runs from about here," I pointed to the location of Paw's house, "to here, doesn't it?"

"Right past where that X is."

She was right! There was an X there, and it looked like it had been made with the same pen Paw had used to mark the spot Melanie's car was found.

"If someone was here," I said, pointing to the X for Melanie's car, "the tobacco road would be the quickest way back to town, wouldn't it?"

She nodded. "Depending on traffic, it can be a lot quicker. Now I won't go that way at night, because there's not a soul near there and not the first sign of a light, but Ellis used it all the time. A man doesn't have to worry the way a woman does."

I folded up the map, my hands trembling with excitement. I was willing to bet that somewhere along that dirt road was where Melanie had been killed. That X was marking something. Whatever Paw had seen, he had to have seen it there.

"Aunt Maggie, I love you!" I threw my arms around her and kissed her cheek with an audible smack.

Aunt Maggie stepped back. "Laurie Anne, I think you need to wear something on your head to keep the sun off. It's hotter than the hinges in hell out there."

"I've got to go now, Aunt Maggie," I said. I pried Aunt Nora away from the curtains and pulled her along with me to her car. I think I would have run if she hadn't been with me.

"Can I drive back?" I asked Aunt Nora when we got back to the car.

"If you want to," she answered.

I used every trick I had ever seen used in Boston, including a few that would make a taxi driver blanch, to get back to Aunt Nora's in record time. I didn't know *who* had killed Melanie, but I was sure I knew *where* she had been killed. There had to be something there to lead me to the murderer. As soon as I caught up with Richard at Aunt Nora's, we could go find out.

I turned the corner toward Aunt Nora's house, and saw the empty space in the driveway. "He's not here," I said stupidly.

"Who?" Aunt Nora asked, and then she chuckled. "You mean Richard? Goodness gracious, you saw him just a few hours ago. Anyone would think you were newlyweds."

I followed her inside, hoping for a note from Richard, but was disappointed.

"I guess Buddy and Willis decided to go watch the ball game with the boys after all," Aunt Nora said after checking around. "Thaddeous isn't here either, but he said he had a couple of errands to run."

The next hour was endless. Where was Richard, anyway? What was taking him so long? I shouldn't have let him go alone. He was probably lost. I thought I was hiding my agitation but Aunt Nora finally said, "Laurie Anne, what's the matter with you? You're acting as nervous as a long-tailed cat in a room full of rocking chairs."

I put down Thaddeous's bronzed baby shoes, with which I had been fidgeting, and smiled weakly. "Sorry, Aunt Nora. I'm just waiting for Richard to get back. There's something we need to do this afternoon."

"I'd think you'd be better off waiting until later this evening."

"How come?"

"Haven't you heard the thunder?"

I pushed the curtain back to look out the window, and realized how dark the sky had become, changing from sunny to cloudy as it only could in summer. Dark bundles of grey clouds were rolling in, and as I watched, a triple flash of lightning forked across the sky.

"Oh lord. Not yet!" Those clouds foretold at least an hour of hard, pounding rain that would dig rivulets in the red clay, and meanwhile destroy every bit of evidence that might be left along the tobacco road. There wasn't time to wait for Richard.

"Aunt Nora, can I borrow your car?" I tried to think of what else I might need. "And your camera? And do you have any baggies?" I brushed off my aunt's concern and gathered up all the sandwich bags in the house, Aunt Nora's camera, and a pair of tweezers.

"What is going on?" Aunt Nora asked.

"Aunt Nora, I've got to go out."

"Now? It's fixing to storm."

"That's why I've got to go now. If Richard gets back before I do, give him this." I took Paw's road map out once again, and drew in the tobacco road in red felt-tip. Then I drew arrows pointing to it to make sure he would know that this was where I had gone.

"Tell him to come meet me here."

"What on earth for?"

"There's no time to explain," I said and headed for the door.

"Is this about Paw's death?"

"I think so."

"Then wait for Richard! Or I'll track down Buddy and Willis to go with you."

"I can't. There's no time."

"At least take a raincoat." Aunt Nora reached inside the coat closet and pulled out a bright yellow slicker. "Take Thaddeous's."

I shoved my arms into it and left her watching me through the open door.

CHAPTER 37

The storm was threatening to break at any moment as I climbed back into Aunt Nora's Buick. I drove as fast as I could, not even looking at Paw's house as I turned down the tobacco road. The rutted dirt road was barely wide enough for the car, and looked more like a seldom-used driveway than a road.

The dark clouds looked even more ominous out in the open, looming over the dusty, brush-covered fields. Trees had encroached onto the once-clear ground, blocking the view. Though I knew there was a busy, friendly neighborhood just behind me, it still looked as if I was in the middle of nowhere. The only structure visible was the weathered, grey tobacco shed up ahead.

The murderer would have been coming from the other direction, of course, driving toward Byerly instead of away from it, and the tobacco shed would have been the marker that he was about to reach Gilmore. Either Thaddeous or Arthur would have known that. So logically, if he was planning to attack Melanie, he would have driven no further than the shed.

The road widened slightly as I approached the shed, and I stopped the car and got out, stuffing camera, baggies, and tweezers into the pockets of the raincoat. There were tire tracks all around. I tried to decide how fresh they looked, and wished I had paid more attention to tracking in the Girl Scouts. To my untrained eye, it looked as if there were at least two sets of tracks.

That fit in with what I suspected. One set would have been the murderer's, and one set Paw's. Paw drove up, stopped, and saw. . . . I still didn't know what he had seen. I took pictures of both sets of tracks, and stepped carefully over them.

Now, where were the driver and Melanie when Paw arrived? In the truck? No, Paw would have seen them struggling and he would have done something. Think it through, I told myself. I'm Melanie, and the man who picked me up has parked his truck and now he's making a pass. What would I do? Jump out and make a run for it. I looked at the ground on the passenger side of both sets of tracks. Was that a footprint? I couldn't tell for sure, but I snapped a picture of it anyway.

Where would Melanie have run? Down the road? No, the driver could have caught up with her in the truck. Across the field? Maybe, though according to Aunt Maggie, there wouldn't have been a single light to guide her. What about the shed? Would Melanie have realized that it was abandoned, that she wouldn't find any help there? Maybe not. If she were panicked, and goodness knows she had reason to be, maybe she would have thought it was someone's house.

I looked up at the shed unhappily, not wanting to go inside. It never had been a very sturdy-looking building, and it looked even worse today, swaying in the wind. I didn't much care for the idea of it collapsing with me inside. The shed had been built to lay burley tobacco to dry out, so the roof was good tin but the floors were just rough planks and the walls had gaps between each board that had grown larger as the wood rotted.

Another grumble of thunder made the ground tremble, and the wind was blowing up to whip my hair in front of my face. Now was not the time to be squeamish. I had to look inside.

The door into the shed was around the side, and as I walked toward it, I found a whole footprint. It looked like a man's shoe, but it wasn't Paw's. His feet hadn't been much bigger than mine, but the shoe that made this print was two inches longer than mine, I took another picture, then tore one of the plastic bags open to lay it carefully over the footprint and weighted the makeshift tarp down with a couple of rocks. It probably wouldn't do any good, but it was worth a shot.

I went on a few more steps, then saw a tiny scrap of green cloth caught on a plank that had half-fallen off of the wall. Hadn't Richard said that Melanie had been wearing a green shirt when she was last seen? I took another picture, used Aunt Nora's tweezers to retrieve the scrap and place it into a baggie, and stuck the baggie into a pocket. Then I poked another bag on the end of the plank as a flag to mark the spot, winding it tightly and hoping it would withstand the coming rain.

At first I thought the door was open, but then I saw it was hanging on one hinge. It had been intact the last time I saw it, but I couldn't honestly say how long ago that had been. Had it finally given way, or had it been burst open? By Melanie? Or by her pursuer? I took a deep breath, and stepped inside.

I waited a minute for my eyes to adjust to the gloom, and jumped when I heard a loud crack. It was just the wind breaking off yet another fragment of wood. Though the shed masked some of the sound of the wind, the weird whistles and howls as the wind ripped through gaps were hardly comforting.

Now what? I didn't see a thing. No, that wasn't completely true. There were random pieces of wood and rusty nails scattered about, and dust everywhere. Except over there. In one corner, the floor looked relatively clean, I went closer, and amended my thought. The floor in that corner might be clear of dust, but there were dark brown stains that had seeped into the wood.

I fought the churning in my stomach as I recognized the stains for what they were. Blood. Melanie's blood.

I returned to my mental reenactment of Melanie's flight. Melanie hadn't gotten far before her attacker caught her. This must be where he had pushed her onto the floor, pinning her to the floor so he could rape her. Then he killed her. The picture of Melanie's body lying there was suddenly all too clear.

A thunderclap startled me out of my imagination, and reminded me of the coming storm. I steadied my hands enough to take several pictures of the stains, thankful that I had remembered flash bulbs.

I heard a sharp ping on the tin roof, followed by another. The rain was starting, but I no longer cared about it. The roof would preserve the evidence long enough for me to call the police.

The stains were something concrete, something I could take to Junior. Then she and the county police could find out who the murderer was.

I took a deep breath, and realized I was actually relieved. Let the police figure out who had killed Paw and Melanie. They would be avenged without my having to play Judas. With luck, and Junior's cooperation, no one would have to know how far I had gone toward implicating one of my own family.

I turned back toward the doorway, eager to get to a phone, but then I saw the shadow of someone standing outside the door.

"Richard?" I said, but he wasn't tall enough to be my husband. I moved back a little and called out, "Who's there?"

The man stepped forward as if to answer me, but didn't say anything. When I saw the rifle he was carrying, a chill ran down my spine, the sensation Paw had always said meant that someone was walking over my grave.

"Uncle Loman?" I said. "What are you doing here?"

Uncle Loman looked around the shed. "Where's your husband?"

"He's not here," I said. What was going on? Uncle Loman couldn't have killed Melanie. He had been at the lodge and then with Uncle Conrad. Then I remembered what Richard had suggested about two men working together. Only it hadn't been Arthur and Thaddeous — it had been Loman and Conrad. All the bits and pieces I had been collecting finally made sense.

I should have been scared out of my wits, but I was too mad to be scared. "You son of a bitch! You killed Paw! That's what I couldn't figure out. You couldn't have killed Melanie because you were at the lodge Friday night, and Conrad couldn't have killed Paw because he was home all day Sunday. But Conrad could kill Melanie, and you could kill Paw to cover it up!"

Loman spat onto the floor and said, "When you started asking questions, I figured Ellis must have told you something. I've been keeping an eye on you ever since he died, but I didn't think you knew enough to matter until I followed you here. I guess you're smarter than I thought."

Maybe I should have kept quiet, but anger carried me recklessly on. "Paw called Conrad, didn't he? He saw Conrad's truck here that night. When he started to figure out what Conrad had done, he called him and told him."

Loman didn't look much interested in my narrative, but he didn't interrupt.

"Conrad must have put him off somehow, and then called you," I continued. "You got to the house in time to see him driving to the mill, and while he was at the security booth, you drove over behind the mill and snuck in that hole in the back fence. You're a supervisor, so you must have a key to the door. You waited for him, and you hit him from behind like a . . ."

My voice cut off in a gasp. I didn't know a word low enough to describe what he had done. "He treated you like his own family ever since you and Aunt Edna were courting!"

"There's family, and then there's family. It came down to him or Conrad. If he hadn't been messing in things that didn't concern him, nothing would have come of it."

"What about Melanie? Was she nothing?"

"You're as bad as Ellis, aren't you? I knew he'd never let go until he put Conrad in jail and no blood kin of mine is going to jail, for not giving some tramp what she was asking for in the first place. I should have made sure he was dead in the mill, but as old as he was, I didn't think he'd live long enough to tell anybody anything."

"You bastard!"

"I didn't think you'd understand. All them college degrees of yours don't mean spit! Blood's what's important."

"Paw was my blood!"

"And Conrad's mine." He hefted his rifle. "Now you walk in front of me and get into the truck. We're going to go find your husband."

I knew he was planning to kill me and Richard, but I didn't move.

"I said, get in the car. You mind me, hear?"

"No, Loman. If you want to shoot me, you're going to have to do it right here."

Deliberately he lifted the rifle and brought the sights to bear on my forehead. "I'll do what I have to."

"You're pretty good with women and old men," a voice said from behind Loman.

"How are you with a healthy man, Uncle Loman?" Thaddeous was standing in the doorway with Great-Great-Uncle Thaddeous's shotgun perched on his shoulder.

Loman turned just enough to see him, but didn't move his aim from me. "Boy, you put that down," he said.

"No sir, I won't. You killed Paw, but I'm not about to let you kill Laurie Anne."

"Are you going to let your Uncle Conrad go to jail? For her? Her and her computers and her college professor husband — she's never had any use for any of us. Are you going to let our family get smeared all over the papers because of her?"

"Conrad stopped being any kin to me when he hurt Melanie, and the same goes for you. Now put that gun down before I show you how *my* family deals with trash like you."

There was a deadly pause, then Loman swung toward Thaddeous. I screamed a warning, but it wasn't needed. Without seeming to react, Thaddeous squeezed the trigger and the report of Great-Great-Uncle Thaddeous's shotgun shook through the shed. Loman dropped his gun, staggered, then fell back. With a crack of thunder, the rain poured down.

CHAPTER 38

"Are you all right?" Thaddeous asked.

"I think so." I looked down at Loman's body. It looked so odd to see his eyes open and unblinking. I realized that I was wobbling, and turned away.

"Come on," Thaddeous said.

We walked back to the road, where Thaddeous's and Loman's pickup trucks were parked behind Aunt Nora's car, and he helped me into the cab of his truck. Then he walked around to the other side, and carefully hung Great-Great-Uncle Thaddeous's shotgun on the rack at the back of the cab before climbing in himself.

He started the engine, clicked on his CB radio, and twisted the knob to station 9. "Breaker, breaker. I've got an emergency. Are there any Smokies out there with their ears on?"

Almost immediately, a voice replied, "This is Deputy Trey Norton of the Byerly Police. What do you need?"

"Trey, this is Thaddeous Crawford. Do you know the old tobacco road that runs by my grandfather's house?"

"I know it."

"There's a dead body in the tobacco shed out here."

"Jesus! What happened. Thaddeous?"

Thaddeous ignored Trey's question and added, "That shed is also where Melanie Wilson was killed, so you better bring whatever you need to check it out."

"Me and Junior will be right there. You just stay put."

Thaddeous shut off the radio, and put the truck in gear.

"Where are we going?" I asked.

"I heard part of what Loman and you were saying, but now I'm going to find Conrad and hear it all. Are you coming?"

I knew I'd never be able to talk him into waiting for the police, and I wasn't about to stay there alone. "Let's go."

He drove slowly through the pouring rain until we hit Gilmore and turned toward town. A minute later one of Byerly's police cruisers zoomed by, followed closely by a county police car, but they took no more notice of Thaddeous than he did of them.

"How did you find me?" I asked.

"I got home and Mama was all upset that you had run out like that. She kept talking about Paw having been murdered. I looked at the map you left for Richard, and thought you might could use a hand. I didn't know what was going on, but I brought the shotgun, just in case. I guess it's good thing I did."

He didn't speak again during the fifteen minutes or so it took us to reach Conrad's house. I had no idea of his intentions and was afraid to ask. We pulled up in front of Aunt Ruby Lee's house, and Thaddeous got out and walked toward the back, shotgun in hand. I followed him.

Thaddeous didn't go to the front door, but instead walked across the soggy lawn toward the open garage door where I could hear the sound of hammering. Conrad was placing a two-by-four into place on a half-finished picnic table. He saw us, and smiled.

"Hey there Thaddeous, Laurie Anne. Come on in out of the rain. Ruby Lee and the kids went shopping, so I could use some company." We stepped in, and then Conrad saw what Thaddeous was holding. "What's the shotgun for?"

Thaddeous said, "Loman's dead."

Conrad let the board fall onto the concrete floor and turned white as a sheet.

"I want you to tell me what happened to

Melanie and Paw," Thaddeous went on.

I watched as Conrad's usually cheerful face crumbled. "Oh Lord, Thaddeous, I didn't mean for it to happen, not any of it. You've got to believe me."

When Thaddeous's expression didn't change, he directed his words toward me. "Where do you want me to start?" he asked uncertainly.

"You better tell us everything, from the beginning," I said gently.

He swallowed hard, and then began. "I was up at the lodge, and we had been drinking, maybe a little too much. When we ran out of beer, I went to get us some more. I was about halfway to the 7-Eleven when I saw her by the side of the road. Melanie, I mean.

"She said she was out of gas. I told her I'd take her to a gas station, but she said she'd rather I take her home, that her Daddy would come pick up the car later. I'd known Melanie since she was just a little thing, but I don't think I ever noticed how pretty she was until she got into the truck beside me.

"We were driving along and she smiled at me, so I put my hand on her knee. When she pushed it off I just thought she was playing hard to get, you know how women are sometimes. By then we were on that old tobacco road by Ellis's house, and I pulled off the road and put my arms around her, just to get a little kiss, but she shoved me away and jumped out of the car."

I was chilled, hearing how close my suspicions had been to the truth.

"She ran into the tobacco shed, and I was afraid she'd get hurt in there as dark as it was, so I followed her. I tried to tell her I wasn't going to hurt her, but she screamed and hit me.

"I got mad and grabbed hold of her arms to stop her from hitting me, and with the booze in me, I just got carried away. I didn't hurt her none, but I pushed her onto the floor, and, well . . ."

"Finish it," Thaddeous said.

"Afterwards, she was crying, and I was trying to tell her I didn't mean to hurt her and that everything was all right. Then I heard Ellis yelling for me. It scared me as much as if the Lord himself had called my name, and I didn't want him to find us like that.

"She was going to scream, so I put my hand over her mouth to stop her. She was fighting me, and then she bit me so hard I couldn't think straight. I reached around with my other hand and found a board or something, and I hit her with it. She quit fighting me, but it wasn't until after I heard Ellis drive away that I realized that she wasn't breathing anymore."

Conrad's knees buckled as if they could no longer hold him, and he sagged onto a cedar bench, flinching when Thaddeous took a step closer.

"Then what?"

"I didn't know what to do. I drove up to the 7-Eleven and called Loman at the lodge. He told me to go back to the shed and wait for him. When he got there, he said we'd have to move her because if she was found there, the police would suspect everyone connected to the Burnettes. He put her in the back of his truck. She was all limp, and I started shaking when I saw her. Loman told me to clean myself off, and then he went back into the shed to see if he could find anything to show we had been there. He found the board I hit her with and said he'd burn it, but we couldn't get the stain out of the floor. He said we'd put her in Marley so everyone would think the niggers did it. I thought that was real smart — Loman's always been smarter than me.

"I didn't want to take her clothes off and leave her naked like that, but Loman said we had to get rid of everything in case there were any traces of me. He made me do it while he kept an eye out. She was still warm, and for a minute it looked like she was still breathing." He wrung his hands. "Loman said he'd burn the clothes later, and then we drove over to Marley. We made sure there wasn't anyone watching, and then I carried her over to the Dumpster and put her in."

He looked beseechingly at me, but when I didn't even try to hide my revulsion, he went on. "I wanted to go home after that, but Loman said we had to go get the beer I'd been sent for, and then we picked up my truck so I could follow him back to the lodge. He told everyone I had had car problems someplace miles away from where we'd been and nobody thought anything of it. We thought they'd find the body right off, but when they didn't, Loman called the police and told them where to find her and that niggers had done it."

"What about Paw?" I asked.

"Loman was as mad as a wet hen when he found out about that. I was so scared that night that I forgot to tell Loman that Ellis had seen my truck. Then, that Sunday, Ellis called me. He'd come by and looked for me, but then he saw Melanie's pocketbook where she had left it in the front seat of my truck. He thought I was out there fooling around on Ruby Lee, so he left as soon as he saw it.

"He hadn't decided whether he should talk to Ruby Lee or not, but then he heard about Melanie being missing. The paper told what Melanie's pocketbook looked like, and Ellis knew it was the one he had seen in my truck. He asked me straight out if I knew where Melanie was.

"I couldn't lie to him. I had to tell him what happened." Then he held his head up a little. "Only I didn't tell him about Loman. I didn't want to get him in trouble."

He sounded just like a little boy who had been caught cheating and wouldn't tell who his co-conspirator was.

"Ellis said I was going to have to go to the police, and if I didn't, he'd call them himself. I told him I had to talk to Ruby Lee first, and he said he'd wait until that evening, but if I hadn't turned myself in by then, he'd go see Junior Norton himself.

"As soon as Ellis hung up, I called Loman, and he said we'd go talk to Ellis together. Only Ruby Lee wouldn't let me go. Loman said for me to just keep my mouth shut and he'd take care of Ellis."

"Then you knew what he was planning to do to Paw?" I said.

"No, I swear I didn't. I thought he was just going to talk to him. When I heard about Ellis getting hurt, I never thought that Loman could have had something to do with it. When I asked him later on if he talked to Ellis, he just told me to shut up."

"You're lying," I said. "You didn't care whether Loman killed Paw or not. You wouldn't have called Loman like that if you hadn't expected him to do something."

Conrad drew his hand over his forehead, and brought it down wet with sweat. "I swear I didn't know. I never meant to hurt nobody."

Thaddeous slowly lifted his shotgun, and aimed it at Conrad's midsection. Then he stared at Conrad for a long time. I'll give Conrad credit. He didn't even flinch. Finally I touched Thaddeous's arm.

"Thaddeous, why don't you go call the police?"

He hesitated a minute longer, then lowered the shotgun and said, "I believe I will." I wasn't sure who was more relieved when he went into the house, me or Conrad. Maybe it was Thaddeous himself.

CHAPTER 39

The police showed up quickly, and after volleys of questions, they bundled Thaddeous, Conrad, and me into squad cars to drive us to the station. I saw Aunt Ruby Lee and the kids arrive just as we were driving away, and thanked the powers that be that I didn't have to be the one who told them what had happened.

The three of us were separated as soon as we reached the station. I was led to a tiny room with a coffee machine and a tiny refrigerator. And questioned by a dyspeptic looking county policeman equipped with a legal pad and a tape recorder. I told him everything, from the time Paw had first told me that his accident was an attack to Conrad's confession. Although he asked for clarification on a few points and seemed bewildered by all the names, he mainly just nodded and scribbled. Once I finished, he said, "I think that's all we need," and left the room before I could ask him anything in return.

Now what? Was I going to be arrested?

Probably not, because they hadn't read me my rights. Did that mean I couldn't use the phone? What about Thaddeous? I didn't know whether or not what he had done had been strictly legal, but Loman had been about to shoot me, so that should count for something.

The door to the room opened, distracting me from my questions. It was Richard. The two of us held onto each other for a long time.

"What are you doing here?" I finally asked.

"I got back to Aunt Nora's house about an hour after you left. She was all upset, and told me you had gone out, followed shortly thereafter by Thaddeous. So we went after you."

"Aunt Nora came, too?"

"I didn't want her to, but I didn't have a choice. All of you Burnettes are as stubborn as mules. Anyway, we couldn't get to the tobacco shed. The police had it blocked off. I tried to tell them that my wife was in there, but they just brushed me off. Then we saw them carrying off a body on a stretcher, and no one would tell us who it was.

"That's when Aunt Nora took over. She said to tell Junior that she was her mother's best friend from high school, and if Junior didn't come over, Aunt Nora would tell her mother. Junior was there in less than a minute."

"I'm not surprised. I've met Mrs. Norton."

"Anyway, Junior tried to calm Aunt Nora down, but Aunt Nora demanded to know what had happened to you and Thaddeous. Of course, Junior didn't know where you two were. When she told us that it was Loman's body that had been found, we didn't know what to think. That's about the time the call came in from Aunt Ruby Lee's house, and we followed Junior back here."

"Do you know about Conrad?" I wasn't going to call him "Uncle" anymore.

"Most of it. Conrad killed Melanie, and Loman helped him cover it up and killed Paw to keep him quiet."

I nodded, and told him the rest of the story, concluding with, "I'm sorry I gave you such a scare. It never occurred to me that the murderer would come after me. As a detective, I'm a decent computer programmer."

"You did fine. I'm just grateful that you're all right."

"What happened with Arthur?" It

seemed like forever since I had suspected him. Or Thaddeous.

"Though it hardly matters now, he and Thaddeous were together Friday night for a perfectly innocent reason. One of Arthur's regular customers is a jeweler who is giving Thaddeous a good deal on a brooch for Aunt Nora's Mother's Day gift in return for a generous trade-in allowance from Arthur. They went to the jewelry store Friday night to negotiate, but since Thaddeous wanted it engraved, Arthur had to go back on Sunday to pick it up."

"So why didn't Arthur tell Vasti where he had gone?"

"Would you tell Vasti a secret?"

The county policeman came back in, looking happier with his digestion, and said, "You're free to go. Your story checks out." He escorted us to the front desk, where we found Thaddeous arguing with a young deputy I recognized as Trey Norton. Aunt Nora and Junior were looking on in exasperation.

"I've got a permit, don't I? It's my shotgun, and I mean to take it home," Thaddeous said.

"It's evidence," Trey replied, "and it's not leaving this station."

"Then I'm staying, too." Thaddeous

showed every sign of abiding by his decision, while Trey looked just as determined to prove him wrong.

"Thaddeous, you let me handle this," Aunt Nora said. She turned to the police chief. "Junior, you know that shotgun has been in my family for generations."

"Yes, ma'am."

"I want you to swear to me that it won't be hurt, and that you'll return it *personally* when all this is taken care of."

"Yes, ma'am. I'll take care of it."

She nodded. "Come on, Thaddeous. Let's go home." She turned and saw me and Richard.

"Laurie Anne?" she said cautiously. "Are you all right?"

"I think so." We hugged, and Aunt Nora kept her arm around me as we walked through the rain to the rental car. I let Thaddeous ride in front with Richard, while I climbed in back with Aunt Nora.

"Junior said they'd bring Thaddeous's truck and the Buick over to the house this evening," Aunt Nora said.

"I suppose you want to know what happened," I said.

"I know most of it already," Aunt Nora said, "but there is one thing I wanted to ask. When you and I talked the other night, did you know it was someone in the family who had killed Paw?"

"No, ma'am, not then. I don't think I could have gone through with it if I had known sooner."

She nodded.

"I'm sorry, Aunt Nora."

"What on earth for? You did what you had to." She patted my leg.

"I know, but I didn't know how it was going to come out."

"Of course you didn't. There was no way you could have known." Aunt Nora paused, and then said, "I should warn you. I talked to Buddy before we left the station, and he said that everybody is over at my house waiting for us."

I felt my stomach tighten.

"If you want, I'll do the talking," Aunt Nora offered.

I was tempted, but I took a deep breath and said, "No, I have to tell them myself."

"Are you sure?" Richard asked.

"I have to face them sooner or later. They're my family." I just wasn't sure that they'd want to claim me anymore. Aunt Nora must have known what I was thinking, because she put her arm around me and kept it there until we got to her house.

CHAPTER 40

As we approached Aunt Nora's house, I saw that the driveway and the street in front of the house were filled with Burnette cars. I tried to steel myself as we went toward the door, but even so, I nearly turned and ran when we walked in and saw every adult member of the Burnette clan. Except Conrad and Loman, I reminded myself. And Paw.

Aunt Nellie had her arm around a red-eyed Aunt Ruby Lee in one corner, while Aunt Daphine was comforting Aunt Edna in another. Uncle Buddy, Willis, Uncle Ruben, and Sue seemed to be trying to calm down a wildly gesticulating Linwood. Vasti, Arthur, and the rest of the cousins were standing in an uncomfortable knot. Only Aunt Maggie, rocking slowly in Aunt Nora's rocking chair, seemed at ease. It was she who saw us first and said, "Here they are now." Everyone stopped talking, and turned toward us.

Aunt Nora went to Uncle Buddy, who in a rare public display of affection, kissed her. Thaddeous went and sat on the couch, saying nothing.

I stood looking at and being looked at by them all, feeling like a stranger. Richard put his arm around me protectively.

"Well, Laurie Anne," Aunt Maggie prompted. "Are you going to tell us what happened?"

I swallowed hard and said, "I guess y'all know most of it."

No one responded but Aunt Nora, who attempted an encouraging smile. I went on to give a bare bones description, trying to spare Aunt Ruby Lee, Aunt Edna, and their children as best I could, but knowing that there wasn't a whole lot I could do. "That's what happened," I said finally.

"You're lying!" Linwood said.

I flinched, but said as evenly as I could, "No, Linwood. I'm sorrier than I can say, but that is what happened."

"You killed my daddy, that's what happened!"

"I'm the one who shot him, not Laurie Anne," Thaddeous said quietly.

"Maybe you're the one who pulled the trigger," Linwood said, "but she put you up to it. Sticking her nose where it didn't belong, stirring up trouble. She deserves just what that slut Melanie got, if you ask me, and —"

"Linwood!" Aunt Edna said. "You watch your mouth!"

He turned to his mother, his eyes filling with tears. "But Mama, she killed Daddy!"

"Your father killed himself when he refused to put his gun down. Thaddeous shot in self-defense," Aunt Nora said firmly.

"But if *she* had left well enough alone, it wouldn't have happened. Daddy would still be alive."

"If Conrad hadn't killed that girl, none of it would have happened. Why don't you blame him?" Aunt Daphine said.

Linwood looked at me, then at his feet, but said nothing.

"I blame Loman," Aunt Edna said dully.

"Mama, how can you say that?" Linwood asked, aghast. "He was your husband."

"And Paw was my father! Loman killed my father! He hit him, and then sat with us at the hospital, waiting for him to die. He dressed in his best suit to come to the funeral, put out some of his precious money to buy flowers for the grave, even comforted me when I was crying. That bastard took what Paw left him in his will! I took a lot from that man because he was my husband and your father, but I can't ever forgive him that. I'd tell Loman that to his face if he were here. Maybe it's just as well he's not."

"Mama!"

"Linwood, Paw was your grandfather. Don't you see? Loman killed Paw!"

The two stared at each other until finally Linwood lowered his eyes. "But he was my Daddy," he said with a sob. He pushed past me and Richard, and ran out the door.

Aunt Edna started to follow.

"Leave him be, Edna," Sue said without moving. "He's going to have to work this one out on his own."

Aunt Edna sat back down, and a minute later we heard Linwood start up his pickup truck and drive off with tires squealing.

Sue caught my eye. "Like Linwood said, if you hadn't started asking questions, Loman would still be alive. Maybe he wasn't the best father in the world, but he was the only one Linwood had. That's neither here nor there. It did happen, and I don't think that there's anything you could have done different. I guess you were doing what Paw wanted you to, and I can't fault you there. I think Loman would rather have died that way than to go to prison anyway."

I looked at the other aunt I had somehow deprived of a husband. "Aunt Ruby Lee?"

Aunt Ruby Lee sniffed loudly. "I don't know what to say. I feel like I brought this on us all."

"Ruby Lee, don't say that," Aunt Nellie said, holding her tightly.

"It's true! I should have known somehow. I guess I never was any good at picking husbands. You'd think I'd learn sometime." She wiped her eyes. "I went down to the police station to see him, but I just couldn't stand to be in the same room as him. I knew Conrad could be weak, but I never knew how weak. You say he was drunk when it happened?"

"Yes, ma'am," I said. "He said he didn't mean to hurt anyone."

"That's something, anyway. I don't blame you, Laurie Anne, really I don't, but it's hard to understand it all. So much has happened."

I nodded. "I know. I'm sorry."

"There's one thing I want to know," Aunt Maggie said. "Why didn't you tell someone what you were up to?"

"I tried to," I said, and Aunt Nora and

Aunt Daphine nodded. "I was afraid no one would believe me, or that you'd think I was trying to make trouble."

"That's my fault," Uncle Buddy said. "Laurie Anne tried to tell me what she was doing, but I wouldn't listen. If I had, things might have turned out different." He looked down at his hands, as if embarrassed at making such a long speech.

"If I hadn't stumbled around like an idiot, I know things would have turned out differently," I said miserably. "I really messed things up. I'm sorry."

"Well, just stop being sorry," Aunt Daphine said crisply. "This is going to be hard on all of us, but we'll get by just the same."

I was still standing at the door. "Do you want me to leave?"

Surprisingly, it was Vasti who said, "Laurie Anne, that is the silliest thing I ever heard! Now come on in here and sit down."

I never lost the sensation of walking on eggshells that night. We all knew that it was going to be a long time before life felt normal again. Still, mostly what I felt was relief that despite everything that had happened, I was still family. Or maybe I was finally family.

CHAPTER 41

"Richard, will you *please* let go of my arm?"

"Not until we're home. This is the only way I can be sure you'll stay out of trouble."

"Are you going to come into the bathroom with me?"

Thaddeous snickered.

Reluctantly Richard released his grasp. "I'll be right here," he said.

I sighed in mock exasperation, then went into the airport ladies' room. Ever since we had returned to Aunt Nora's house, Richard had not let me out of his sight. Two days had passed since Loman's death and Conrad's arrest, and I was hoping that the worst of it was over. Thaddeous, Richard, and I had attended Melanie Wilson's funeral on Monday, but would not be attending Loman's on Wednesday.

Now Thaddeous, Aunt Nora, Uncle Buddy, and Aunt Maggie had come to the airport to see us off. I finished in the ladies' room and went to join the others at the gate.

"They said boarding would begin in a minute," Richard said. "We better start on the good-byes now."

I started hugging necks, with Richard following along behind me.

First Uncle Buddy who, to my surprise, added a kiss on my cheek.

Then Aunt Maggie.

"You take care of yourself up there, hear?" Aunt Maggie said.

"I will."

She lowered her voice a bit. "Now Laurie Anne, I can see why you didn't want to tell any of your aunts about what you suspected, not when you didn't know whose husband or son was a murderer, but why didn't you tell me?"

"I was afraid you'd be upset with me," I said sheepishly.

"Why in the Sam Hill did you think that?"

"You said once that only trash would turn in their own family."

"Good Lord, child, I was talking about stealing, not murder. Do you really think I'd want my own brother's murderer left out on the street? You did good. Ellis would be proud of you. Now don't take so long coming home next time."

Aunt Nora was already sniffing, tissue in

hand. "Laurie Anne, I'm sorry things went the way they did, but it's been awfully good seeing you. You let us hear from you."

"I will." Feeling tears welling in my own eyes, I hugged my aunt tightly. "Let me know how you're doing, too."

"I will. I've got a right to call my own niece once in a while," she added defiantly. She looked pointedly at Uncle Buddy, who actually nodded.

"Are Aunt Edna and Aunt Ruby Lee going to be all right?" I asked.

"You know, I think Edna is going to come out of this better than she went in. It's kind of shook her out of herself. Besides, she's got Reverend Glass to help her through."

"I didn't think Reverend Glass would have much use for her since he didn't get Paw's house."

"But she still makes the best ginger snaps around."

"What about Aunt Ruby Lee?"

"She's in pretty bad shape. First Paw dying and now Conrad in jail — it's hit her hard."

I nodded.

"She'll divorce Conrad, of course. He's already said he won't fight it, which helps.

Daphine is staying with her until she gets over the worst, and I hear that Roger Bailey has been coming round to comfort her."

I smiled. Roger was a stubborn soul.

"They've started boarding," Richard said.

There was one last good-bye. "Thaddeous . . . ," I began, then gave up and stretched to throw my arms around him. He turned bright red.

Then Richard took his hand and shook it thoroughly. "I can't thank you enough, Thaddeous."

"It wasn't anything that anyone wouldn't have done," he said.

"The heck it wasn't," Richard said.

"You come up and see us, and let us show you around Boston," I said.

"I just might do that," he said. "I'd kind of like to ride in those boats sometime."

"Boats?"

"Those pretty bird boats in the pond. You sent me a postcard with them on it."

I was momentarily transfixed by the imagined spectacle of my cousin wedged onto one of the Swan Boats in the Boston Public Garden lagoon.

"It's a deal," Richard said solemnly. Then, to me, "We better get on board."

There was a chorus of final farewells as

he handed the attendant our tickets, and I turned to wave furiously.

"Now, if you need anything, anything at all, you just call," Aunt Nora called after us. "Collect!"

The employees of Thorndike Press hope you have enjoyed this Large Print book. All our Thorndike and Wheeler Large Print titles are designed for easy reading, and all our books are made to last. Other Thorndike Press Large Print books are available at your library, through selected bookstores, or directly from us.

For information about titles, please call:

(800) 223-1244

or visit our Web site at:

www.gale.com/thorndike
www.gale.com/wheeler

To share your comments, please write:

Publisher
Thorndike Press
295 Kennedy Memorial Drive
Waterville, ME   04901